A GAME OF TRUE OR FALSE

"Sir, I appeal to you! This is unseemly," Sophia declared with all the conviction she could muster as Lord Ramsey clasped her about the waist.

A candle flame flared in the breeze, then died, but not before Sophia had caught the fervid gleam of Lord Ramsey's eyes. "This is more so," he said.

She read his intention and put her hands against his broad chest and pushed. "No! No, you could not! You will not!"

"Don't you want me to kiss you?" he inquired.

"No, of course I do not."

"Liar," he said softly, pulling her deeper into the shadows. . . .

How could she deny it—or him. . . ?

A SERVANT OF QUALITY

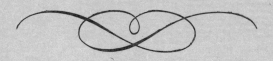

by
Eileen Jackson

A SIGNET BOOK

NEW AMERICAN LIBRARY

SIGNET TRADEMARK REG. U.S. PAT. OFF. AND FOREIGN COUNTRIES
REGISTERED TRADEMARK—MARCA REGISTRADA
HECHO EN CHICAGO, U.S.A.

SIGNET, SIGNET CLASSIC, MENTOR, ONYX, PLUME,
MERIDIAN and NAL BOOKS are published by NAL PENGUIN INC.,
1633 Broadway, New York, New York 10019

First Printing, July, 1988

1 2 3 4 5 6 7 8 9

PRINTED IN THE UNITED STATES OF AMERICA

One

Lady Sophia Clavering delved into her pocket and searched wildly for her purse.

It took only a moment for her to discover that it was gone. Her fingers went on searching frantically, uselessly. She needed time to gather courage to face the innkeeper, who had just set out a jug of ale and a pork pie on the plain table at which she sat.

Her first impulse was to thank God that she had not touched the victuals when she no longer had the means to pay for them; the second to wish that she had assuaged her piercing hunger before discovering the theft of her money. She looked at the food and drink and her mouth filled with juices. She was accustomed to food being brought by soft-footed servants at regular intervals, and her stomach was outraged at having today received only two pieces of toast and a buttered egg many hours ago. She had to fight an urgent impulse to grab at the pie, as she inwardly cursed once more her stupidity, as well as her total lack of decorum, in having left her home so precipitately and so ill-prepared. It was February, unbelievably cold, with not a sign of spring even in the south. It was said that the Thames was frozen right over and for weeks her guardian had allowed her out of doors only when she was swathed in furs from head to toe. Garbed as she was now, her feet wet with the snow that had dribbled into her shoes, the intensity of the cold had made her feel quite ill.

Lady Sophia was exceedingly vague on the subject of punishments ordained for those who tricked innkeepers. Would an offer to assist in the kitchen be of use? She looked up at the innkeeper, whose smile was becoming a trifle forced. He had already argued with his wife, who clearly ruled the roost and had not welcomed the entry of a young woman so ill-favored and badly dressed and clearly of the lowest of the laboring class. She was a large, frowning woman in a bright orange gown and a long white apron—not a person with whom one trifled lightly—and she was advancing rapidly toward the table.

Sophia decided to tell the truth, or at least as much as possible in the circumstances. She remembered to keep the country burr in her voice as she said, "My money's been stolen. I was jostled by some young shavers a mile or so back. They took my necklace and earrings, but I thought they'd missed my purse."

Sophia felt her color rise as she met disbelieving stares. "It's the honest truth—" she began.

She stopped speaking as the innkeeper's wife pointed at the door. "Out!"

"But, ma'am, I haven't eaten since this morning. This bitter cold will destroy me if I don't eat. I'll send you money, I swear."

"That's a tale we've heard afore. Be off with you and think yourself lucky we don't call on the village constable. Robbed, indeed! Huh! What would you have worth stealin'? Necklace and earrings! I s'pose they was diamonds!"

Sophia rose with as much dignity as she could muster, looked for a longing moment at the food and the fire that roared up the wide chimney, pulled her heavy black cloak around her, and made for the door.

It was blocked by a man who did not move.

"Allow me to pass," she commanded, forgetting for the moment her role as a humble woman.

The man's brows rose over his dark eyes. "Return to your food," he ordered. He waved imperiously in the direction of her table, saying to the innkeepers, "She's only too right about the cold. Feed the wench. I'll pay her shot."

Sophia's first reaction was puzzlement. Nothing in the seventeen years of her cossetted life had prepared her for such a situation.

The man's eyes traveled over her, from her heavy black leather shoes to her bottle-green worsted gown, to her face.

Sophia's hands itched to touch her skin, to make sure that the sallow-colored *pomade à baton* had not run and that her large mob cap continued to conceal the curls that a beau with a poetical turn of mind had described as the color of ripe horse chestnuts.

Her mind was whirling. If she were truly the person she pretended to be, she would have no hesitation in accepting charity from a gentleman. Her appearance, rendered as unappealing as possible, could scarcely be a temptation to him.

What had he called her? ". . . the wench . . ." Wench indeed! How dare he! But she remained silent. If she was to travel the remaining miles to London, she must eat. Everything was going dreadfully wrong, but at this moment she was being offered warmth and food and her world could encompass nothing else.

She reseated herself at the table and took a large bite of the pork pie. It was succulent and the pastry melted in her mouth. A few more bites and a drink of the ale comforted the worst of her hunger and she stole a glance at the man who had rescued her.

He sprawled on the cushioned windowseat, his long, booted legs stretched straight in front of him as if to ease their cramp. His muscular figure was impeccably garmented in a long-tailed dark green cloth coat over a white waistcoat. His breeches were black, his cravat had been tied with flawless skill, though it was now slightly crumpled, and his leather driving gloves lay beside him. As he waited for his meal he looked at his fob watch, his heavy black brows drawn together in a frown over his strong nose, and his mouth set in grim lines. He pored over a traveler's guide, unfolding a map, his frown deepening. Sophia wondered if he was merely concentrating or was as angry as he seemed. She would not care to cross such a man. He glanced up and caught her watching him and a brief smile softened his harsh, swarthy features, though it did not reach his eyes. Sophia wished she were not indebted to him.

Even so, he looked remarkably interesting. What a pity that she could not have met him while occupying her proper sphere, dressed in her favorite pale green muslin with flounces and the wide pink sash that set off her creamy and rose-tinted complexion so well. Would he like her hair if it were properly displayed, the curls drawn up into a fashionable Grecian knot and secured with a bandeau of silk flowers and pearls? Would he admire a pair of pink satin slippers on her dainty feet?

She banished such wayward thoughts. Her first duty to herself and her relatives and friends was to reach the safe haven of her cousin's house.

She felt a sharp stab of remorse. Would Miss Anne Sheffield, her dear governess-companion, suffer for permitting her charge to abscond? Before leaving she had tried to write to Anne, who for nine years had all but taken the place of a mother to her, but in the end she had left only brief notes for Edwin and her guardian. She had believed that she would be in a position to send them details of her whereabouts within a few hours. She had not expected to be stranded like this.

She had realized almost from the first that this whole adventure was hazardous and exceedingly improper. But what else could she have done? And if she returned, they would only go on with their plans.

No one had meant to be unkind to her. They had simply smiled indulgently at her protests, telling her that all young women felt fluttery at the idea of marriage and that once wed she would laugh at her fears. They had continued to make their arrangements until she felt as if she was about to be smothered in a landslide. All her arguments were brushed aside as if she were a child whose every movement must be guided and ordered. That, she had discovered, was exactly how they regarded her.

Lady Fothergill, Edwin's mother, had gently pointed out that it was not as if they had chosen a stranger for her. No, indeed. Edwin was as well known to her as if he had been a brother.

When Sophia said wildly that that was probably the trouble, that he was *indeed* as a brother to her, they shook their heads and smiled and made comments about marriage being a union between men and women of similar breeding and interests, and elders knowing best. Such tender, loving tyranny was impossible to fight.

Sir Edwin Fothergill's estate marched with hers and plans, all complete and tidy, had been evolved for them years before. They had simply been brought forward. Edwin and Sophia would marry and she would take up residence with Edwin's widowed mother and together they would await the completion of his education at Oxford University.

She and Edwin had been reared together, were taught side by side in the schoolroom of Edwin's large house, and when an epidemic of malignant fever had carried off his father and both her parents, had wept together and shared the devotion of his mother. Sophia felt a stab of remorse at the way she was treating a lady who had shown her nothing but kindness, but she knew she could never marry Edwin. For whatever reason her instincts recoiled from the idea. And besides, she wanted a little fun, a little romance in her life before she settled into marriage, with its inevitable motherhood.

She looked over at the man again and once more he seemed to feel her eyes upon him and looked up, this time frowning a little, though whether at her or his thoughts she had no means of guessing. She resolved to keep her gaze down.

The landlady bustled in carrying a covered dish, followed by a maid with a tray of more dishes, and a pot boy bearing ale.

The man rose, stretched, seated himself at the table, and the landlady removed a cover to release a rich savoury smell. "Your broiled beef steaks, my lord. Put the vegetables on the table, girl," she snapped to the maid. "There's turnips and onions, and some roasted potatoes, my lord, and I ventured to bring broccoli with eggs, a specialty of my own, and I've a capon and a fine turbot with oysters in the kitchen if you should want them. I've just made an apple pie and there's a Hanover cake if your lordship's taste runs to sweet things. My husband is bringing bottles of hock and port from the cellar."

"I'll just take the ale and some cheese to finish," said

his lordship, his crisp tones permitting no argument, "but I daresay the young woman would enjoy a slice of pie, or a piece of cake. Women like sweets. What say you, girl? Is your appetite satisfied?"

What was there about this man that so rasped Sophia's nerves? Possibly the realization that he could read her so clearly. She had finished the pork pie and her stomach still felt empty. She wondered if he had heard it gurgle. Well, what matter? They'd not meet again.

"I'd like a bit o' pie," she said, in her assumed rough tones, "an' I wouldn't mind tasting the Hanover cake. My c—" she stopped herself just in time from referring to her cook— ". . . cousin makes a very nice Hanover cake."

The landlady glowered at her, shooed the servants away, poured his lordship a mug of foaming ale, heaped a dish with beef, and left, turning in the doorway to bestow a benevolent smile on the impervious nobleman and a scowl on Sophia.

Scents of apples and cloves wafted from the pie and the cake smelled deliciously of almonds. The little maid who brought them handed her a dish of cream. "Take some and I'll top it up with milk, dearie. She'll never miss it." She giggled and the man paused in the act of conveying a piece of beef to his mouth to survey the two girls.

Then Sophia and the man were alone. They chewed in silence for a while. Sophia finished all the food and drink and sat on, wondering what to do next, wishing she did not have to leave the warmth of the inn for the perilous open road. The man was still studying his book which he had propped against the ale jug.

He spoke suddenly. "Have you eaten your fill?"

"Yes, thank you, sir."

"Good."

Sophia felt it incumbent upon her to show a little interest in the charitable lord. Her governess-companion had instructed her that gentlemen liked to be thought interesting to females, even when they were exceedingly dull. In fact, especially then. "Have you far to travel, sir?"

To her intense annoyance the man slid his long white

fingers down a black ribbon until they reached an eyeglass which rendered his eye huge as he stared at her coolly. "If I had surmised that my intervention on your behalf would provoke vulgar curiosity, you may be sure I should have allowed you to go hungry."

Sophia swallowed her spleen. She hoped she might one day meet this boorish fellow on common ground. She'd teach him to behave so superciliously. "I was just showin' a bit of interest, my lord."

"Indeed!" His lordship cut himself a piece of cheese. "Have you come far?" His strong voice demanded a reply.

"From Exeter in Devon. I'm on my way to London."

"You would appear to have strayed somewhat from your path."

This was an irrefutable fact. Sophia discarded all the explanations that crowded into her mind and, unable to tell the truth, said nothing at all.

The sudden decision of Mr. Plerivale, her guardian, to see her married at once to Sir Edwin Fothergill had been inspired by the way she and Edwin had bickered their way through his vacation last summer from Oxford and the recent Christmas festivities. Edwin was willing to marry at once in spite of their arguments and quarrels. He had accepted the explanation that they arose from a too-long betrothal and would cease upon marriage.

Lady Fothergill had confided to Mr. Plerivale, "Only let them be properly united and the animosity will cease as if by magic. Within a year they will probably have set up their nursery and Sophia will have more than enough to occupy her."

Mr. Plerivale had lived in Sophia's house for twelve years, tending her estate, the only one left to her after three dedicated and sadly unskilled gamesters in a row had lost all the other family properties. Clavering Hall and its farms and lands needed constant supervision and improvement to bring in a sufficient income for the daughter of an earl. Now a comfortable fortune had been amassed and Mr. Plerivale saw the union as ideal. Sophia would have a well-born, wealthy husband; Edwin would have an equally well-born, accomplished, handsome wife; Lady Fothergill would get the genteel daughter-in-law and the grand-children she longed for, and she and Edwin would see to it that Sophia's land was kept productive, while he could return to his extensive library and erudite pursuits in peace. What could be better?

Sophia sympathized with Mr. Plerivale even as she argued with him. "Dear Guardian, you may return home. I am seventeen, no longer a child, and I have Miss Sheffield to take care of me. You've always said she's a woman of sound sense and great reason."

"And I hope she'll consent to remain as your loyal companion after your wedding," said Mr. Plerivale, his pale blue eyes lighted by a kindly smile. "But she can never be the same comfort and protector to you as a husband. No, Sophia, my dear, I am resolved that the wedding must take place."

Lady Fothergill said, "How fortunate that you have that sweet new white muslin, Sophia. It will look enchanting with a silver shawl and your pearls, and Edwin can wear his pale gray velvet coat and his buckskin knee breeches. You'll make a splendid couple." Lady Fothergill's eyes had misted over with sentimental tears. "If only Edwin's dear papa and your dear parents were alive to see this day. You know the joining of our two houses in this way was their fondest wish, do you not, Sophia?"

As Sophia had been barely five years old at the time of their deaths, she felt she could scarcely be expected to understand anything of the sort. In her bedchamber she paced the floor, bursting with futile fury. Miss Sheffield had expressed no opinion on the matter, but even had she sympathized with her she would not have felt it proper to argue with Mr. Plerivale or Lady Fothergill.

No one seemed to realize that Sophia's life, which had been so tranquil and happy in the gentle pursuits of the countryside—picnics, exploring outings, parties, amateur theatricals—was to be ruined. It was useless for them to tell her that things wouldn't change. Having a husband cut her off instantly from unmarried friends. And what about her first Season in London? Her future mother-in-law assured her that she would be presented as a married lady and that was just as exciting.

It could not possibly be! All her female acquaintance looked forward to their come-out. They talked and giggled about the gentlemen with whom they would flirt, whose hearts they would break at the assemblies, the balls, the card parties. They sighed for the opportunity to wander through Vauxhall Gardens beneath lamplit trees, listening to music, taking supper, showing off their gowns and hair styles, teasing beaux, their eyes full of laughter over their fluttering fans. They enthused about the theaters and the famous players they would see.

Now she would perhaps have to wait until Edwin left Oxford. Two whole years before she tasted the joys of society.

Her friends would have such gay times in London while she would rusticate in the country. Above all, she longed for the theater. Amateur dramatics were her favorite recreation and she was always given a good part because of her acting ability. Must it all cease? Sophia swept back and forth in her room until her anger and frustration grew quite unmanageable. She decided to run away. Not in any stupid way so that she'd be stranded on the road like a bird-witted heroine in a novel, but in a properly planned and ordered manner that would permit her to arrive at the door of her distant elderly cousin Pamela, Lady Stoneyhurst. Her ladyship had quarreled years ago with her family, but she had entrée to the best houses, even to Carlton House, wherein dwelt George, Prince of Wales, Regent during his father's dreadful illness.

Cousin Pamela would most likely enjoy chaperoning her into society if by doing so she could annoy the relatives with whom she had been at outs for years. Sophia had congratulated herself on remembering to "borrow" this ghastly gown from a laundrymaid—large enough to allow for thick padding beneath her shift—leaving a pretty wool frock in its place, and had removed the fortunately heavy cloth cloak from the theatrical box. She was inordinately pleased with the skill in stage make-up that had enabled

her to change her perfect, fair skin to an unbecoming
sallowness. She darkened her brows and walked, when
observed, with a slight shuffle, her shoulders bent. She had
made her way on foot and by carrier's cart to Exeter where
she could catch the London coach.

The horses were already being whipped up when she
arrived and it was a shock to discover she should have
booked herself a place, but she was lucky enough to be
offered the seat of someone who had not turned up. The
fare would leave her with a frighteningly small sum of
money and she had hesitated while the guard tutted
impatiently, and the driver bellowed a request to be
h'informed what was a'olding up the stage which was
bound to arrive late in this wicked weather, but he for one
wasn't goin' to wait for no one, king nor commoner.
Sophia half-leapt, was half-pushed by an ostler up the
steps and into the coach where she found a small space
between a bony cleric and a fat merchant's wife. Her small
valise lay on her knees. She had been unable to carry much
with her, but Cousin Pamela was rich enough to buy her all
she needed and Mr. Plerivale would surely send on her
gowns and allowance when he saw how determined she was
to reject Edwin. The coachman shouted instructions, the
guard blew a fanfare, the horses' hooves struck sparks
from the ice-cold cobbles, their heated breath steamed into
the chill air, and the heavy coach rattled out of the Half
Moon Inn yard.

What a good thing she had made herself look so
unattractive. A young gentleman seated opposite took one
glance at her, grimaced slightly, and thereafter ignored
her.

She was dismayed when she discovered that the coach
had engaged to take her only to Lobcombe Corner, where
two folk had booked their seats, and she had to get out
near a sign post that informed travelers that it was seventy-
two miles to London.

She did not have enough money to try another coach. If
only she had not frittered away her generous pin money.
Just a few shillings more and she could have been safe on
another coach.

Sophia recalled that his lordship had asked her a question. "What did you say?" she inquired. "I've forgot."

His lordship had given up waiting for an answer and was marking his map.

"What? Oh, er, yes, I remarked that you are out of your way."

"That's true," agreed Sophia, thinking up and discarding a variety of excuses. After she had been deposited on the highway she had turned her face to London. Ice and drifting snow had rendered the roads dangerous and she had fought her way forward, thankful that the active life ordered by Miss Sheffield had given her good health and robust endurance. She had spent two miserable nights in poor quality inns, wrapped in her cloak, partly for extra warmth, partly as protection against the bugs and flea-ridden mattresses, depleting her money even more. The snow often obliterated the road, rendering it indistinguishable from a cart track in places and some time during the afternoon she had mistaken her way and struggled two miles off the post road to this inn.

As she passed through a stand of close-packed trees, their frost-laden branches clattering in the icy breeze, increasing the darkness caused by lowering clouds that threatened more snow, she had been terrified when a number of ill-clad youths surrounded her.

They had opened her small valise and extracted her amber necklace and earrings and thrown her other possessions into the woods. Then they had surged off, laughing, into the gloom, leaving Sophia, lips pressed tight with anger and a determination not to weep, to pick up what she could find.

Now that hunger had ceased to dominate her, she was able to give her full attention to her predicament. It was past six o'clock. She wondered if the landlady would give her a bed in return for work, but decided it would be useless to ask a favor of such an unpleasant woman. She must make her way back to the post road and offer her services at inns along the way. London was now much nearer than her Devon home and eventually she would arrive at Lady Pamela's Grosvenor Street town house. All she needed were courage and resolution.

The man watched her for a moment, then shrugged and picked up a newspaper which he continued to peruse as Sophia put on her cloak and drew the hood over her head. She stopped by his table. "Sir, thank you for your help. I was very hungry."

He nodded and made an inarticulate sound without looking up.

Sophia, at a loss to know how to deal with a gentleman who remained seated in her presence, could not think of a way to terminate the scene.

The man glanced at her, then slid two fingers into his pocket and pulled out a half sovereign. "I am not usually so lax. You must excuse it. My mind is running on other matters. Take this. It'll make certain that you eat on your journey."

His manner was dismissive and Sophia wanted to fling the money into his indifferent face, but her newborn sense of self-protection came to her aid. And she had a small, gleeful moment when she congratulated herself on the excellence of her disguise.

She curtsied her thanks. As she reached the door the man spoke again. "I suppose you haven't come across a very pretty young lady with gold curls, traveling with as addlepated an elderly woman as it has ever been my misfortune to encounter."

Sophia shook her head.

The man's eyes swept over her. "No, I don't suppose you would frequent the same inns. Well, if you happen to see her—" He rose and walked across to her. "Take my card. If you *should* meet with them, I would be vastly obliged if you would send word to my house in Berkeley Square. Oh, but I daresay you cannot read or write.

"Yes, I can, sir."

"Good. If you discover their whereabouts for me, you'll be well rewarded."

Sophia glanced at the card and curtsied again. She kept her eyes down, tucked the card into her pocket, and for the first part of her walk was occupied with the knowledge that she had chanced upon Hugo, Viscount Ramsey, noted for his dissolute behavior. Prudent mamas warned their daughters never to become entangled with him unless it should be within the sanctity of an approved marriage.

Sophia had envisaged the viscount as an elderly painted rake, not a powerful, strikingly impressive man of about thirty. Of course, Lord Ramsey could not be held to have any attraction for a gently reared young lady, but he was decidedly not the licentious old roué that she and her friends had sometimes giggled about. And he had made no attempt to molest her. She had forgotten for a moment her sallow skin and her hideous gown. When she did recall them, she wondered just what would have happened had she appeared in her usual beauty, and the thought sent a regrettably excited shiver through her.

Two

Viscount Ramsey stared at the closed door for a few moments after the maid had left, wondering why she thought fit to cover her face with *pomade à baton*, make her brows heavy with some dark substance, and drag back her hair beneath a dreadful cap, leaving a fine scar visible almost on the hairline. Possibly she was pimpled and pock-marked and scraggy-haired. Women! Well it would be scarce worth her trouble to try to make herself attractive when she had such a shambling gait and ungracious manners.

He put her out of his mind without difficulty and finished his meal, damning the rogue who had sent him to this inn by swearing he had seen the two ladies he described enter it. The scoundrel had pocketed the two shillings reward with a respectful touch of his hat, and all the time he had been lying. When he found Charlotte she would feel the length of his tongue. Not that it would make any difference to her. He was weary of rescuing his sister from one predicament after another, all caused by her remarkable beauty, her unremarkable intelligence, and her predilection for imagining herself crazily in love with some man or other who was always so damned unsuitable.

The viscount swore that before the end of the Season he would marry her off to the first personable suitor who presented himself and be relieved forever of having to sort out her amatory tangles. God knew, there were enough gentlemen swearing eternal devotion to her. They swarmed like bees around flowers whenever the Honorable Miss Charlotte Ramsey appeared. There need be no concern over money; to be well-born was enough, for Charlotte was an heiress in her own right.

The coming Season was to be her first, and he vowed it would be her last as his responsibility. He would get her wed if he had to carry her to the altar in a sack over his shoulder, so he would be free to follow his own pursuits.

Viscount Ramsey had no illusions about himself. He knew that the dowagers called him selfish and rackety, a positive rakehell, and warned their pretty little virgin charges against him. He grinned humorlessly. Just let him offer marriage to one and she would find herself in church as soon as her guardians could get her there. What made them all so vitriolic was the fact that he preferred to have women of a certain class in keeping and refused to bestow his attentions and his large fortune on any of the worthy, pure young ladies paraded Season after Season in the Marriage Mart.

The viscount paid his shot, buttoned up his many-caped long coat, pulled on his gloves, and rammed his beaver hat on his head. He was in no mood to remain at this putrid inn and even in the present atrocious conditions, he preferred to keep his precious pair of horses moving rather than leave them stabled in the draughty outhouse. His progress would be even slower now the light was so poor. His high-bred cattle must pick their own cautious way along the execrable track.

His small tiger-groom, his long coat swirling around his ankles, muffled to the ears in a scarf, and his hat jammed down so far it reached his collar, settled himself in the rear seat and folded his arms. His private opinion was that the viscount was mad to risk his horses for a woman, even his beautiful sister, but he would have sat as imperturbably if his beloved master had been driving into hell itself. Ever since he had been rescued from a brutal chimney sweep, he had regarded the viscount as his god.

The cold was biting and a few snow flakes were beginning to float down and melt on the horses backs. They tossed their heads, flinging steam into the air, peevish at being kept from a warm stable and good food and Jemmy grinned behind his scarf at the language which emanated from the straight-backed man in front.

Lord Ramsey controlled his horses on a gentle rein, still thinking of his sister. He had no fears for her physical safety, surrounded as she was by trustworthy servants. It was her reputation he was out to guard. Dainty hooves stepped as carefully as a lady in high-heeled shoes between ruts, and the curricle moved slowly forward.

Was ever a man so unfortunate in his female relatives? wondered the viscount morosely? His mother had not seen fit to inform him that Charlotte's trusted governess-companion—her sixth, or was it seventh?—whom he had picked a year ago from a dozen applicants, had left to marry her long-time sweetheart. And what in heaven's name had prompted Lady Ramsey to engage a bird-witted rattle like Miss Thomasina Hill as female companion for her equally bird-witted daughter?

It would have been the easiest thing to do at the time, reflected the viscount, his mouth set in grim lines. He had just returned from an exhausting visit to Charlotte's Scottish estate, left her by a distant cousin, where he had settled quarrels between the villagers and the gamekeepers to everyone's satisfaction. Before leaving, he had escorted his sister on a journey to visit an extremely conformable family in the country where a party of young people had gathered. Safe enough, Hugh had assumed. He should have known better. Where Charlotte was concerned nothing could be taken for granted.

Lady Ramsey had retired to her bed the moment she received her daughter's tear-stained letter apprising her of her intention to return home instantly, her heart having

been broken forever by her discovery that her latest
favored beau wore a wig to cover his balding head. "And
he but four and twenty," ran the letter, "and wigs not in
fashion for ever so long. We were frolicking outside and it
came off when I knocked off his hat with a snowball. The
wind took it and he chased after it. Everyone knew I
enjoyed his attentions and I feel so mortified I could die.
How can I care for a man who has made me a tease of our
whole party?"

The short time of peace among his friends that the
viscount had promised himself before the new Season
began was destroyed. He had set off at once to scour the
post road on which his sister would travel home. Pray God
she actually was returning home. By now she could have
fallen in love with someone else, in which case her behavior
might grow even more erratic. He must discover
Charlotte's whereabouts before even a whiff of scandal
could leak out. Even the presence of Miss Hill, her
personal maid, their chief coachman, the head footman,
and two trusted postillions would not be enough to prevent
tongues wagging were it ever to be learned that such an
irresponsible girl as Charlotte Ramsey had spent whole
days and nights abroad without a member of her family in
attendance. She would find herself in society but not
completely of it. A woman could never be too careful
where her reputation was concerned, and most servants
enjoyed tittle-tattling, vying one with another as to whose
family was most interesting.

Lady Ramsey would, she had conceded with a resigned
sigh, accompany her daughter into society—"As far as my
health permits, you comprehend"—but her chief
preoccupation would continue to be the diagnosis and cure
of her many indisposition. She would never lack for these
since several physicians were kept busy supplying her with
new ones. She would, she explained languidly, do her best,
but Hugo must be on hand to help her.

The viscount had considered various female relatives
who might assist his mother and decided that not one of
them was to be trusted in the matter of bringing order to
Charlotte's wayward life. The duty rested upon him to

guard her from the worthless fortune-hunters who would be lured by her wealth.

The curricle lurched in and out of frozen cart tracks and potholes, the snow flakes grew larger and the cold more intense, and Jemmy bared an ear to hear with greater clarity as his master's language grew more choice.

So absorbed did the viscount become in his acerbic musings that he uncharacteristically lost his concentration and his wheeler, startled by the swoop of a white owl, balked and slid on a patch of ice, dragging its partner into a deep pothole and sending the light curricle veering into a ditch with an unpleasant sound of splintering wood.

The viscount and his greem were fully engaged in calming the excited cattle, his lordship's language reaching new transports of invention while Jemmy inwardly deplored the whole female sex.

Caspar, the wheeler, was lamed and the curricle was partly blocking the road. Although it was unlikely that anyone would be mad enough to attempt to drive or ride fast along this apology for a highway, Lord Ramsey could not risk someone's being seriously injured by a collision in the dark with his smashed vehicle. He removed the harness.

"Keep the lantern, Jemmy, and remain alert. I'll lead Caspar and send help as soon as I can. I shall be at the nearest post house."

The viscount rode his sound horse bare-back at Caspar's slow pace. He must find a warm stable where the horse's injury could be treated and where he could be left in safety. He would then have to hire a coach to continue his journey, though there could be nothing to compare with his own made-to-order curricle. He'd not even looked at the damage to its elegant frame. For all he knew it might be beyond repair. What dire sin had he committed to be burdened with a pack of idiotic females?

He arrived back on the post road and, after a mile at less than walking pace during which he removed his greatcoat to cover Caspar, he arrived at a posting inn. The ostlers ran out when he called and passed admiring comments on a gentleman who was prepared to freeze for the welfare of

his cattle and who actually knew how to prepare a poultice
and apply it to an injury that proved thankfully minor. A
postboy was sent to engage the help of a local farmer's
work horses to deal with the damaged curricle.

Caspar and his companion were fed and watered and
bedded down and Lord Ramsey was welcomed into the
warmth of the kitchen where he swallowed two glasses of
spiced mulled wine to complete his thaw. The necessity for
speed was gone. He had seen Charlotte's horses munching
contentedly in the big stable, and a look into the coach
house had revealed the two traveling coaches required for
herself and her retinue.

He glanced into the common bar where her two
postillions and a senior footman in the Ramsey livery were
downing draughts of ale, while William Noakes, head
coachman of many years to the Ramseys, sat in a chimney
seat smoking his pipe, florid-faced and clearly replete after
a meal.

The viscount walked back along the stone-flagged
corridor, preceded by the innkeeper who had instantly
recognized his client's worth and was explaining that he
could offer him a very good bedchamber, though not the
absolute best as a lady had arrived earlier and taken it, and
his other rooms were full of travelers on this dreadfully
cold night, though a fire had already been lighted in his
lordship's room and his groom, when he arrived, could
have a bed in the kitchen, and the horses would be looked
after with all the care bestowed upon newborn babes.

Lord Ramsey heard little of the diatribe. There was a
flurry of rustling skirts and a woman who had been
peeping into the dimness of the passage began to run
lightly up the stairs. She had not made her escape quickly
enough.

The viscount was galvanized into action. Watched by a
scandalized innkeeper, he chased after her. "Charlotte!
Come back! I know it's you."

A couple of bedchamber doors opened and faces peered
out curiously. The viscount stopped running and shouting,
and his mouth set in grim lines. By God, not in any one of

his many amorous adventures had he been detected in such grossly juvenile behavior. He gave the watchers a glare that made them withdraw quickly and walked to the door that had just been slammed. He knocked. There was no reply, but he heard whispers.

He put his face close to the keyhole, conscious of the people who were undoubtedly listening, and said in as beguiling a tone as he could manage, "Charlotte, my dear, pray open the door. I want to talk to you."

"You'll not be at outs with me?" His sister's voice was quavery and an elderly gentleman, his nightcap askew as he pressed his ear to his bedchamber door, shook his head. "Young folks today," he muttered, returning to his bed.

"Such unseemly goin's on," voiced a female who had followed the viscount up the stairs. His lordship turned and stared hard at her and she entered her room hastily.

"Do I have to remain knocking on your door all night?" demanded the viscount.

"You *are* at outs with me! You sound dreadfully cross. I thought I recognized your voice in the yard and crept down to make sure. Do go to bed, Hugo. They'll find you a room. The landlady is ever so nice and kind."

"*Will you open this damned door?*" demanded the viscount through his teeth.

There was a brief lull during which all movement in Charlotte's bedchamber was suspended, then the door opened and his sister stood framed for a moment. Even after weeping she still looked lovely, she being one of the rare and fortunate females whom distress frequently caused to appear more fragile and beautiful. Her small lace cap was perched above glossy golden curls, her deep blue eyes with their long lashes beneath delicate brows begged for sympathy. Her shapely figure was swathed in a white muslin wrapper.

Her brother bowed. "May I come in?" he asked, his voice as chill as the ice outside.

Charlotte stood back. The bedchamber looked like a rag shop. At least, it would have done if the clothes scattered around had not been so costly.

"What in God's name is your maid about?" asked the viscount harshly. "And where's that woman? Miss Hill? Are you hiding? Come out at once!"

A small thin woman dressed in brown, her gray hair pulled into a wispy knot, crept through an inner door. "I beg of you, don't scold, sir. Tell him, Charlotte. Pray, tell him. I was against this journey. Do, pray, tell him." Her voice quavered and her nose went red.

The viscount closed his eyes. He knew he was being unjust to feel hostility to this lachrymose female and he answered in a voice of controlled calm, "You have no need to tell me so, ma'am. I am well aware of my sister's *penchant* for falling head first into one imbroglio after another."

"But truly, she's such a sweet innocent . . ." Miss Hill's voice quavered to a stop at a glance from the viscount.

Charlotte pouted her soft lips and slumped into an easy chair by the fire, the only chair not concealed by clothes. The viscount swept a jumble of slippers, shawls, and lacy garments to the floor and sat opposite her.

"My best shawl," shrieked Charlotte. "It'll get torn."

"Perhaps your maid, madam—"

Miss Hill gave a small wail and held a phial of hartshorn to her pointed nose, and Charlotte said, "Kate's gone. It's not our fault that she fell in love with the pot boy at the inn where we spent last night and decided to elope. When I woke this morning, she was gone back to him." Her voice softened, a smile curved her delectable lips, and her blue eyes became misty. "I have to admit, Hugo, that I am touched by the romance. The pot boy was uncommon handsome. I remarked so at the time, did I not, Miss Hill, and you said—"

The viscount breathed heavily. "Did she create this chaos before she fell victim to her touching romance?"

"What? Oh, no, Miss Hill and I have been looking for things. I did so want to wear my blue merino gown with the pale yellow knots of ribbon tomorrow. It is bad enough having to put on such thick clothes in this dreadful weather, but at least it will look well beneath my dark blue cashmere pelisse—it reaches to my ankles, you know, so *à la mode*—and I purchased a sweetly pretty velvet hat to match.''

Charlotte leaned forward to scrabble about in a large portmanteau. ''I have ribbons here of exact matching shades. If I could but find them, I could show you . . .''

She looked up, gauged her brother's mounting fury, and said quickly, ''Oh, I collect you do not wish to see the ribbons. Don't worry about the room. It will soon be cleared because I have only this past hour engaged a new maid and she will bring the room to rights—and she is cunning with her needle, too. I know she will make an excellent maid because—''

''A new maid? Within the past hour? Here?''

''Come down from your high ropes, Hugo. I am persuaded that she is respectable.''

His lordship held out his hand and asked with deceptive calm, ''May I see her references?''

''That is not possible because the poor soul has lost them. She is not gowned like a lady's maid, I must confess, so I set her a little test. You know my sweet yellow satin opera hood—oh, well, I collect that you do not—it got torn and she mended it so that no one could ever tell—''

''Where is she? Is there another room through there?''

''No, it is a closet, but huge. Big enough to hold a truckle bed that the landlord is going to send up and Susan will lie there tonight while Miss Hill shares my bed. I do hope somewhere may be found for you, brother.''

''Do not disturb yourself on that score, madam.''

Charlotte pouted in a way guaranteed to send her many male admirers into frenzies of apologies, but which had no effect on her brother. There were sounds from behind the closet door indicative of silver tissue being folded.

''Is one permitted to view this paragon?'' asked the viscount. ''She seems reluctant to appear.''

''Come out, Susan,'' called Charlotte.

The sounds stopped abruptly, there was a brief silence, then the maid walked into the room.

''You!'' exclaimed the viscount. He turned to his sister. ''I met this female earlier under the most inauspicious circumstances. She's little more than a vagrant.''

Lady Sophia pressed her lips together, buttoning up her fury at the insults. A half-formed impulse to confide in Charlotte and ask for assistance died. She could not chance her good name with such a goose and most likely her autocratic brother would consider the tale to be well worth repeating to his cronies. Charlotte rose to stand by her. "Dear Susan arrived at the inn and heard me asking for help from the innkeeper, but the chambermaid was too busy and there were only two greasy skivvies in the kitchen. Susan offered her assistance and truly, Hugo, she is so good. Pray do not be angry with me. She will produce references. You will, won't you, Susan?"

Lady Sophia nodded, feeling this to be less of an untruth than speech.

Lord Ramsey was not satisfied. "Where is your luggage? Most domestics seem to travel with trunks big enough to live in."

Sophia pointed to her small valise.

"Is that all? And why don't you carry your precious references with you—if, that is, you ever had any."

"When my belongings were thrown into deep snow when I was robbed, my lord, the ink ran. I must write for new references."

The viscount stared at her. "How am I to trust you? What of your promise that you would send word if you found my sister?"

Charlotte turned huge, shocked eyes on her new maid. "Susan, you didn't!"

"I saw no reason not to, Miss Charlotte," replied Sophia. "I hadn't met you then and didn't know how sternly you're treated by your—er—that's to say . . ."

"I suppose my sister has told you a dozen Banbury stories concerning her wicked brother who threatens her with bread and water if she disobeys—"

"Oh, Hugo, I didn't," cried Charlotte.

"Did you not? You amaze me."

"You won't send Susan away, will you, Hugo? I cannot manage without help."

"That is all too revoltingly obvious. Well, she may

remain with you tonight at least. Tomorrow, we set out for London.''

"That's where Susan wants to go. Surely she can accompany us. It's above sixty miles further, you know.''

The viscount bowed his acknowledgment of the information, his mouth set, his eyes glittering.

"And poor dear Susan has no money at all. She was robbed by footpads and *dreadfully* abused—''

"Were you?'' asked the viscount with spurious composure. "You made no mention of it before.'' He raised his eyeglass and peered at Sophia. "How were you abused?''

"Where did you meet?'' inquired Charlotte interestedly. "How fascinating it all is. Pray tell me.''

"Oh, God! Charlotte, will you keep silent,'' begged the viscount, "if only for a moment.''

Charlotte shrugged and frowned. "It is only natural for me to be interested.''

"I met Susan in an inn earlier this evening. She left shortly before me.''

"*Shortly* before you?'' cried Charlotte. "Where have you been these past hours?''

The viscount's breathing grew heavy. "One of my horses is lamed. Jemmy is attending to the removal of my carriage from the highway and one can only pray he will find his way here. My new curricle is probably broken beyond redemption—''

"You didn't surely have an accident! And you such a famous whip. Whatever were you doing?''

Lord Ramsey spoke distinctly. "I was searching for you, my dear sister, after being misdirected by a son of Satan over one of the worst roads it has been my misfortune to meet to an unspeakable hostelry. There was a barn owl—''

He stopped. Three pairs of eyes were regarding him. Miss Hill's, damp and pale blue, were expressionless as if years of weeping had washed out their power to express emotion. His sister's, a deep, cornflower blue, were opened wide in wonderment.

It was the third pair that gave him a shock. It was not so

much that Susan's hazel eyes were unexpectedly large, luminous, and undeniably beautiful, but that they held an expression of almost wicked amusement.

Three

Sophia sat in a corner of the well-sprung traveling carriage with her back to the horses. Her feet were cozy against a warm brick; a fur travel robe lay over her knees. The viscount had asked for these comforts and Sophia had accepted them as her due. She realized her behavior had not been that expected from a humble domestic when Miss Hill, her eyes filled with grateful tears, babbled an endless story of past employers who had shown her no such consideration. Sophia immediately joined her thanks to the elderly companion's and tried to ignore the skeptical look given her by Lord Ramsey.

She kept her eyes firmly toward the window, half afraid to look at the viscount who sat opposite her. Last night she had been foolish to reveal her amusement. She was under no illusion that his lordship had not interpreted her emotion correctly. Those dark eyes were far too searching, his mind far too quick to be deceived.

Charlotte had insisted that her new maid travel in the coach with her. "I might at any time feel the need of succor," she insisted. "My nerves are never of the strongest and, as you know, dear Hugo, I get so sick if the coach sways a lot and it must do when the roads are so hard with ice."

The viscount's heavy brows had climbed high. "Your nerves, my dear, are about as fragile as my boots. However, I admit that you are a poor traveler and if you feel the need of Susan's assistance, I shall not argue."

Sophia had counted on traveling with the servants and was dismayed by Charlotte's insistence when she discovered that Lord Ramsey, unable to find a saddle to fit exactly his uninjured horse, had tethered him to the leading coach while he joined his sister.

Sophia did not wonder at Lord Ramsey's continued irritation. No doubt he had had to cancel several interesting engagements of the kind indulged in by gentlemen of fortune and breeding to pursue Charlotte, his new curricle had been pronounced irreparable, his horse was lamed and had to be left behind in Jemmy's care until he was fit to be ridden home, and another groom would need to travel to the inn with a saddle.

Charlotte jumped when her brother made a sound. She said rapidly to her new maid, "Susan, pray hand me the hartshorn. I vow I begin to feel queasy. I think I should not have eaten so heartily at breakfast."

She realized as she began to speak that the viscount had merely given way to a discreet yawn. He turned a sardonic gaze upon her. "I agree, Charlotte. And I must confess to a feeling of surprise that one so lately crossed in love could actually consume three large slices of ham, two eggs, three pieces of toast and conserve, and two pears."

"Oh, don't mention food!" begged Charlotte. "Good heavens! I had no idea you watched me so closely."

"Only to ascertain that your health has not suffered beneath the recent cruel blows of fate."

"My dearest brother cares so well for me," said Charlotte, her voice taking on a sarcastic note. "Does he not, Susan?"

Sophia was obliged to look round. "How comforting that must be," she said, and was dismayed to hear that her voice was almost as acerbic as the viscount's. She must keep a better guard on herself. Last night she had scurried about tidying Charlotte's bedchamber, had cossetted poor Miss Hill who now shared her seat with backs to the horses, a handkerchief soaked in lavender pressed to her forehead, and generally busied herself too thoroughly to give an opportunity to Lord Ramsey to ask her more questions.

But he was not a man to give up easily and this morning he had demanded once again to know why she traveled with only a valise.

"My employer is to forward my trunk when I have found a new position—sir!" she added hastily.

"She must be an unusually kind person."

"Who?"

"Your late employer. I take it you were employed by a female since you have proclaimed yourself to be a lady's maid."

"Ah, yes, sir."

"You dress so simply that one could take you for—for what, I wonder? All the lady's maids I have seen have been gowned as well as their mistresses. Some even better, and often to far greater effect."

"Indeed, sir. I decided to wear these rather unbecoming garments to save myself from—from—"

"From what?" inquired the viscount in silky tones.

"From rapacious gentlemen, of course," said Sophia.

The viscount looked her up and down. "I see. Have you had much to do with rapacious gentlemen, Susan?"

"One must always be on one's guard, sir."

"A tactful and somewhat evasive answer. I look forward to seeing you transformed when we reach London."

At Sophia's inquiring look he said gently, "When your trunk arrives, or when my sister outfits you in something pretty. That is, of course, if—I beg your pardon, when— your references prove satisfactory."

"For pity's sake, Hugo, do not bait her," said Charlotte pettishly. "As soon as we arrive in Berkeley Square I shall send out for muslins and ribbons. You sew so well, Susan, and you will soon have something pretty to wear."

"Thank you, ma'am."

"And you can write at the next inn to your former employers asking for a reference," said the viscount.

Sophia was feeling increasingly uncomfortable and worried. She had thought the offer of a position and a passage to London a gift from God. She was still grateful to the ingenuous Charlotte, but guilt and Lord Ramsey's cutting questions threatened to swamp her fragile calm.

And it was not only guilt that tormented her. The previous evening after she had retired to her truckle bed in the closet Lord Ramsey had visited his sister and sent Miss Hill to join the maid for a while.

At first the viscount's tones had been kept so low the two women could hear only a murmur. But when Charlotte began to protest and weep loudly, Lord Ramsey had spoken over her sobs. Miss Hill, crouching on a small stool, instantly covered her ears, but Sophia was mesmerized by his reproaches, which concerned his condemnation of Charlotte's action in absconding from her hostess.

"What will the other guests make of it?" he demanded. "And just how did you escape Mrs. Fairley's vigilance?"

Charlotte's sobs and protestations grew louder. "Everyone went on a visit to a neighboring estate. I said I was not well and would rest. She almost canceled the outing because she did not wish to leave me and would not allow the others to go unchaperoned, but I insisted that Miss Hill and Kate would look after me. And Miss Hill has, though Kate ran away. But that was not my fault, and surely Mrs. Fairley will not gossip."

"Everyone gossips! And the other guests are of your generation. They will not be reticent. And what of the servants? Oh, for God's sake, cease that caterwauling, Charlotte. It does no good."

Charlotte's sobs decreased and the viscount's tones were once more low. The words that seeped through made Sophia squirm. "Your reputation . . . idle talk . . . ruined . . . honor . .. come-out . . . Almack's . . . great hostesses . . ." Then followed names of ladies she had only read about—Lady Jersey, Lady Sefton, Princess Esterhazy. Charlotte fell silent and her brother left her. Miss Hill climbed into bed beside her charge and Sophia heard her faint snores, but sleep was long in coming to her in spite of her weariness.

She knew she had blundered dreadfully in running from her home, but had tried to block out the truths her conscience was trying to tell her. Now her mind became crowded with horrors. She heard Miss Sheffield's firm, but gentle voice. "A woman's most precious possession is her honor, Sophia. Do not forget it. Never permit yourself to be placed in a position where *anyone* can cast aspersions upon you. Be you ever so innocent, loose tongues will make all appear lewd. Once a woman's honor is lost, she too is lost—as far as society is concerned. One day, my dearest Sophia, you will grace the *beau monde* with your lively manner, your pretty looks, and your charm, and you will enjoy your first London Season greatly because your decorous behavior will have gained respect from everyone of consequence.''

Sophia tossed and turned. If Lord Ramsey considered that Charlotte had damaged her reputation by running away accompanied by a whole retinue of servants, what would be said of a girl who had taken to the road alone and indulged in such an escapade as hers?

She recalled what she had heard of Lord Ramsey. Words such as *rakehell* and women of a certain order tumbled around her mind. Words which she and her companions knew to depict something reprehensible. There were whispered stories of once-respectable ladies who were utterly ruined, (though not by Lord Ramsey), and the ruin had everything to do with the lost purity of their persons by the breaking of a strict code of honor for ladies.

Good God, if ever her escapade came to the notice of anyone of influence she may as well return to the country and rusticate forever. Edwin or his mother—especially his mother—or, recalling Edwin's earnest attitude to life, maybe especially Edwin—would probably reject her. Perhaps they had already done so. She wondered what was happening at home. She prayed that Miss Sheffield and dear Guardian had managed to keep the affair secret. But the servants would know. Servants always knew. And servants tittle-tattled incessantly.

Just let her get to London and Susan, the maid, would disappear as if she had never been. She would escape and run to her cousin, Lady Stoneyhurst. Whatever her ladyship thought of her relatives and of her niece's behavior, she would surely put family honor above all and take her in.

Charlotte must never know the truth because she would

undoubtedly consider it extremely diverting and, however much she might protest her ability to keep a secret, she was clearly a confirmed rattle.

At the thought of what Charlotte would say if she knew who her maid really was, her sense of humor and appreciation of the ridiculous took over for just an instant when she wished she could share her masquerade with someone who would find her dual role amusing and clever.

She glanced across the carriage at the viscount and was dismayed to find he was watching her. Her tinge of humor died instantly. He looked grim. Ever since he had arrived at the inn, his whole demeanor had expressed profound disapproval of his sister and her new maid, though she had to admit that he was polite to the timorous Miss Hill. He showed a streak of chivalry there.

She was bound to meet him in society after her come-out, if she had one after this. His eyes were so searching; he had such an air of discernment it frightened her. But how would he ever guess that Lady Sophia Clavering, creamy-skinned, beautifully gowned, with a graceful gait and proud head with a crown of rich red-brown hair held high on a slender neck, could ever be associated with Susan, the dark-skinned maid with a scarred face, a clumsy walk, and stooping shoulders? Suppose he did find out. Would he talk about her? He might not. But he would despise her, and she was surprised tolearn that this troubled her.

Was she showing her thoughts on her face? A beau with a poetical turn of mind had likened her countenance to a summer sky, each passing expression to a soft white cloud that with its every shape gave welcome shade from the heat or blessed rain for the earth. He had presented her with a scroll on which he had written a poem expressing these sentiments in flowery language. It was surrounded by falling rose petals, with a picture of a field and a cloud in one corner all painted by himself in water colors. Miss Sheffield had laughed aloud at it, apologized for her rudeness, and laughed again, and Sophia had joined in. But she had been discreetly kind to the young gentleman and he had not been hurt. The glowering man opposite had nothing in common with him or with any man she had previously known.

He leaned forward. "I believe you saw something diverting, Susan. Pray share it with us. It will enliven our journey."

"Oh, yes," cried Charlotte, her voice betraying her relief that her stern brother seemed to be unbending a little.

Sophia was under no such illusion. The viscount's dark eyes taunted her and his mouth was set in a sardonic curl.

"It was only a thought," she said. "One of my—my brothers—, my friends—"

"Are you uncertain?" inquired Lord Ramsey, in spuriously sympathetic tones. "What a host of brothers and acquaintance you must have, Susan, to muddle them so."

Sophia would have liked very much to lean forward and land her hand on the side the viscount's head with a clump that would have wiped the smile from his lips.

" 'Twas a friend."

"So what amused you, dear Susan?" Poor Charlotte sounded hopeful that the disapproving atmosphere could be lifted a little.

Sophia's wits were in tumult. She searched desperately for an anecdote that could have been told by one rural to another and could come up with nothing.

"I've forgot."

His lordship's brows almost vanished beneath the brim of his beaver hat. "Good God, Susan! How dreadful for you to have such a shocking bad memory! I am no longer surprised that you can remember so little about your late employer. How inconvenient it all is."

"Yes! It is!"

It had suddenly dawned on Sophia that a man like Lord Ramsey would consider it beneath him to bait a humble maid. Did he suspect that she was nothing of the sort? Who did he think she was? Or what? Perhaps he believed her to be a criminal and would send for a constable as soon as they reached London. Perhaps the tale of an ill-fitting saddle and his insistence on journeying in the coach were but a ruse to keep a watch on her.

She looked out of the window, sudden unexpected tears threatening to break her brittle calm. How could she continue to tell so many lies? She disliked deceit. For the first time it occurred to her that play-acting had nothing to do with real life. Once she extricated herself from this dreadful scrape she would never confuse the two again. Perhaps she should make her escape at the next post house while they waited the few moments for a change of horses.

Sleet, interspersed with large hail stones, was lashing the coach. She had no money, and no other clothes. Healthy as she undoubtedly was, to try to walk to London in this could easily kill her. Would that matter? Death was supposed to be preferable to dishonor and, while she had not done anything fearful, who would believe her?

If her deception were ever known she would have to live carefully in the country for several years, engage in good works among the poor, and attend church diligently without ever allowing her mind to drift during the long sermons. After that, perhaps a worthy squire would offer for her. It all sounded exceedingly dismal, but better than death.

The weather worsened into thick snow, Charlotte began to feel ill, and the party was forced to put up at an inn for another night.

As soon as Charlotte and Miss Hill were installed in the best bedchamber the viscount called Sophia into their private parlor.

"Here are pen, paper, and ink, Susan. You may write your letter now."

"Letter?"

"Dear me, your memory really is unsound! Your references. You are going to send for at least one regarding the position you have just quit. I realize now that to expect you to recall any other previous employer would be too taxing for your brain."

"Yes. A reference." Sophia felt suddenly extremely weary. Tears threatened again. Normally she was not given to weeping, but she felt she could endure no more of this man's tormenting.

She said flatly, "My employer has gone to—to Jamaica and her address was lost in the snow when I was attacked."

"Jamaica? How interesting. I have estates there. Pray, what is her name? I may know her."

Sophia's despair was dissipated in fury. Her fingers itched to throw the inkpot over him. He was scarcely even pretending now to believe her.

She recalled a name she had heard in connection with Jamaica and took a deep breath. "Mrs. Wetherall," she declared as firmly as she could. "She was my latest employer. In Somerset."

"A charming lady. What happened to Belinda?"

Sophia looked at him blankly. "Belinda?"

"You did say the Somerset Wetheralls, did you not? Since your memory seems to have entirely deserted you at this point, owing possibly to the fright you sustained during the dastardly attack and robbery, I will remind you that Belinda is—or perhaps was—that lady's most devoted maid and has been since she was in the schoolroom. Pray, do not tell me that something dreadful has happened to Belinda."

"Nothing dreadful, sir. She—er—needed a rest so I was engaged for a short time."

"Ah, yes. I see. I must say I am astonished that a lady of over seventy summers would want to go jauntering off to Jamaica. What stout courage! I must congratulate her when she returns. Meanwhile, there is the vexing question of a reference. Can you recall *no one* else who can vouch for you?"

In desperation, Sophia blurted out in as clumsy a country accent as she could manage, "I can't at present. I believe you're right, sir. My memory's been affected by the attack."

"Then you must go to your bed soon. A good sleep may do wonders. In the morning perhaps you can exercise your mind and recall the name of another employer. You cannot have had many. You are not old enough."

Sophia curtsied and fled to Charlotte's bedchamber

to climb into a truckle bed. Again sleep eluded her. Some time in the early hours she decided that she must get away at once, only to discover that Lord Ramsey had taken the precaution of locking his sister's bedchamber door. She returned to her bed, which seemed to have acquired positively malevolent lumps, and dozed on and off until morning.

Sitting up in bed, she glanced at herself in the small looking glass she carried in her valise. She scarce needed maquillage. There were deep shadows beneath her eyes and there actually was a sallow tinge to her complexion. However, she smeared the dark cream over her face and dragged her hair back even more tightly beneath her cap before she called Charlotte and braced herself for a further verbal attack from the viscount. She served Charlotte and Miss Hill their food and then, at Charlotte's insistence, sat on the windowseat to eat, though her appetite was small.

When the viscount entered her nerves were quivering. He looked at her, then peered more closely, and Sophia thought with dread that in her haste she had used the *pomade à baton* carelessly. Oh, God, what would his lordship have to say now?

He continued to subject her to one of his most piercing looks. She kept her eyes on his, but hers fell first.

"Be quick, please, Charlotte," he said. "The snow has turned to rain, which will make quagmires of the road. We need all the daylight hours we can get if we are to reach London tonight."

The journey was monstrously slow. Out of the three ladies in the principal coach, Sophia wondered whose sensibilities were suffering the most torment. Miss Hill appeared to have developed a head cold and sniffed constantly. Charlotte's limited patience was being tried to the utmost and she moved restlessly and grumbled. Sophia did her best to be unobtrusive, difficult when one's knees kept coming into contact with Lord Ramsey's as the coach lurched and swayed.

The viscount kept his eyes closed and she hoped he was sleeping, but it became clear that he was not when a particularly vicious pothole jolted Sophia into his lap. He caught her firmly, laughing down at her, apparently forgetting his spleen.

For an instant she was close to him, close enough to detect a faint hint of sandalwood perfume, to feel the strength of his muscles, to see the real amusement in his dark brown eyes.

Her own laughter bubbled irresistibly to the surface. She could not know that her own eyes were alight with fun and that for the second time the viscount felt oddly fascinated by this ridiculous woman who was entertaining him with some, as yet indecipherable, game of her own.

Four

No one was more relieved than Sophia when the cortege at last drew up in front of the Ramsey town house in Berkeley Square. She threw herself into her role as servant with a frenzy that defied interruption from the viscount, supervising Charlotte's mounds of luggage as they were carried into the house and unpacking them from their silver tissue paper with much rustling and arranging.

Once the first bustle of arrival was past, Charlotte went to join her mother to take refreshment and Sophia had a little time to think and to recognize that her problems had been aggravated by her reaction when she had been held so briefly in the viscount's arms. The tensing of his muscles as he supported her, the scent of sandalwood from his body, his dark eyes filled with humor had given her an insane longing to remain close to him. And not only to remain close, but to embrace him. No wonder the man had so much success with women. Well, whatever his attraction, she would never become weakly entangled with such a rakehell. As soon as it was practical, she intended to make her escape to cousin Pamela's house. She would thoroughly deserve whatever strictures her cousin laid upon her, but she would be in a safe family haven.

Charlotte entered her bedchamber, her tongue wagging almost before she arrived. Sophia was astonished to hear her chatter as easily as if nothing untoward had occurred. "My brother and my Mama fear that I may have jeopardized my position in society. Ramsey fusses and fidgets like an old woman. As if anyone would believe ill of me. Do you think they will, Susan?"

They most decidedly will, thought Sophia. In fact, you and I, Charlotte, could find ourselves outcasts together. Aloud she said, "I pray not, Miss Charlotte. I don't know anythin' about the world, so how can I tell? Has his lordship made any plans for you? I'm sure his lordship knows what's best."

Charlotte sighed, her blue eyes becoming momentarily clouded. "He always *thinks* he does." She took a fan from the mahogany dressing table that matched her elegant bed, and picked absently at the azure-dyed feathers which floated to the floor, appearing, thought Sophia, as insubstantial as Charlotte's wits.

She removed the fan gently and said soothingly, "No doubt Lord Ramsey will ensure that no one oversets you, ma'am."

Her words expressed more confidence than she felt. With every moment that passed, the depth of her own transgression against society's laws appeared clearer.

She was picking the last of the feathers from a pretty pink and blue rug when a footman arrived at the door. He was admirably proportioned and quite handsome in the Ramsey livery of royal blue, silver, and yellow, his hair covered by a white wig. He brought a message that his lordship wanted words with the new maid. He added that she'd best be quick because Lord Ramsey had a short way with servants that kept him waiting.

Charlotte's small hand flew to her mouth. "Oh, heavens, I was meant to tell you an age ago, Susan. Is my brother cross, Tindal?"

"Cross, Miss Charlotte?" Tindal recalled the cold eyes of the viscount and his acerbic tone. "Yes, I think he's cross."

Sophia toyed wildly with the idea of hurrying to the

nearest street door and leaving immediately, but she dared not add to her transgressions by walking the streets of London in the gathering dark, unchaperoned. This was her first visit to the metropolis and she had already decided that the teeming, noisy thoroughfares were bewildering and unfit for a lone gentlewoman during the day, leave alone at night. It was bad enough to have wandered unaccompanied as she had in the country, but a woman alone in the city, any woman, even one who appeared as unattractive as she, was fair game for the numbers of mischievous apprentices and rollicking bucks and dandies. She followed the footman, remembering her stooped shoulders and slightly shuffling gait as she was ushered into the library where his lordship stood near a blazing fire, leafing through a magazine.

He had changed for the evening and for a moment Sophia stared in open admiration. Never before had she met a gentleman whose powerful form was so much enhanced by clothes intended for formal evening wear. His long-tailed, dark blue coat covered his wide shoulders with not a trace of a wrinkle, and his knee breeches and white silk stockings showed his muscular legs to advantage.

Forgetting her role entirely, Sophia said, "How very smart you look! And your cravat is so beautifully tied—if you don't mind my saying so, my lord," she finished, endeavoring belatedly to appear humble.

Ramsay's brows climbed. "I daresay a man should feel gratified to receive praise from any female, but I have not so far desired the approbation of a servant. Always excepting, of course, my valet."

Sophia remembered to curtsy. "I beg pardon, sir—my lord, I mean. I haven't been a servant very long."

Ramsay's dark eyes raked her from head to foot. Sophia almost cringed. She felt his penetrating gaze was reading all the secrets of her soul. She would not be able to deceive this man for long.

"Do you wish to sit, Susan?"

Sophia moved to an easy chair near the fire, where she waited, hands in lap, eyes cast modestly down.

"How different you are, Susan, from the usual maid. Most would have declined to sit in my presence, or, at the very least, would have picked a hard chair."

"Oh! Well, I would usually, naturally, but I'm enervated by the journey," muttered Sophia.

"Enervated? There are occasions when you have a somewhat advanced vocabulary for a ladies' maid."

"I—I lived in—I worked for a lady—that is to say, Mrs. Wetherall is quite a bluestocking," blurted Sophia.

"How interesting. Then she will have no difficulty in writing a reference. You could receive one within a matter of two or three days."

"No, I couldn't. Remember, sir, she's gone to—" Sophia stopped. Had she previously given Jamaica or America as Mrs. Wetherall's destination?

"Jamaica," supplied the viscount urbanely.

Sophia glanced at him and looked quickly away. She could swear that a brief amusement had danced at the back of his daunting eyes.

"I had no notion that the Somerset Wetheralls had spawned a bluestocking. In what branch of learning was your mistress interested?"

Sophia gritted her teeth. "Mathematics," she said.

"Mathematics! What an unusual female she must be. Most ladies of my acquaintance cannot add their pin money correctly."

"Perhaps your lordship should cultivate a different sort of lady," snapped Sophia.

The viscount walked across the room with catlike grace and stood looking down at her. "Susan, I have a theory about you," he said.

"Indeed, my lord?"

"Indeed, Susan. I suspect that you cannot write for a reference because you were dismissed by your previous employer for undue familiarity. If your attitude to me is anything to go by, it would not surprise me."

After her one glance Sophia had intended to keep her gaze fixed firmly on the fire, but irresistibly she found herself raising her eyes to look into the viscount's face. The flames that danced in the coals were no brighter, or more scorching, than the ones in his eyes. She searched for something to say, but her brain appeared to have stopped functioning. She had become suddenly a creature of flesh. A creature who wanted above all else to reach out to the man beside her and hold him and be held by him. She was bewildered by the power of a need so totally unfamiliar, and frightening. She looked away, but not before she suspected he had begun to diagnose the shaming message in her face.

She must say something to fill the silence, which was growing almost tangible. Nothing original occurred so she fell back on the viscount's suggestion. "You're right, my lord. I was thrown out of my place at a minute's notice for, er, what you said."

Ramsey's tone was harsh. "Dismissed without a reference! And you dare to inflict yourself upon my sister!"

Sophia forgot her sallow face, her hideous mob cap, her shambling gait, and her accent, and sprang to her feet.

"Inflict myself? How dare you!"

Her words seemed to echo around the library, bouncing from the leatherbound books to the reading chair to the molded ceiling, and back to her own horrified ears.

She flopped into the chair, her legs feeling too weak to support her. "I beg your lordship's pardon. I forgot myself."

"I would put it stronger than that. You were insolent. Disgracefully so!"

Sophia suddenly saw a way out. What an idiot she was! All she had to do to escape was to give his lordship more sauce and he would dismiss her. She could then go thankfully to her cousin's house and remove the disguise which, since she had made the acquaintance of this autocrat, had become shockingly irksome.

She searched in her brain for something really outrageous with which to administer the *coup de grace* to her masquerade when Lord Ramsey spoke again. He said softly, "Let us forget the past moments, Susan. You have had an exeedingly trying time of late. I wish to discuss your wage. I am sure that my dear, scatter-brained sister will not have negotiated terms with you."

Sophia experienced a curious mixture of regret and elation. She longed to end her pretense, yet a part of her rejoiced in the evidence of the viscount's kindness to a humble, unattractive, and none too polite domestic. She ventured to look at him again and saw that the devilish amusement was still lurking in his dark eyes. Was he simply playing a game with her? If his reputation as a rake were true, and she had looked pretty, he might be trying to play a very different game with her.

"Miss Charlotte said nothing about a wage, my lord."

"How odd of you not to have asked. Most servants are very particular about money. I daresay you were too over-wrought to consider it and possibly so thankful to find shelter it entirely slipped your mind."

"Yes, my lord," said Sophia, unable to dredge up anything else.

"Yes, to what, Susan?"

"To all that you said, my lord."

The viscount regarded her for a moment before walking to a large writing table. Seating himself in a wide elbow chair, he withdrew a black book from a drawer and mended a goose quill with an ivory handled knife. His hands were white and might have been mistaken for soft, had Sophia not felt their power when he held her. His long fingers were sure as he used the sharp blade.

He dipped the quill into a cut-glass inkpot. "Your name?" he asked.

"You know it, my lord. Susan."

"Susan what?" inquired the viscount, glancing at his fob watch with a small sigh that infuriated Sophia.

"If your lordship has an engagement, we could do this tomorrow," she suggested.

"Your thoughtfulness touches me," Ramsey said. "Your name, Susan. I take it you had parents. Or that someone endowed you with more than a forename."

Sophie gave him a glare which he did not see, his eyes

still on the book, his pen hovering. "C-C-Crocus," she stammered, her eyes on the Chinese bowl of flowers on the mantelshelf.

"Crocus! How unusual. I vow I have never heard it before."

"Not crocus," said Sophia desperately. "I was thinking of—of my father's garden. The flowers made me remember it."

"In what part of Britain is it, Susan?"

"In Devon, my lord. But it's not his garden now. He's dead. So's my ma," she concluded, recovering her country accent.

"My sympathies," said the viscount, with a small, seated bow.

"Thank you, my lord."

"Have you recalled your name yet?"

"Crocker, my lord."

"Ah, yes. Crocus and Crocker—so alike—so easy to make a mistake."

Please God, let this stop soon, prayed Sophia. Either I shall fall into hysterics or hit him with the poker.

The viscount wrote, then looked up. "What was your former wage?"

Sophia's shoulders sagged. She had only the vaguest memory of Miss Sheffield's attempt to teach her mathematics and economy. Once, after Sophia, at the age of fourteen, had purchased for twelve guineas an Italian fan for which she could have no immediate use, her governess-companion had rebuked her for extravagance and revealed that her yearly wage was eighty pounds. This, she had explained earnestly, was a great deal more than most genteel ladies received when employed as governess-companions in the houses of the wealthy and was indicative of Mr. Plerivale's honesty and appreciation. At the thought of Miss Sheffield's and her guardian's distress at her behavior, Sophia almost broke down in her need to confide in someone and ask for assistance. But she must not permit herself such an indulgence. Surely no gentleman, even one who was showing such untoward magnanimity to her, would be able to keep such a good story to himself. It would circulate the clubs and coffee houses and her reputation would be in shreds. She would write home as soon as she reached the safety of her cousin Pamela's house and beg forgiveness.

The viscount said. "Will you daydream all day, woman? What was your former wage?"

A lady's maid would not receive as much as a governess, reflected Sophia. What wage did Effie, her own maid, get? Was it nine pounds a year, or nineteen? Or twenty-nine? Effie was only twenty and fairly new, the elderly lady who had maided Sophia and her mother before her having recently retired. Sophia wished she had paid more heed to these matters, but truth to tell, she was one of the females referred to so scathingly by his lordship who never could quite balance her generous pin money against her expenditure.

"My wage was—was nineteen pounds a year," she said as firmly as possible.

The viscount bestowed a ferocious frown upon her. "*How much?*"

Sophia licked her lips. "Nine pounds a year," she amended.

His lordship's dark eyes rested for a moment on Sophia's face, which she could feel was crimsoning beneath the maquillage. He seemed about to speak, but to her relief he glanced once more at his watch and wrote in the book.

He closed it and said, "I'm sure my sister will find you a decent gown until your trunk arrives, but as you were robbed and have no money, you will need to purchase various articles necessary for female comfort."

Sophia felt her blush deepening. She had never in her life discussed with a member of the opposite sex details of her feminine needs, not even as a child with Mr. Plerivale. "I beg your pardon?" she said, for want of anything better.

"Until your trunk arrives," reminded Lord Ramsey evenly, brushing a tiny speck of dust from his sleeve. "The one containing all your worldly goods."

"Oh—yes, my lord, but I cannot accept money for—for personal items from you."

The irritating eyebrows rose again. After a slight pause he said, "I truly never thought to come upon a serving wench quite like you, Susan. Have you a particular reason for not accepting my money? The servants in my household must uphold the dignity of the family; I do assure you there is no obligation attached."

Sophia's fists were clenched in the folds of her gown. "I didn't assume that there was."

"Did you not? You truly must be new to the position of lady's maid. I believe many young servant girls constantly guard against what they call 'being taken advantage of.' "

"Your experience is clearly greater than mine, my lord." Sophia stopped. No wonder those infuriating dark eyes were regarding her with suspicion and, she realized with futile fury, a lurking demon of amusement. "I'll be grateful for your help, my lord," she finished.

The viscount pulled a cashbox from another drawer and drew out two gold coins. "Take these and tomorrow buy what you need, and pray do not feel the least alarm. You may, if you prefer, consider the money to be an advance on your wage."

Sophia's face and neck were now fiery. She had to force out her hand to take the money. One of the first instructions received by any young lady of *ton* was never to take gifts from any man, save a close relative, and never, ever, money.

"You look dreadfully uncomfortable, Susan. Are you not well?"

"Perfectly well, I thank you, my lord."

He nodded at her. "You may go."

Sophia rose and fled to the door, where, remembering her place, she turned, dropped the viscount a small curtsy, and hurried back to Charlotte's bedchamber.

As she scurried through the passages she wondered if the viscount was simply amusing himself, or if he was unmindful of the fact that his sister was a petite five feet two inches tall, while Sophia was five feet six and apparently quite plump, due to her padding, and could never get into one of Charlotte's cast-off gowns. She came to the conclusion that he was precisely the kind of man who would know to a degree the size of gown worn by any woman and was therefore amusing himself at her expense. She looked forward to the day when she could meet him on an equal footing and treat him with the scorn he deserved. If that day ever dawns, she thought grimly. As matters lay at present, she would far more likely end up rusticating forever.

Charlotte listened to Sophia's account of the interview with her brother, an account which omitted the wrangling. Sophia groaned inwardly at the network of lies in which she was becoming entangled. Pray God she could go to bed early, rise at dawn, and make good her escape. She wondered if she would ever again be willing to take part in theatricals. It was simplicity itself to act before an uncritical assembly of friends; it was unbelievably difficult to play a part in the real world.

Charlotte stood before her breakfront wardrobe and pensively chewed on a dainty forefinger. "I cannot think what my brother is about, Susan. He must know that you are too big and tall for one of my gowns. But wait a moment. I've an idea. You are a splendid needlewoman. Here is a gown I bought, but found it did not suit me. We are somewhat similar about the bodice and you could let out some of the tucks and add a frill to the skirt. Yes, I'm sure that will answer."

Sophia hated herself more than ever for her deception. She had no need of Charlotte's gown, even an unwanted one. Tomorrow, once her cousin Pamela had recovered from the vapors which Sophia's present predicament and attire would undoubtedly induce, she would send out for a regiment of mantua-makers to attend her. "Thank you, Miss Charlotte, but I'm happy to remain as I am at present. Your brother has very kindly given me two pounds in advance. I shall—er—purchase material and make a gown for myself."

Charlotte stared at her with wide blue eyes. "Two pounds for a gown! I'm sure I cannot think how that may be contrived. It buys me only three or four pairs of silk stockings, and my last gown—a heavenly one in the palest green with spangles—cost, as I recall, thirty guineas, or was it forty? I never can recall the cost of anything. But you must let me assist you because Mama has asked to see you and if you go to her dressed like that she might fall into a fit of hysterics.''

Sophia felt helpless in the face of the ever-increasing complications, and accepted the proffered gown. It was of a somewhat harsh pink shade that would clash horribly with her hair. The fact that she kept on the dreadful mob cap made no difference to her sensibilities. To wear this gown would be an offense against her taste, but she had no choice. She snipped open a few tucks, gathered into frills the length of white muslin produced by Charlotte, drew it into a deep flounce, and stitched it hurriedly to the hem. The gown barely stretched over the pads she had sewn beneath the hips and bosom of her shift.

"Dear Susan," exclaimed Charlotte, "you look almost transformed, but must you wear that unbecoming cap and hide your hair? Why, I do believe you could appear quite pretty if you took a little care. For instance, you could easily cover that scar with curls."

Sophia's hands went to her cap to defend it. "No, Miss Charlotte. I pray you, don't insist. Fancy styles don't suit me at all."

"If you truly are set on wearing it—how did you come by the scar?"

Sophia had sustained it during a mad ride with Edwin through the woodlands on his estate, when a whippy branch had caught her. It would not do to say so. "I forget," she muttered. "It was long ago. I'm well used to it."

Charlotte sighed. "We had better repair at once to Mama's sitting room. We have already kept her waiting too long. She has no more patience than my brother."

Sophia stood as still as possible beneath the scrutiny of a pair of eyes as blue as Charlotte's. Lady Ramsey reclined on a daybed in an undress gown of pink satin with many tiny ribbon bows. Her hair, as gold still as her daughter's, Sophia suspected by artifice rather than nature, was dressed loosely and curls clustered around her pink and white face. A small table holding many bottles and phials

stood within reach. Her maid, elderly, but fashionably
dressed, hovered by and gave Sophia an occasional
contemptuous glance.

Lady Ramsey finished studying Sophia. She murmured,
"Oh, my God," and her white hand reached for her
hartshorn. The maid threw Sophia a resentful glare as she
administered the restorative.

"Thank you, Nell," Lady Ramsey whispered, then said
faintly to her daughter, "I was informed that this girl—
Susan, is it?—was traveling alone without luggage and that
you engaged her on the spot as your maid."

Sophia, the subject of the conversation, felt as insignificant as a piece of minor furniture as Charlotte replied
effusively, "Yes, Mama, and she has been of such value to
me. Do you recall my sweet yellow satin opera hood?"

Lady Ramsey's intelligence was instantly lively in the
face of a question of such immense consequence. "I do,
indeed. Such a pretty headdress."

"Well, it got torn—" Lady Ramsey emitted a small
scream— "and Susan mended it so minutely that I defy
any mantua-maker to do better. I cannot even find where
the tear was."

The viscountess gave Sophia another long scrutiny.
"She does have a good point then."

"Yes, indeed, Mama, and more than one. You must
know that when I first engaged her, she put my bedchamber at the inn to rights in an amazing short time and
you know how I am unable to sort out my clothes. When
Kate ran away—"

"I was informed she went back to a previous inn to
marry a pot boy. Was the wench being foolish?"

"Oh, no, indeed, Mama, she was not. He was *very*
handsome."

Charlotte's sigh was echoed by her mother. "If only
some of the *ton* gentlemen were as well set up. So Susan is
to send for references? Your brother dwelt on that with
somewhat tiresome vehemence."

"Just as soon as we supply her with paper and ink."

"Do so quickly," said Lady Ramsey. "A friend of my
youth—" she paused for another, deeper, sigh— " once

engaged a maid without a reference purely out of the
goodness of her tender heart and do you know how the
wicked girl repaid her? She opened the front door one
night and admitted robbers who took all dear Lady Betty's
jewels and much of the family silver. Of course, the maid
was never seen again. I suspected at the time that she wore
some kind of disguise. I said so, but Lady Betty paid me no
heed.''

"And deserved what she got,'' muttered Nell.

"Susan isn't like that!'' protested Charlotte.

Speech deserted Sophia. To be sure, she had no
intention of permitting robbers to harm this family, but
she *was* disguised and living a lie which, if it were
discovered, would make Charlotte a target for the wrath
and scorn of her loved ones. With every moment that
passed she was inflicting more harm on a girl who,
although feather-headed, was treating her with exceeding
kindness.

Lady Ramsey said, "I delight to know how experienced
a seamstress you are, Susan. There is a gown of mine, a
sweetly pretty peach silk, that I long to wear. I thought it
beyond repair, but—''

Her maid snorted so loudly that her ladyship jumped
and almost dropped the fan she had begun to waft with
languid grace. "Come now, Nell, you must not mind. We
both know your eyes are no longer sharp enough to sew so
finely.''

Nell shot a look at Susan which made her thankful she
would not have to fulfill the role of maidservant in this
house for much longer, but she sympathized with her and
said placatingly, "Nell, I can sew, but I know little of
London fashion. You must please to tell me how to go
on.''

Nell's stare grew, if anything, more malevolent. "Don't
know about London fashions, eh? Lot o' good you'll be
maiding Miss Charlotte.''

Lady Ramsey said, "Nell speaks truth. Yet you say that
Susan is so useful. Oh, dear, I vow such problems are too
distressing.''

The viscountess gained the full attention of her maid and

daughter. "Mama, you must not permit your nerves to be overset."

"My lady, remember your state of health."

Lady Ramsey shaded her eyes with a soft white hand. "Indeed, I do often forget my weakness, especially where folk needing help are concerned. Pray, do not be cross with me, Nell. I depend on you utterly. You will always be first with me, but," she continued, in a sudden surprisingly firm tone, "Susan shall mend my gown. It is one of my favorites."

Five

Viscount Ramsey was not proving his usual good company, and all the humorous insults hurled by his fellow card players had little effect. Mr. Barnaby Chatteris, a congenial companion and friend, watched in disbelief as his lordship lost fifty guineas three times in a row by backing almost sure losers in a game of *Vingt-Un*.

Mr. Chatteris persuaded the viscount to halt for refreshment and sipped his brandy thoughtfully and a trifle nervously. Ramsey never displayed emotion during games of chance, losing or winning with equal grace, and he was not a man who cared for criticism even from his closest acquaintance, but Mr. Chatteris felt that someone should point out that the viscount was simply throwing money away. Mr. Chatteris was also irresistibly curious about the reason for the viscount's abstraction.

He said, "Ramsey, dear fellow, no wish to tread where I ain't wanted, but your play tonight—your wagers . . ."

The viscount appeared not to be listening. Barnaby tried again. "Hugo, we've been friends for a number of years . . ."

Ramsey turned, his brows raised. "What? I have never disputed it."

"No, no, of course not. But as your friend, I think I

may be allowed a trifle of leeway in my speaking to you."

"You do?"

"Er, yes, I think so. I've been watching you play tonight—"

"Yes, and damned annoying I found it to have you standing over me sighing heavily. Pray, don't do it again."

"Can you blame me when you wager fifty guineas twice on sixteen and once even fifteen, and give prodigious satisfaction to that dandified snake, Crawley."

"I did that?"

"Yes, indeed. Are you ill? Permit me to escort you home."

The viscount laughed. "What a good man you are, Chatteris. No, I'm not ill. My mind is vexed by a problem. A female."

Barnaby heaved a sigh of relief. If a woman was distracting Ramsey, she would engage his attention for only a brief time. His amorous adventures with the most beautiful of both the *ton* and the *demimonde* were a source of envy to many and fascinated Mr. Chatteris. He himself enjoyed only modest success, being six inches short of six feet, a trifle weighty, and—his chief disadvantage—having little more than a comfortable income.

"She must be a veritable goddess to make you forget your play. Have you conquered her yet? When may I make her acquaintance?"

"Never, I think. I have not conquered her, nor have I any wish to do so. She appears ill-favored and wears the worst gown I ever saw. Sometimes, but not always, shuffles along with a slight stoop and seems to possess a figure which can only be described as lumpy."

Mr. Chatteris would have spoken had not amazement imprisoned his tongue.

Ramsey accepted a glass of brandy. "She is my sister's latest maid. Charlotte engaged her at a moment's notice during . . ." Ramsey paused. Barnaby was trustworthy, but the viscount still did not know just what stories would circulate about his sister's foolish escapade and he preferred absolute discretion. ". . . during the past week."

Mr. Chatteris sipped reflectively. Ramsey would not

normally give a woman such as he had described a second look. It was very puzzling and there was something odd in his friend's tone. He ventured, "You said this girl *appears* ill-favored and *sometimes* has an ungainly walk and *seems* lumpy."

"I did, indeed."

Silence fell and Barnaby waited. The viscount looked as if he had fallen into a trance.

"Shall I return to the card table?" asked Mr. Chatteris.

Ramsey nodded and Mr. Chatteris left, feeling frustrated, but not daring to venture further.

The viscount was feeling increasingly perturbed. There was a mystery about Charlotte's new maid that intrigued him. He had studied her unobtrusively, but thoroughly, during the journey to town. Susan's features beneath her maquillage were regular, her hazel eyes were luminous and capable of expressing a wide range of emotion. Her manners were, in turn, haughty and deferential. She was perfectly capable of walking properly yet, when she knew herself to be observed, affected a stoop and a shambling gait, and when he had held her so briefly in the coach, his experienced hands had encountered padding beneath her gown. The situation had begun by amusing and interesting him, but now he wondered if he were being a complete fool. Who in hell was she? And why had she inveigled her way into Charlotte's entourage? Stories of robberies and violence connected with evil servants had begun to invade his mind. He could be exposing his female relatives to harm and, although he found both his mother and sister intensely trying and utterly vain and preferred not to be in their company more than was absolutely essential, he cared for them and was their natural protector. He stood so abruptly he caused an elderly gentleman in an armchair to start.

"Dammit, sir! Must you leap like that? I almost spilled wine down my new waistcoat."

Ramsey did not hear and the gentleman passed a few choice animadversions on the conduct of the younger generation. The viscount called for his carriage and within minutes was entering his house.

"Where are the ladies?" he demanded.

Lorimer, the portly butler, being used to the fits and starts of the nobility, answered equably, "Lady Ramsey is in her sitting room with Miss Charlotte, who is, I believe, recounting the events of her visit to the country."

Ramsey glanced sharply at Lorimer. Was there extra meaning in his voice? Servants always knew everything and Charlotte had made no attempt to hide her indiscretions. He wished she were young enough to spank. What an imbroglio she had landed them in. He took consolation in the knowledge that, under his roof, at least, the upper servants would forbid gossip by the lower.

"Where is Susan?" he asked.

Lorimer looked blank. "Who, my lord?"

"Miss Charlotte's new maid. I wish to know where she is."

Lorimer's breast swelled with indignation. "I could not say, sir. I leave the females to the control of Mrs. Parrock, our worthy housekeeper."

Ramsey frowned. "Then go and ask her. No, tell her to attend me in the library."

Mrs. Parrock, her arduous duties for the day finished, had been relaxing in her private parlor while the maids laid the table for the servants' supper, and was indignant at being summoned at a time when his lordship knew full well the head footman and some of his minions were on duty. "Susan?" she replied. "I would suppose she is making Miss Charlotte's room ready for her to retire. Do you want me to send a footman to find out?"

"Yes! No! I'll inquire myself."

Mrs. Parrock frowned at him. She had been in service with the Ramseys as long as Lorimer. "That would be most inappropriate, my lord. I'll go." She left without waiting for a reply. A full five minutes passed before she returned.

"What an age you have been," rasped his lordship. "What happened?"

"I'm sure I beg your lordship's pardon for keeping your lordship waiting," intoned Mrs. Parrock, unmoved by her master's irritation. "It seems that Mrs. Hill has the headache and Susan was bathing her forehead and putting a hot brick to her feet. Naturally, I never thought of looking there, Miss Charlotte's maid not being engaged to wait on her companion.''

The contempt in Mrs. Parrock's voice irked the viscount. He had seldom questioned the behavior of the below-stairs inhabitants, preferring simply to enjoy their ministrations and leave the running of his establishment to the senior domestics. Now he suddenly saw Miss Hill as more than a lachrymose female who inadequately guarded his sister, and had a vision of the life of a timid creature from a genteel home dropped into a situation where she was respected by no one. He also felt unaccountably glad that Susan was kinder than the others. He dismissed Mrs. Parrock with thanks and an order that Susan was not to be reprimanded.

Sophia drew the covers around Miss Hill, made sure that the lavender water was within reach, and removed a medicine phial and the bowl that had contained gruel she had persuaded Tindal to extract from the kitchen. She had an uneasy feeling that the footman wanted something in return. He surely could not be attracted to her person. She decided to develop an occasional squint in an effort to appear even more unprepossessing.

The night was chill and she piled coals generously on the fading fire, then dropped an impulsive kiss on the companion's forehead, extinguished the candle, and crept away, the atmosphere around her warm with Miss Hill's gratitude.

The moment she had been dreading had arrived. She must descend into the servants' hall for supper and she had not the least idea of how she was expected to behave.

She was conscious first of the scrutiny of a number of domestics who stood behind their chairs at a table set with places in almost as grand a manner as the upstairs dining room. On a side table there was a large dish of cut bread, slabs of butter and cheese, a broiled ham, and a stuffed rump of beef. On the table was a tureen from which drifted a savory smell and Sophia realized she was very hungry.

She attempted a small smile that was returned only by
Tindal. A pretty maid actually scowled at her.

The hall was tiled and the bright firelight was reflected in
copper gleams from the pots and pans and danced on the
many hanging utensils required by a cook for the feeding
of a noble family.

Sophia walked to the table. "Where am I to sit?" she
asked.

Lady Ramsey's maid, Nell, whose blue gauze gown did
not suit her years, sniffed. "Where lady's maids always
sit."

There was a silence broken by the nervous giggle of a
little girl whose red hands proclaimed her position as
scullery wench.

Sophia stared at Nell, then walked firmly to the head of
the table and took a place behind the chair opposite
her.

The butler and housekeeper arrived, moving in a stately
manner that could rival a duke and duchess, and Sophia
had to hide a smile. She turned aside and Tindal caught her
eye and winked. The pretty maid's scowl deepened.

Lorimer moved to his place between the two lady's
maids and Mrs. Parrock walked to the other end of the
table. A gnarled old woman on her right mumbled a grace
and the servants seated themselves and, waited on by a
junior maid and a footboy, proceeded with their meal with
such extreme ceremony that it might have affected
Sophia's appetite had the food not been so delicious.

Tindal said, "I vow, Mrs. Powell, that your mutton
broth gets more appetizing than it's ever been before."

The plump cook beamed. "Thank you, Mr. Tindal, I'm
sure I do my best."

"We need no assurance of that," said Lorimer.

"It's kind of you to say so, Mr. Lorimer."

The old lady mumbled something. "Mrs. Garnet wants
more butter on her bread," announced a thin
chambermaid.

A young footman poked the kitchenmaid in the ribs.
" 'Ere that, girl? Take the butter to Mrs. Garnet and
spread 'er bread. You know better than to make old Nurse

wait. 'Er ladyship would be angry if she thought Nurse wasn't treated with the respect due to 'er.''

Sophia ate steadily, her eyes down, speaking only when she needed something. The hostility wafting at her from Nell and the pretty maid whose name was Kitty grew more potent as the meal progressed.

Kitty asked, "Is that some new fashion you've got on, Miss Crocker? I declare I've never seen its like."

Sophia continued eating until a nudge from a housemaid reminded her of her assumed name.

"No," she said shortly. She glanced up to see all eyes upon her. "I was robbed of my belongings and my trunk hasn't come yet. I must to make do with what I can get. I wore this gown for traveling. I didn't want to attract attention from—er—" Sophia foundered in a quagmire of words. Who would pay her unwarranted attention the way she looked now?

Tindal said gallantly, "From young sprigs o' the nobility what might take liberties."

"Yes," agreed Sophia. "I mean to say, you never can tell."

Kitty's snort was, felt Sophia, well deserved. She decided to end the topic and assert herself at least a little in this unusual company. "Fortunately," she said firmly, "I am skilled with my needle."

She had picked the wrong escape route.

"Oh, *yes*," declared Nell, her thin nose wrinkling, "she believes herself a cut above me in her sewing and she's not got a *single* objection to pushing herself forward."

"So you was sayin', Miss Price," said Kitty. "Very forward, I call it, to be settin' 'erself above you what've been with the family for this age past."

"*I* heard she mended a gown so you couldn't see the stitches," put in Tindal.

Kitty glared at him. "Miss Price can do that easy. For my part, I can't abide females what shove themselves in where they're not wanted."

"But she was wanted," pointed out a small, thin man with gray hair, brown eyes, and easy manners. "Isn't that so, Miss Crocker?"

"You don't know nothin' about it," said Kitty.

"That's no way to speak to his lordship's valet," reproved the butler.

Sophia wanted to scream. Who could have guessed that a servants' hall could be so crammed with formality and traps?

She opened her mouth to defend herself when she caught sight of Kitty's face. It was suffused with pink and her eyes were shiny with moisture as she stared at Tindal. Good God, the girl's in love with him, thought Sophia. No wonder she is so overset. She wished she could reassure Kitty and explain that tomorrow Susan Crocker would vanish forever.

She was brought abruptly from her musings by raised voices and realized that she was the subject of further acrimony and that she was being regarded by eyes that expressed various emotions, including fury and incredulity from the seniors and admiration and disbelief from the juniors.

"*Miss Susan Crocker,*" said Mrs. Parrock. "I can scarce credit my senses. You *ordered* gruel for Miss Hill from Mrs. Powell's kitchen without so much as a by your leave from me? And fetched more coals for her fire. Coal's given out once a week to servants, and must suffice."

"I asked Tindal—I mean, Mr. Tindal—to bring some gruel, yes," said Sophia. "The poor lady is most unwell. And I have to confess that I removed some pieces of coal from Miss Charlotte's room." She decided not to reveal that she had also purloined a little lavender water.

"That's stealin'," said Kitty.

"No, it ain't," said Tindal. "It weren't for herself."

"Tell that to a judge an' jury!" snapped Kitty.

Sophia was alarmed. The newspapers were full of accounts of dreadful sentences passed upon people for purloining very little.

"Be quiet, the pair of you," ordered Lorimer. "It isn't your place to do any of that," he continued portentously. "You should have made a formal request to our head housemaid who would have passed it to Mrs. Parrock who, in turn, would have given the request to Mrs. Powell.

Mr. Tindal knows better than to assist you in wrong-doing.
I shall want words with you later, Mr. Tindal.''

"What about Miss Charlotte's coal?'' asked Mrs.
Parrock.

Lorimer said, frowning heavily, "Her scuttle must be
refilled directly after our meal.''

Sophia sternly repressed the desire to hammer on the
table with her fists. She could scarce wait for morning
when she would escape from this prison-like place. Never
again would she view her servants casually. They lived lives
of intense and harrowing competition that would be a
lesson to an army officer. She bent her head meekly and
apologized.

Supper over, the juniors began their task of clearing up
and Sophia hurried up the back stairway to make her way
to Charlotte's room. She pushed open the door leading to
the upper quarters and scurried along the candle-lit
corridor. She turned a corner and bumped into someone.
Her senses told her instantly that she was once more in
close proximity to Viscount Ramsey. She muttered an
excuse and tried to pass him, but he held her arms. For an
instant Sophia felt explosively angry. Hot, furious words
flew to her tongue and were suppressed. She must get
through this night without further incident. Just this night.

"You appear to be in a hurry, Susan.''

The hard hands released her and she retreated and
curtsied. "Yes, my lord. I have eaten supper and I must
prepare Miss Charlotte's bed and—'' She tried again to
pass the viscount and again he prevented her, this time by
barring her way by leaning in front of her with his out-
stretched arm against the wall. Forgetting herself entirely,
Sophia ducked under and began to run. His lordship ran
after her and caught her and whirled her around to face
him. They had reached a place where a branch of candles
affixed to the wall gave out generous light and the viscount
held her with a vicelike arm and tipped her chin in strong
fingers. She immediately lowered her lids.

"Look at me,'' Lord Ramsey commanded.

"Go to hell,'' muttered Sophia.

His lordship laughed softly, an ominous sound that sent

shivers down Sophia's back. "What are you doing here? What game are you playing? I am not so easily taken in as my womenfolk."

"Let—me—go!" Sophia's teeth were clenched in fury.

"It's useless to struggle."

"I'll scream."

"Pray do so, if you wish to make a scene for the whole household."

Sophia stopped fighting.

"That is much better. I await your explanation." Footsteps sounded ascending the nearby main staircase. "Hold hard. I think we shall do better if we are somewhere private."

The viscount urged Sophia along the landing, turned a handle, and kicked a bedchamber door open. His valet looked around, eyebrows slightly raised. "You may leave us, Dunlop," said the viscount.

Dunlop bowed, looked at Sophia without expression, and left, closing the door quietly behind him.

A vast four-poster bed with gold and crimson hangings and bedspread seemed to Sophia to dominate the room and sent shivers of apprehension through her. Who was to stop this man from having his way with her? The household was completely under his rule. Ramsey's eyes went from Sophia to the bed and back to her reddening face.

"I assure you I have no intention of ravishing you," he said, a sardonic smile curving his mouth.

Sophia folded her lips and clasped her hands before her, willing herself to maintain command over her feelings. Ramsey's nose and chin were too strong, his complexion too swarthy for him to be called handsome. He was more than that. His body emanated a quality previously unknown to her, one that held a terrifying attraction for her.

"Pray, permit me to leave, my lord," she said, wishing her voice did not shake. Fear had ironed out all trace of country accent, all evidence of servility.

"Who are you?" demanded his lordship harshly.

"You already know, my lord."

"Are you aware that for the past five minutes you have walked and run upright and that your countrified accent comes and goes like rain in spring?"

There was no answer Sophia could make so she made none.

"And why that ridiculous paint on your face? And what is the reason for the padding beneath your gown?"

Sophia felt her whole body must be crimson with shame. "How dare you, sir," she flashed. "And how do you know. . . ?" She faltered to a halt.

The viscount grinned, revealing his strong white teeth. "I am accustomed to the contours of women."

Sophia's fear increased, but she held her chin high. "Are you indeed? I dare swear it must give you much pleasure to boast of that in your cups—sir," she added, not troubling to hide her scorn.

She had scored a hit, but she had not been wise. The viscount's face was dark with sudden rage. "I never talk of ladies in public."

A devil goaded Sophia on. "Ladies? I did not know we spoke of ladies. I am but a humble serving wench. I've heard tell that gentlemen frequently assault such as me and make sport of it in their clubs."

"My God, but you are an insolent wench." The viscount moved swiftly to her side and his hand went up. Sophia gasped as her mob cap was dragged none too gently from her head. She put her hands to her hair, but he tore at pins and ribbons with ruthless fingers and within seconds the full beauty of her chestnut curls was revealed.

"Delightful," said the viscount, "though it needs to be shorter for fashion. And it goes damned ill with that gown."

Sophia stood still, hot with fury.

"Now, wash your face," commanded Ramsey.

"I'll do no such thing."

"Then I'll do it for you."

"I don't doubt it, my lord. You, sir, are a bully to treat a helpless woman in this fashion."

Inside Sophia there were warning voices that urged caution, but she had now tumbled completely out of her role of servant and met his lordship's furious eyes with all the dignity and wrath to be expected of Lady Sophia Clavering.

"My God," said Ramsey softly, "do you truly expect me to believe in your act of servant? Who are you? You *shall* tell me."

Social disaster faced Sophia. Let this cruel man once know who she was and all *ton* doors would be closed to her. And no matter what he did to her, no one would blame him. They would say she had been asking for trouble. She looked wildly about her. Ramsey stood between her and the door. Even if she escaped, where would she go? No one in this house would, or could help her.

She said impetuously, "I was destitute, my lord. I am an actress out of a place—"

"A stage player?" The viscount's face grew grimmer, his eyes colder, and belatedly Sophia recalled some of the scurrilous tales she had heard whispered of actresses. Many a sprig of nobility who wanted a pretty mistress might turn to the stage for her.

"Yes," she said pleadingly, "but a highly respectable one, I do assure you."

"Have I suggested otherwise?" The viscount's manner was even more suspicious.

"No, sir. What you thought was implicit in the way you looked at me."

"Well, well, your accent has entirely vanished. But I daresay you have learned to ape the ways of a lady for your stage roles."

Sophia nodded.

"Is Susan your real name?" he snapped.

"No! Yes! It is the one I use for—for acting. To tell truth, my lord—" which is something I shall always do in future, she vowed silently— "I come from a respectable family and they wouldn't hear of my becoming an actress so I—"

"Ran away? And discovered that the world is a cruel place for a woman alone?"

"Yes, my lord." At least that was true. "And I wish I

had stayed at home. At least, I think I do—'' Sophia did not realize that her voice had taken on inflexions that reflected her distress compounded by the memory of an almost forced marriage, penitence at having caused hurt and dreadful anxiety to those she loved, and regret at deceiving Charlotte.

Ramsey said in a gentle voice that unnerved her far more than his derision, ''Won't you permit me to contact your home and return you there in a respectable way?''

Sophia came to her senses. If she were sent back now, Lady Fothergill and Mr. Plerivale would proceed with the marriage preparations. Or more likely her ladyship would spurn her for her outrageous behavior and refuse to chaperone her into society. She could be trapped in the country until another suitable sponsor had agreed to present her, or if no acceptable lady would, maybe forever. Sophia felt as if she were in a self-induced quicksand of deceit and trouble, and every step she took dragged her further down.

Ramsey quickly seized her arm and pulled her toward the bed. Sophia was wondering if emulating a stage play by falling to her knees and begging for mercy would save her when she realized that he was making for the washstand. He dipped a washrag in the warm water that his valet had prepared and handed it to her.

''Take that paint off your face. I want a proper look at you.''

Six

Sophia discarded the notion of an impassioned plea for mercy. She had the impression that the viscount would regard such melodrama with grim amusement. She felt desperate. It was bad enough that he had seen her hair, but to remove all the deceptive shadows and blemishes on her face would finally ensure that she would never be able to enter her own sphere of society. Too much had happened;

she had been in too many compromising situations. She must get to Lady Stoneyhurst, who would surely be more than ready to hush any possible scandal by asserting that Lady Sophia Clavering had arrived, fully expected, on her doorstep, the same day she had left home. Families must hold together in the face of imminent danger.

She stopped struggling and, when Ramsey's grip relaxed, launched herself forward, grabbing at the sides of the bowl. It tipped and water cascaded down the viscount's knee breeches and into his silver-buckled shoes. He cursed and released her and she made a frantic dash for the door and, her skirt held above her ankles, raced along the corridor.

Then for the second time that night, she was caught and held by a strong pair of arms.

She struggled feverishly, "Let me go, my lord, release me."

"Oh, ho!" said a voice that was decidedly not Ramsey's. "Like that, is it? His mighty lordship's been tryin' to seduce a poor serving girl."

"Tindal! Please let me go. I must prepare Miss Charlotte's bedchamber for the night."

"Let you go? All right, but there's a price to pay."

"What?"

"A kiss, to be exact. Just one kiss an' you're free." Tindal's brown eyes were mischievous.

He was flirting with her, thought Sophia, and could not imagine why, with a kitchen full of pretty girls to choose from, he should want to.

"You've lost your cap, Susan, an' a good thing too. You've got lovely hair, really you have. You ought to let it show." Tindal ruffled her curls and bent his head, obviously with the intent of kissing her. Sophia was at the end of her endurance. She drew back her arm and slapped the footman hard. He swore, but released her. "You think you're high an' mighty don't you, just because you're a lady's maid." His voice became ingratiating. "Well, a girl's allowed a slap, I suppose. I'm glad you ain't cheap, Susan. One day I want to be a valet. You could teach me a lot about upstairs life. His lordship's valet don't have much to say to me. Jumped-up devil, he is, just because his father's a boat-builder who's done well for himself."

Sophia had a sudden inclination to laugh. She, daughter of an earl, was being wooed by a footman because he believed she could have influence with a valet.

Tindal's grasp on her shoulders reminded her that matters were not so funny. She pushed his hands off, gently but firmly. "Not now, please. I truly must be about my duties."

As she turned to go, Tindal landed a slap on her buttocks. Sophia almost froze with indignation. She turned angrily and saw the viscount outside his bed-chamber door, quite still, watching her. She was acutely embarrassed and stalked away feeling glad that water still dripped into his shoes from his spoiled breeches, and wondering if anything she encountered in the polite world would prove as harrowing as her experiences below stairs. She had a fleeting wish that she could share it all with someone who could laugh with her and decided that it was an impossibility. Society, she had been instructed, took matters of etiquette very seriously, as was proper when it existed for members of the *ton* to meet one another with a view to enjoying the benefits of expensive aristocratic frolics, and making financially rewarding marriages.

Sophia sped to Charlotte's bedchamber without further interruption, flung herself inside, and slammed the door, leaning back against it. Her sense of security was soon dispelled by the thought that at any time during the next hours either Tindal or Lord Ramsey could resume their separate campaigns. A wicked little smile broke through her confusion at the thought of what Ramsey's reaction must have been when he had discovered that he was rival to one of his footmen. The smile died quickly. Of course, the viscount would think nothing of the sort and she was fully persuaded that Tindal's attentions would disappear like ice in the sun if he believed he was in danger of angering his employer.

Sophia was abruptly tired, worn out far more by the emotional havoc of the past hours than the physical exertions. Her constitution, in fact, was excellent, but not even a day's hard riding or a long exploratory walk had made her as exhausted as she felt at this moment. In fact, she had the beginnings of a headache, a rare occurrence with her.

Was it possible for her to leave the Ramsey house tonight? A burst of raucous merriment answered by the wild shrieking laughter of some women of the night ascended from the street below the windows reminding her that the dangers lurking outside outweighed those inside. Or did they? She put a hand to her forehead and groaned, then realized that her suffering gave her an answer to her problem. She would tell Charlotte she was ill and this time she need not lie. The pain in her head was increasing and flashes of light in one eye foretold a megrim.

Charlotte was all consideration. She was a nice girl, Sophia decided, for all her frivolous, foolish ways.

"Poor Susan, how I sympathize. I detest the megrims. First poor Miss Hill and now you. Maybe it was the traveling. I detest it. Go to your bed and Nell shall maid me."

Truly in deep pain now, Sophia gave merely a passing thought to the fury of Nell and probably the rest of the servants that the pushing new maid should expect to be cossetted on her first night in the house.

Someone sent the little rough-handed skivvy to show her to her bed in the attics. "You should 'ere the row goin' on downstairs, Miss Crocker. Miss Price is 'avin the vapors sayin' she don't see why she should 'ave double the work because o' the likes o' you, no, not if you was dyin', and Mrs. Parrock and Mr. Lorimer is sayin' the magistrate ought to be sent for on account of they've 'eard from the 'ead coachman when the outside staff came to supper that you're no more than a beggar off the streets, an' Kitty's 'avin the 'ysterics cos she says that you're tryin' to take Mr. Tindal from 'er, though 'ow that's possible, she don't say, 'er bein' so pretty and you so—well, anyway, it's all 'ullabulloo downstairs. This is your room, Miss Crocker. You're lucky. You got one to yourself, bein' Miss Charlotte's lady's maid. I got to share a bed with three others, an' I fall out as often as not on account of I'm the smallest, an' . . .''

Sophia thanked the girl and closed the door of her room. It was smaller than her gown closet at home and contained only a chest of drawers with glass marks spoiling its once shiny surface, a narrow bed, a nightstool, and a basin-stand with a towel, soap and washrag, and a chipped jug of cold water. Sophia pulled off her clothes, almost too weary to think, and washed herself as best she could. She had no nightgown. One of the youths who attacked her had taken it—for a lady friend, no doubt. Well, she could sleep in her shift as she had at the inns. Soon, thank God, she would be able to take a long bath in scented water before a leaping fire, and get at her money and purchase all the soft cotton and linen underclothes she needed. Memories of what her life should be, and would soon be again, made her ache for tomorrow when she could return to it. There was a knock and the little maid trotted in, her eyes wide. "Mr. Dunlop gave me your mob cap to give you. He said you'd dropped it! And Miss Charlotte's sent you a clean nightgown and cap an' a draught of medicine. She's a good sort, ain't she?''

She is indeed, thought Sophia, as the laudanum began to take effect. She tied the long ribbons on the pretty lace-trimmed cap, then snuggled down inside the sweet-smelling, soft linen gown with its high, frilled neck and long sleeves that protected her from the rough sheets. As she slid into welcome unconsciousness, she felt safe for the moment from male attentions. She wondered if Lord Ramsey believed she had encouraged Tindal. An odd wisp of regret floated free from her euphoria.

When she awoke she lay still in a shaft of wintry sunlight that held dancing motes of dust, unable to recall for the moment what had happened. Remembrance rushed in and she sat up so fast she felt giddy. Thank heavens her head was better, but what time was it? She had the feeling that the dawn in which she meant to make her escape was long past.

There was a gentle tap at the door and Miss Hill entered,

bearing a small wooden tray. "How are you, Susan? Better? I'm so relieved. I too am well, thanks to you. When I rose this morning I felt quite overset by the realization that you had waited so kindly on me when you were ill yourself—"

"I wasn't—"

". . . and I volunteered to bring you a dish of tea. So reviving, I always say. And I persuaded Mrs. Powell to let you have two slices of bread and butter. I do hope you can eat it. Mrs. Parrock would have insisted that you attend breakfast with the others hours ago."

Sophia sipped the tea with real gratitude. "How many hours ago?" she inquired, breaking into Miss Hill's flow.

"Oh, an age. It is now eight o'clock and the servants begin breakfasting at six. But Miss Charlotte gave orders that you were not to be disturbed. Such a sweet young lady, though distressingly headstrong and—"

"Eight o'clock! So late!"

"Yes, my dear, but it is of no consequence. Miss Charlotte is still abed. It is her practice to lie there until ten o'clock breakfast, though once the Season starts she may well not rise till noon—"

"Is Lord Ramsey about?"

". . . the Season being so enervating, even for young ladies. Lord Ramsey?" Miss Hill looked vacant. "I'm not altogether sure, though I did hear something. Now what was it? Ah, yes, Mr. Dunlop, that's his valet you know, such a kind man, almost a gentleman in his behavior, sent down early for coffee and his lordship has gone riding in Hyde Park and will not return for an hour or more and—"

Sophia threw back the covers and leapt from the bed.

"Susan, my dear, pray be careful. I have known the megrim to return if an attack is followed by undue activity."

Sophia crammed bread and butter into her mouth and finished the tea, and Miss Hill looked disappointed. "You are but a serving girl, after all. Somehow I had the idea—well, no matter."

Sophia felt contrite. "Forgive me, dear Miss Hill. Thank

you for your kindness. I must rise quickly. I can't explain.
Pray, do leave the tray and I'll finish the food."

Miss Hill smiled, her thin face relieved of some of its
gloom, her washed-out eyes attaining a slight shine. "You
know, my dear, I prefer your looks without the
maquillage." Then she left.

Sophia wished that ladies could curse as roundly as men.
She had not meant a soul to see her unpainted and she had
completely forgotten her assumed accent. She threw on her
clothes, tying tapes and fastening buttons with fingers that
seemed almost unwilling to obey her brain. She took out
her *pomade à baton* and smoothed it over her face,
grudging the lost time. Then she crammed her mob cap
down over her hair, put her cape over her arm, and picked
up, then put down, her small valise. What use was there to
take it? It held nothing of value. Just a few minutes of luck
and she would be out of this house.

She opened her door and listened. Very distantly she
heard the murmur of servants' voices from below. She
walked quietly to the back stairs, at the foot of which she
knew there was a tradesman's entrance, and began the
descent. Once, further on down the narrow staircase, there
was the sound of footsteps as a servant went to the family
rooms. Her heart was thundering in her ears as she crept
on down, passing door after door in the tall house.

At last she arrived at the street entrance. She turned the
key and pulled back the bolt. She was outside and almost
collided with a woman carrying a basket which her nose
told her contained fish. The woman stared at her before
hammering with the Ramsey kitchen door knocker and
Sophia ran around the nearest corner into the next street.
She paused. She had no idea how to get to her cousin's
residence, but she had a tongue in her head and she asked
directions from a passing urchin.

"Dunno 'ow to get to Upper Brook Street! You must be
a proper Jilly-raw." But he gave her instructions, and
Sophia gathered enough information through his cockney
accent to find her way along Mount Street and Park Street
to Upper Brook Street, her ears ringing with the noise of

carriages, carts, and wheelbarrows rumbling over cobbles, the cacophony of street cries, the shouting of apprentices and the barking of dogs. She stood for a moment looking along the rows of dwellings with their variety of architectural styles, catching her breath and wondering which of the elegant houses belonged to her cousin.

A sweep approached her, attended by two boys, all three caked with soot.

Sophia asked in as broad a country accent as she could summon, "Sir, can 'ee tell me which 'ouse be Lady Stoneyhurst's?"

The sweep looked her up and down and his small assistants stared up, the whites of their eyes startling against their engrimed skin. "Goin' as sarvant, are ya?"

Sophia nodded.

"She's in the fifth along from 'ere, but she don't want no sarvant." The sweep roared with laughter, which was taken up in shrill squeaks of mirth from his undersized climbing boys, their teeth shining, their eyes crinkling into the dirt.

Sophia was puzzled, but thanked him and hurried to the house he pointed out. As she stared at it she realized with horror the reason for his amusement. The knocker had been removed, the windows boarded over. Lady Stoneyhurst had clearly not yet returned to London for the Season.

Sophia had to fight an overwhelming need to weep as she turned aside. What could she do now? She knew no one else. She walked away, not needing to simulate a stoop, feeling utterly dejected, knowing that the only place where she could find refuge was in the house owned by Viscount Ramsey. And perhaps not even there if her absence had been noted and resented.

For the first time she really saw the street vendors. Some looked quite prosperous, others, like a scrawny woman with three hungry urchins clinging to her skirts, were half-starved as they attempted to interest passing folk in their commodities. The ragged woman had a tattered basket of wild flowers and herbs. A pretty girl in a soiled white gown and tobacco colored shawl held out a handful of paper strips to three gentlemen evidently only now returning from their nightly revels. "Buy a new love song, good sirs. Sing it to your ladies."

One seized the girl around the waist. "A kiss for a song," he slurred.

The girl laughed. "Two kisses, if you like, but my sheets are still a halfpenny each."

"Hard-hearted wench." The young buck kissed her and took three song sheets, dropping a penny halfpenny into her waiting hand, and the gentlemen went on their way declaiming the love song loudly. The girl's smile disappeared. "Bastards!" she said.

Sophia had wandered along the length of Upper Brook Street. Across the road lay a large stretch of open land where some of the more sheltered trees were winning the battle against frost and were green-tipped with spring growth. There were many riders, their mounts treading delicately over the half-frozen ground, yet stirring it enough to send earth and grass-scented air floating to her nostrils, and reminding her of her own, safe garden in Devonshire. What a fool she was to have ignored all Miss Taylor's strictures on the perils of the world to a lady alone and so casually launched herself into it.

Two girls, their heavy face paint garish in the morning light, their clothes overdecorated with frills and cheap lace, their hats crowded with feathers and ribbons, reminded Sophia that there were far more degrading professions than maidservant to which a penniless woman could sink. She stared after them as they made their weary way back to whatever hovel or house of disrepute they occupied. The sight of them, the noise, her recent exertions, the smell of hot pies from a pie man's barrow, all combined suddenly to cause an attack of sick dizziness that had her leaning against a wall, her eyes closed. Miss Hill was right, of course. Her headache was beginning to nag again. She knew there was only one thing she could do. She must return to Charlotte. She thought of Lord Ramsey and the way he battered at her senses. He would resume his demand that she find a reference from somewhere. He had every right. Damn him! she muttered. She was beginning to wonder if there ever would be an end to this self-inflicted torment. She stood upright, her chin high, and turned in the direction of Berkeley Square when, as if conjured by her thoughts, she heard a voice she recognized.

"Susan! What a pleasant surprise!"

She whirled around and stared up into the viscount's mocking eyes. He sat astride a horse whose shining coat and steaming breath spoke of healthy exertion. The green space opposite must then be Hyde Park. She curtsied, searching her mind for something coherent to say, wishing she could be as publicly uninhibited as the seller of ballads.

"Lord Ramsey!" she acknowledged.

He frowned in spurious concern. "If you are shopping for Miss Charlotte you are on the wrong tack. Bond Street, both old and new, lies east of Berkeley Square, and the Oxford Street emporiums are streets away."

"Thank you, my lord."

"Though, I cannot think why Charlotte should send you out when her chief pleasure lies in shopping. She must be desperate for some article. Or maybe you are looking for cloth for yourself. That gown truly is an assault upon the senses. You should wear the one my sister gave you while you spend your guineas."

Sophia had carefully left the two guineas donated by his lordship, and the half guinea he had given her at the inn, wrapped in a screw of paper addressed to him, and placed on Charlotte's folded gown on the chest of drawers in the attic room. Pray God no one had yet discovered them.

"Nothing to say to me, Susan? You are always silent except when it pleases you to talk. An unusual quality in a female."

His acerbic tone brought the angry color to Sophia's face, but she checked her impulse to tell him to go to the devil. She needed the shelter of his roof.

"I—thought I would slip out and get some cloth before Miss Charlotte needed me," she said, grudging the further lie which she blamed on his curiosity. She had no idea that gentlemen baited their maidservants this way. He wore leather breeches and a dark gray riding coat and she could see her reflection in his highly-polished boots. She glared up into his arrogant face with its swarthy complexion and dark brows and wished she could control the inexplicable frisson of excitement that ran through her.

"I think you had best return, Susan. Miss Charlotte will surely be missing you by now. Maybe she will take you around the warehouses, the silk mercers, the haberdashers, and all the other places in which ladies delight to spend time and money. The Season will soon begin in earnest and she must have a complete wardrobe. As, indeed, must Lady Ramsey. The house will be buzzing with seamstresses and hatters and shoemakers and a dozen other trades-people and there will be shrieks of dismay if some frill is too short or too long." His brows drew together above his dark eyes in a fearsome frown. "Please God, my sister will get betrothed in her first Season, or it will all have to be done again next year."

"She's so pretty, someone must surely fall in love with her."

The viscount brightened. "That is true, Susan. Are you not just a trifle jealous of her? Many lady's maids are jealous."

"Your lordship appears to be intimately acquainted with the emotions of lady's maids?"

She expected another frown, but the viscount laughed loudly, causing his mount to strike sparks from the cobbles with his stamping hooves. "What an astonishing wench you are, Susan. I would like prodigiously to talk to you further, but most postpone the pleasure. Can't keep this prime bit of blood and bone standing any longer."

The viscount trotted off, leaving Sophia staring at his back. As he reached the corner he turned unexpectedly, his hand touched his gray felt hat in a mock salute, and Sophia realized that he had known she would be watching him and could have stamped as hard as his horse at giving him the satisfaction of being right.

Sophia got back into the Ramsey house unobserved and raced up to her room. No one had been in it and she put on the muslin gown and was ready when summoned to Charlotte's bedchamber.

Her mistress was sitting up in bed, exquisite in a pale pink bedgown with white satin ribbons, her golden curls clustered beneath her cap, her deep blue eyes gleaming with happiness as she contemplated the day ahead.

"Susan, are you well now? I am so glad."

Sophia thanked her for her thoughtful kindness.

Charlotte smiled. "I always sympathize with anyone who has the headache. So distressing! Today I shall purchase pretty stuffs for your gowns and caps, but in the meantime, won't you please remove that awful mob cap and wear one of mine."

Sophia shook her head, smiling in an effort not to appear insolent.

"I won't take no. I insist you wear something pretty. You know that one of your perquisites is to take my cast-off garments. It's a pity you are so tall because I have a good number of gowns I shall no longer wear. But caps are different. Come now, I positively insist! You must obey me!"

Sophia had to give way and Charlotte handed her mob cap to a housemaid with instructions to "put this in the kitchen range" and Sophia's tightly bound chestnut hair was crowned with a confection of cotton with eyelet embroidery and yellow ribbons.

"That is so much better!" exclaimed Charlotte with truth, as Sophia had to admit. "And later, dear Susan, you shall have gowns to suit your station as my personal maid and you must go on a reducing diet which will improve your figure as well as your complexion. Did you know that some doctors believe that certain foods can clear the skin? Are you so very pimpled that you need to paint so heavily? Poor girl. I do believe you could be almost pretty if we took some care of you."

Sophia, half sick with remorse at her deception, helped Charlotte into a pale pink muslin gown with an embroidered hem, a brown cloth pelisse trimmed with white fur, and a sweetly pretty brown silk-plush poke bonnet. She watched from an upper window as Charlotte

and Lady Ramsey left in a closed town carriage driven by
the senior coachman and attended by two footmen who
clung to the back and she was assailed by a sudden ache to
return to her proper sphere and follow their example. She
had thought of Charlotte as bird-witted, but she had not so
flagrantly disregarded society's laws as she. She leaned her
hot forehead on the windowpane, dejected and
disheartened by the tangle she had got herself into. All her
life she had looked forward to her first Season. She
wondered now if her dream would ever materialize, or if
her childhood companions would dance away the weeks
while she stayed lonely in the country in disgrace. She
prayed that Lady Stoneyhurst would return before long.
How would she know? She could not go daily to Upper
Brook Street to see if the house was opened up. Then she
recalled that in her guardian's newspaper there had been a
column listing the names of the *ton* who had arrived in
London for the Season, and remembered seeing several
newspapers on the Ramsey library table. Her heart
misgave her at the thought of an illicit visit to a part of the
house which was none of her business. What new heights
of sarcasm would the viscount reach if he caught her? She
set her lips in determination as she began to tidy the chaos
left by Charlotte. Let him think or say what he pleased just
as long as she discovered the right moment to make a
successful escape.

Seven

Lord Ramsey sat longer than usual over his breakfast, then
made for his library with an abstracted air that caused
speculation among the upper servants. Something, they
assured one another, was up.

The viscount threw himself into his comfortable high-
backed chair by the glowing library fire. For the first time
in his life he wondered exactly who lit the fires in the house

and at what hour. He had never before considered
domestic details, apart from ensuring that proper wages
were paid.

The advent of Charlotte's unusual maid into his life was
having an odd effect upon him. He could not get her out of
his mind. What made the memory of her so damned
intrusive? He wondered how she was faring in the kitchen.
Acquaintances would advise him to throw so strange a
creature from his door, yet he could not convince himself
that she was a danger to his household. She intrigued him.
Perhaps her eyes held the answer. They were large, thickly
fringed by brown lashes, a radiant hazel that changed with
her moods. Sometimes they reminded him of ocean pools,
at others of a clear sky. Her delicately arched brows were
fine and no paint could disguise her mouth with its sensual
lower lip.

"For God's sake," he said aloud. He recalled with
shame his mishandling of her when he tried to wash her
face, then frowned at the memory of his spoiled breeches.
The next moment he envied a nobleman of old who could
force her to wash the paint from her face, yes, and strip,
and reveal herself to him in all her naked beauty without
those idiotic pads. Many members of high society would
do just that, Ramsey reflected. Beauty? Yes, he was sure it
lay somewhere hidden.

He sank further into his chair. He had played deep until
the early hours of the morning, finally rising from the
hazard table at three o'clock. After a short sleep he had
exercised his favorite horse. Now he was replete with food,
and warm, and his eyelids grew heavy.

He was only half awake when the door opened and
closed and a light footfall crossed the room to the big
library table. There was the rustle of paper and he opened
his eyes a crack to see Susan hurriedly turning the pages of
the newspapers, muttering to herself. She slapped the
Times on the table with an exclamation of irritation then,
hesitantly, pulled open a drawer. Lord Ramsey's eyes
opened and disappointment flooded him. Was she just a
common thief after all? She gave a sigh and removed a

single sheet of writing paper, a small bottle of ink, and a quill pen. She turned to leave and stopped abruptly at the sight of her employer sprawled in his chair, staring at her from beneath his heavy brows. She put her hands behind her back, her face crimsoning. The viscount waited, but she continued to stare at him, her eyes wide, as if mesmerized.

"We meet in strange situations, do we not?" inquired the viscount pleasantly. "This is not your domain, Susan. Why are you here?"

She gestured behind her at the scattered papers.

"Ah, yes. You appeared to be searching for something. What was it? Some item of news? Pray, share your need with me, I may be able to help."

"I don't need help, my lord."

"Perhaps you were seeking the names and products of warehouses, on behalf of your mistress," suggested Lord Ramsey.

Sophia nodded, hating to give even silent credence to another lie, but desperate for an escape.

"How thoughtful of you, and how clever of me to guess. Do not you think I was clever, Susan?"

She might have known he was taunting her again.

"You have no need to trespass in the library. Lady Ramsey has her own newspapers delivered daily. Also a number of the weekly and monthly magazines, filled with fashions and therefore a most necessary expense. I take my own papers. I prefer them with the pages in their proper order and without the embellishment of coffee or chocolate stains."

"I beg your pardon. I didn't know. I'll not enter the library again."

"Wait!" The girl stopped, her back to him, the paper, bottle, and pen now clasped to her bosom. He could almost feel the tension in her.

"Now you are over the shock of the attack upon your person, have you recalled the names of any of your former employers?"

She looked at him over her shoulder and the viscount

almost gasped at the fury in the hazel depths. He rose and said, "You have purloined a sheet of my best paper, a bottle of ink, and a pen."

Sophia stood very straight, her head high. "Oh, no, not purloined! I've only borrowed them and intended to replace them. Except the paper. I was to keep only the paper, my lord. Just one sheet. I didn't think you would mind."

"My mother or sister could produce all you need for you. Your theft is unnecessary."

"I am *not* a thief! Such a fuss over a sheet of paper."

"Nevertheless, it belongs to me and you should have asked my permission to take it, especially as it involved searching in my desk. Lady Ramsey and Miss Charlotte would not dream of doing such a thing, yet you, a mere serving wench—"

Her eyes flashed sparks and she drew in her lower lip with her excellent white teeth.

"Are you afraid of me, Susan?"

"No, my lord!"

"Good! You may write your letter here. I assume you are sending for a reference." He walked to his desk and drew back the chair for her.

"Please, my lord, I'd best not while you're watching. You'll make me nervous. And anyway, a letter's private."

"I see. Very well. Bring it to me when you've done and I'll have it franked."

"That won't be necessary, my lord."

The viscount threw up his hands in spurious horror. "Have you considered the cost to the recipient?"

"It doesn't matter." Her eyes were glowing now with rage.

Ramsey almost laughed. He walked to the door and stood with his back to it. She faced him and he had a flash of admiration at her courage as she met his stare unflinchingly. He stepped closer and she held her ground.

"Susan, I must tell you how pleased I am that you have entered my life. You are a constant source of amusement and interest to me."

Those expressive eyes grew glacial. She surprised him by

dropping into a low, graceful curtsy, lifting the side of her skirt with one hand while the other remained firmly clasped around the things she had taken. "How gratifying that must be, my lord."

"Oh, it is. I shall watch your career with keen enjoyment."

She nodded and smiled, but the smile would not have looked out of place on a duelist. Ramsey stepped aside and allowed her to leave, wondering how a girl found wandering the roads alone could curtsy with the assurance and grace of a duchess.

Sophia walked from the library fuming with frustrated anger. She scarce knew how she had kept her temper. She ached to tell the viscount exactly what she thought of him and his tormenting. She went straight to Charlotte's room and wrote a letter to Mr. Plerivale, begging his and Miss Sheffield's forgiveness, telling him she was safe with a lady and that she would communicate further quite soon.

She managed to slip out of the house and find the nearest inn that took in mail. The letter would require Mr. Plerivale to pay a shilling and eightpence. No wonder there was a brisk illegal trade in franking.

Charlotte and Lady Ramsey returned home four hours later and their carriage was unloaded of its many boxes and bundles by a stream of servants.

Charlotte called Sophia to her mother's room, which resembled a floral garden of muslins, silks, and satins of every imaginable hue, while hats and bonnets, fans and reticules, silk stockings and shoes, all breathtakingly pretty, made Sophia's mouth water. Thanks to her guardian she had an excellent income and she longed to take part in such delightful extravagance.

"Susan," cried Charlotte, "see what I have purchased for you. Blue and yellow muslins that will enhance your hair, fine cotton for morning wear, linen for aprons, and plenty of ribbons and some lace for decoration."

Sophia hardly knew how she thanked her pretty benefactress. Her guilt weighed down her spirits. She had gone into the adventure so carelessly, never dreaming how many people she would involve.

"A mantua-maker will be here later," explained Charlotte, "with her retinue of seamstresses, and she can measure you after she's finished with Mama and me. There is cotton and cambric too for your chemises and bed-gowns. It is all so diverting! Our first engagement is a dinner three nights from now, and a noon breakfast party the day after. Soon, when everyone has returned to town, we shall have many engagements in one day and I shall scarce have time to rest. Think of the gentlemen I shall meet. We will dance and talk and tease." She twirled around the room to the warning shrieks of her mother, fearful that the fine silks and laces might get torn.

Nell hurried in from the dressing room. "My lady, are you ill? Have you got the headache?" Lady Ramsey touched her head and sighed and Nell produced a phial of hartshorn, giving Sophia a dark look, as if she alone were responsible for the riot of untidiness in the room. "I'll clear all this away in no time at all. You must rest. Shall I fetch a cup of tea? Or coffee?"

"I'll have ratafia, Nell, and you may leave the stuffs. The women will be here soon to measure us, though to tell truth, I do not believe my figure varies from last Season by an ounce."

"No, indeed, my lady. You will outshine everyone just like you always do. Please take tea, my lady. Ratafia will make your headache worse."

Lady Ramsey was petulant. "Take the hartshorn away and bring me what I order. I have not *got* the headache, but I shall surely get it if you don't stop vexing me."

Nell's face reddened and she looked near to tears. Sophia threw her a sympathetic glance and received a vicious glare for her pains.

Sophia made several journeys to take Charlotte's shopping to her bedchamber. Miss Hill was there, sitting near the window, mending a cotton stocking.

She jumped to her feet when Sophia entered and her needles and threads were scattered. "Oh, Susan, I thought it was Miss Charlotte. I'm supposed to mend my clothes in my own time, but truth to tell I have little of that and I'm only really free in the evenings and my eyes hurt if I sew by candlelight and—"

Sophia had knelt to pick up the companion's belongings and she handed them to her with a smile. "I cannot think that Miss Charlotte would insist on something that damanged your vision. You should ask her."

Miss Hill went white. "No! No, don't ever tell her. Promise me. It's not that she would be unkind. She's a dear soul, in spite of her waywardness, but Nell would complain and complain about me to Lady Ramsey and she'd turn me off just to stop Nell's tongue."

Sophia said no more. She worked with set lips, tidying the bedchamber and dressing room, aware for the first time how dreadful life could be for a gentlewoman without means. She thought of her own dear governess-companion and had to blink back sudden tears. Would Miss Sheffield be punished for her charge's transgression? Maybe even now she was out of a place and seeking work. If she had had any notion that running away from her home would affect so many people, she would have stayed. Then she thought of Edwin and knew that given the same circumstances she would do the same again. Dear friend though he had always been, she could not marry him.

Her work in the bedchamber done, she went to the kitchen where a light luncheon was being served. The meal of vegetable broth and baked apples was taken with the formality that prevailed in the servants' hall, though upstairs, Sophia knew, the family would be sitting in the morning room picking casually at the midday dainties and probably Lord Ramsey would eat nothing at all at this hour. Gentlemen often did not bother.

Lord Ramsey! How infuriating he could be. He suspected her motives. She had not bargained for having to deal with a man of his keen perception. How long could she keep this masquerade up? And what would happen when she returned to her proper world? She would just be a young girl in her first Season and he preferred experienced women for dalliance. The realization that his indifference would pain her intruded and worried her.

She left the servants' hall thankfully and was followed by Tindal, who caught her up on the first half-landing of the back stairs. "Susan, I bought you a present. Look. Three shades of green ribbons for your cap. They'll go fine against your hair."

Sophia turned and stared at the trailing handful of pretty ribbons. "Mr. Tindal, I know you mean to be kind, but you've no call to be giving me presents. I can't ever be anything to you."

Tindal's face flushed furiously. "Why not? What's wrong with me? Just because you're a top-lofty lady's maid, I suppose you think I'm a nobody. Well, I'll get to the top, too. I'm going to be a valet, maybe even a butler or house steward in a fine house. You'll wish you'd been nicer to me then."

"Please, Mr. Tindal, there's nothing wrong with you that I can see. In fact, you're a handsome fellow."

Tindal's manner changed instantly. "There, I knew you liked me. You're a naughty flirt. Here, give us a kiss." Once more Sophia found herself in Tindal's embrace and this time there would be no Lord Ramsey to stop him. She had never been taught how to deal with such unwanted advances because no one had envisaged Lady Sophia Clavering confronted by such a situation.

Then a shrill voice came from a few feet away.

"You slut!"

Tindal released her and jumped back, almost treading on Kitty's toes. " 'E's mine!" said Kitty to Sophia. " 'E's as good as asked me to marry 'im."

"I'm not a slut!" protested Sophia.

Her voice was drowned by Tindal's. "You got no call to spy on me!" The footman's voice was rising. "An' I don't belong to anybody."

"What about all those things you said when you told me I was the prettiest girl in London. Didn't you mean none of 'em?"

"At the time I sed 'em, yes, but now I've met Susan—"

"You can't tell me that you want that ugly bitch in place of me."

"She's not ugly," shouted Tindal.

"She surely is. 'Er face is enough to turn the milk sour!"

"She's got nice eyes."

"She looks like a bolster and sags like one," shrieked Kitty, "an' she must 'ave a face like a—like a stone quarry to need so much paintin'."

"She talks nicer than you," returned Tindal. "You'll never better yourself if you can't talk properly. I'm not goin' to hitch myself to a girl who'll always stop in the kitchen."

"That's not what you said afore. An' I can learn. You could teach me."

Sophia looked wildly around her. Kitty blocked the stairs leading down and Tindal the ones going up. She was caught between them like a mouse in a trap. The only way out was the door leading to the house and she pushed it open and almost sprang through.

She landed in front of the viscount, who was ready to go out, dressed in a dark gray coat that reached his calves and black boots. He carried gloves and a gray felt hat.

"Good God! Susan! Whatever next? And what's that hellish din on the back stairs?"

"A slight, er, argument, my lord, between a pair of lovers."

The viscount's heavy brows were raised and his eyes held sardonic amusement. "The lower quarters appear to be in a positive ferment. I wish I could stay to share it with you, but I am due at Carlton House shortly. One must not keep His Royal Highness waiting. He desires my opinion on a new scheme of upholstery."

"An important engagement, to be sure," murmured Sophia, dropping a curtsy.

The dark brows rose again and a strong finger tipped Sophia's chin so that her head was forced up.

"Look at me, Susan."

The viscount's only contact with her was his finger beneath her chin, yet Sophia found herself unable to resist his command.

"Such astonishing eyes," murmured Ramsey, then he was gone, leaving behind him a faint scent of soap and clean linen and sandalwood, and Sophia stood for a

moment, touching her chin where the viscount's finger had
rested, trying to deny the pleasure that his nearness had
brought.

The noise from the back stairs had ceased and Sophia
ventured to push open the door. Kitty was in Tindal's
arms, weeping down his livery coat, and he was patting her
back and murmuring something Sophia could not catch.
She wished she could tell Kitty that her lover was in no
danger from her. She closed the door silently and hurried
up the front stairway, unfortunately meeting the indignant
Lorimer, who delayed her with a diatribe about the
insolence of maids who thought themselves too fine to use
the servants' stairs. Unable to cope with another con-
frontation she almost ran from him and his scandalized
voice followed her as she hurried back to Charlotte's
room.

Miss Hill was there. "Oh, Susan, I'm instructed to tell
you to wait upon Miss Charlotte in her Mama's
bedchamber. The mantua-maker has arrived."

That night, as Sophia climbed wearily and thankfully
into bed, she reflected on the day. It had seemed like a
month, with traps laid for her at every turn. She had been
allocated the most humble assistant of the mantua-maker
to measure her and even she had commented on her shape
and advised her to go on a reducing diet. It seemed that in
the Ramsey household whatever she did would interest,
annoy, puzzle, or intrigue someone. She had imagined she
would sink into obscurity here, but she had as well sit in a
fairground booth to be stared at and commented upon by
the passing crowd.

During the next two days Sophia waited on her mistress,
hanging the pretty gowns which arrived in a swift stream,
completed through the days and nights by sewing women
who must be little better than slaves. Sophia's gowns had
been made for her in Exeter, a far quieter town than
London, but even there she had seen rows of girls who
gradually grew paler and more bent from lack of air and
overwork. She was ashamed to recall that she had taken it

all for granted. This journey of hers into the domestic underworld was teaching her lessons.

Into paper-lined drawers she laid Charlotte's new kid gloves, snowy shifts, lacy bedgowns, fans, and shawls. She had surreptitiously returned the viscount's pen and ink to the library, leaving them on top of his desk so that he could have no opportunity for reprimanding her for prying. She did everything possible to keep out of his way and caught only glimpses of him. He seemed to know by instinct when she was observing him and once raised his hand in a mocking wave.

On the third morning, when Charlotte and her mother were visiting a circulating library, Sophia saw the announcement for which she was waiting. Under the heading of "Court News" it was revealed that Lady Stoneyhurst had vacated her country seat in Lancashire and opened up her town house for the Season.

Sophia almost wept with relief. She put her own gown on, left her new ones neatly folded, and placed the viscount's money on top in a screw of paper. To abscond like this went against the grain after Charlotte's kindness, but she had best remain a mystery.

She now knew enough of the house and its routines to make her escape easily and she almost ran toward Upper Brook Street. This time her cousin's house was clearly occupied. The brass knocker gleamed and the front steps had been scoured. She banged on the door loudly.

It was opened by a man who held himself so like a haughty duke he could only be the butler. He stared at her, making no move to ask her in.

"Pray permit me to enter," she said, "and tell Lady Stoneyhurst that—"

"Be off with you!"

"What?"

"Be off with you!" The man's face was crimson with anger. "That's clear enough, isn't it? You've got a sauce coming to her ladyship's front door. If you're here for a purpose, go around the back and talk to the housekeeper."

The door was slammed and Sophia gaped at it, realizing belatedly that the butler could scarcely be blamed for not

recognizing her as quality. She wondered what to do next.
She must get into the house somehow, even if it meant one
last brush with falsehood. She made her way to the back
door where a woman was selling herbs to the cook. When
the transaction was completed she stepped forward before
the door closed.

"If you please, ma'am?"

The cook looked inquiringly at her and smiled, albeit a
little frostily. "So you've arrived, 'ave you? Well, that's
good, though you've took your time about it. Didn't the
servants' registry tell you we was in an 'urry? Well, you're
'ere now, an' the sooner you get to work the better. Come
on in. Mrs. King's upstairs—she's the 'ousekeeper an'
she's always in a right royal mood when we open up the
'ouse. I'm Mrs. Tanner—we're not really missus, we ain't
never been married, but Lady Stoneyhurst's old-fashioned
an' likes 'er servants to be called missus. Mrs. King's some
kind of relative to 'er ladyship, but she's got no money an'
she 'as to eat like the rest of us.'' While she was dispensing
this information, the loquacious cook led Sophia along a
stone-flagged passage. She was rendered speechless both
by the events that were taking her over and Mrs. Tanner's
nonstop flow of talk as she led her into a large, warm
kitchen where already maids were preparing dinner. "Lady
Stoneyhurst is 'avin' guests tonight," explained the cook.
"Now 'ang up your cloak behind the door and go through
to the scullery. The pots an' pans need scouring an' Annie
ain't got time to do it as well as wash all the china. We've
only just got back to town an' everythin' needs a good
clean."

Sophia found herself in a cold scullery confronted by a
large stone sink filled with a variety of saucepans and
skillets that lay in congealing water. She shuddered and
turned away to be confronted in the door by a tall, thin
woman who bore a distinct resemblance to some of the
family portraits at home. Clearly, this was Mrs. King, and
Sophia realized that there were even humbler positions into
which a poor gentlewoman could fall.

The housekeeper looked her up and down with pale,
cold eyes, her mouth a slit beneath a long pointed nose.

"Punctuality is in future to be your first consideration. Proceed at once with your work. Later I shall instruct you fully."

She walked away, closing the scullery door. Sophia leaned on the wall and thought of her dilemma. The crowded kitchen lay between her and her cousin. Even if she managed to leave by a back entrance she would have to try the front door again and a second intrusion would surely cause the butler to send for a constable. The situation was farcical, so much so that she laughed and once begun could not stop. If only she could share the joke. Lord Ramsey would laugh with her, she was positive. What a pity she could never disclose her mad escapade to him. She wiped her streaming eyes, rolled up her sleeves, and plunged her hands into the water. Her disguise must be good, for it had completely fooled Cousin Pamela's servants into accepting her as a scrubwoman.

A sense of unease filled her when she thought of Lord Ramsey. His dark eyes seemed to look deep into her. Would he know her again? Surely not. She felt a sharp stab of regret. She would miss him. There was small chance that their lives would ever entwine. His preoccupations and hers were so different. All humor left her as the cold of the stone floor pierced her shoes, and she shivered.

Eight

Lord Ramsey sensed the excitement that wafted through the house like a breeze. He sighed. Any minute now someone would disturb the peace of his study where, at the behest of the Prince Regent, he was compiling an essay on the cravat. He would not feel it encumbent upon him to write on the subject had not he been commanded, and the words hung heavy. He sighed and sat staring at nothing, his quill idle. He had everything a man could wish for. An ancient and respected title, wealth, and a secure place in society close to the heir to the throne, yet he was increasingly bored by the social round. Another Season was about to begin, filled with simpering misses and ambitious chaperones who, in spite of their whispers about his style of living, would willingly overlook any deficiencies in so eligible and wealthy a gentleman if only he would propose marriage to one of their charges.

Ramsey's friends would have been amazed had they known that if fate were kind enough to send along the right woman, he would welcome marriage. Perhaps he was searching for the impossible. He returned to his essay and was stopped immediately by the peremptory opening of the library door. His mother entered and he sprang to his feet. For her to exert herself to come to him, instead of summoning him by a servant, was so rare that he decided something really dreadful had occurred. His sister followed Lady Ramsey and after them marched a small troop of the upper servants.

"Susan has left," wailed Charlotte, "and I need some different ribbons sewn on my gown for tonight. I cannot conceive why I ever thought that marine blue would go with a violet overdress—"

"I tried to warn you at the time, my love," said Lady Ramsey severely, "but you would not listen to your mama. Violet and marine blue, indeed!"

"Surely you have not disturbed my work to complain about my sister's ribbons," said Ramsey dryly.

"Of course not," said Lady Ramsey, her face growing pink with indignation. "As if we would! It's all your fault, Charlotte. If you had not brought that woman to our home I would not now be frightened out of my wits—"

"Nasty, scheming creature!" snapped Nell.

The viscount tried to sort through these scraps of information as he ushered his mother and sister to a couch near the fire.

"Perhaps if someone told me what's amiss?" he suggested gently.

His mother tried to speak, then raised her hartshorn to her nose and Nell flew to her. "My poor lady—"

"Charlotte?" said the viscount gently. His sister, still

looking affronted at her mother's sudden attack, elected not to hear.

Lord Ramsey turned to the butler. "Be so good as to explain, Lorimer."

"Miss Charlotte's maid appears to have decamped, my lord."

A gust of fury, followed by sharp disappointment, surprised Ramsey.

Mrs. Parrock said, "The person in question can't be found anywhere in the house. Miss Charlotte don't know where she is and I fear for Lady Ramsey's health. She is sure that the girl intends to get us murdered in our beds and then make off with the family valuables, and I must say I wonder if she's not right about that."

"I'm sure I am," moaned Lady Ramsey.

"I always said no good would come of picking up that creature on the road, and she without a reference to her name and no proper luggage either." said Nell in smug tones.

"She's so good with her needle!" Charlotte cried.

"That doesn't mean she's got a good character," said Nell. "But never you fear, Miss Charlotte, I'll do all that's necessary. If Miss Hill had done her proper duty—"

Miss Hill, who was behaving as inconspicuously as possible, flushed at the criticism from an inferior and said defensively, "I cannot be held to account for what happened. I'm sure I did not want Susan to join us. Miss Charlotte—"

"No one is blaming you, Miss Hill," said Ramsey kindly.

"Oh, aren't they?" muttered Nell.

The viscount threw her a glance that closed her mouth. "Is anything missing?"

"Not so far as we can tell, my lord" said Lorimer. "The girl left these behind." He gestured to a footman who hovered in the hall behind him and who now brought forward a small valise, the gown that had been altered for Susan, some lengths of new cloth, and a small twisted package that jingled. Ramsey guessed that the infuriating woman had returned his money.

He frowned and Nell ventured, "Should we send for a constable, my lord?"

"But nothing has been stolen and no damage inflicted. She appears to have left behind even what could rightfully be called her own," pointed out the viscount.

"That's why Mama is so afflicted with her nerves," said Charlotte. "She fears that Susan is part of some dreadful conspiracy and is trying to lull our suspicions. She knows that we have many of our jewels here with us ready for the Season."

"That is so," said Lorimer, "and she had time to discover all she needs to set a group of rogues at us."

"Oh, oh, my nerves! I shall die, I know I shall!" cried Lady Ramsey.

The viscount glared at Lorimer. "If she is in league with rogues, she is behaving in quite the wrong way. She would surely have stayed until they struck and escaped with them. In any event, provided you make sure that all doors and windows are locked and bolted, I do not see how we could be attacked. Besides, Susan will know that we have fire-arms and a number of stalwarts working here. I am persuaded there must be some other reason for her flight."

The viscount paused and the look on his face held the others silent. "Was she being harrassed by any of the male servants?"

Nell gave a snort of derision. "Who's have looked twice at that ugly creature?"

The viscount recalled the scene with Tindal. That recollection was closely followed by the memory of his own behavior and to his anger was added regret and a hope that he had not been responsible for the girl's flight.

He chose to ignore Nell's remark and dismissed the servants. He reassured his mother, placated Charlotte by promising that she could engage a French maid if she wished, then sat alone, wondering if Susan's beautiful eyes hid a dark, criminal nature.

With a large, coarse apron tied around her middle, Sophia washed pots and pans till her arms ached and her hands were sore from scouring.

She shared the servants' midday meal, noticing that the order of precedence here too was strict, though this town house kitchen was not large enough to hold more than one scrubbed table. She was seated lower than the laundry maids and footboy. In fact, she was clearly regarded as the lowest of the servants. Lady Stoneyhurst's elderly maid, gowned in blue, a fine lace cap perched on her graying hair, sat on the butler's right hand.

The kitchen was so hot that Sophia's maquillage was beginning to melt and she made many surreptitious dabs at it, and prayed that soon she would find a way out. There could be no reasonable excuse for a skivvy to go through the door that led to the family quarters.

The meal over, the servants dispersed to their various duties, instructions were given, opinions exchanged, and in the general commotion Sophia pulled open the inner door a fraction and slipped through.

No outcry followed her and none would. The housekeeper would click her tongue over the unreliability of the lowest form of kitchen life and engage someone else. There was no one around and she sped through the corridor and out into the main hall from which several doors led to the family rooms. A staircase with a wrought-iron balustrade curved to a landing with more doors. She had no idea which one, if any, concealed her cousin. The sound of a soft footfall sent her scurrying through the nearest into a small parlor, thankfully unoccupied. She watched through a crack and saw the lady's maid enter a room near the back of the house, and heard the sound of voices, one unmistakably autocratic, and was sure she had found her cousin at last. She hoped Lady Stoneyhurst would be kind. The sight of herself in a gilt-framed looking glass did nothing to reassure her. She looked dreadful—coarse, brown, and ugly, her hair awry beneath her cap.

The maid crossed the hall once more and Sophia waited. When there was no sound of movement, she crept from the parlor. She reached the central rug and stopped to listen, suddenly very nervous. She eased forward, trying to lessen the clatter of her heavy shoes on the tiles, dragging at the strings of her apron and succeeding only in getting them so

tangled she could not undo them. Then the door leading to
the servants' quarters opened and the maid reappeared,
carrying a coffee pot.

For a moment she was speechless with outrage, then she
found her voice. "How dare you, woman! You have no
right to be here. Get back to the scullery this instant!"

Sophia did not waste time arguing. She skipped around
the scandalized maid and entered the occupied room. A
bright fire burned in the steel and carved wood fireplace,
was reflected in the polished floors and gleamed back from
a small table and a sideboard.

A woman who was standing at a window looking out at
the garden turned and stared. She was inches taller than
Sophia, wore a pale yellow wig on which was a large lace
cap with pink ribbons, a morning gown of pea-green
velvet, and heavy pink and white maquillage.

She lifted her eyeglass to stare at Sophia. "Good God!
Who are you? What are you thinking of to come here?
Lockett!" she called, "Jane Lockett, where. . . ?"

"Here, my lady. I cannot think what this creature is
doing. She's the new scullery wench. Get back to the
kitchen this instant minute! I've told you once!"

Sophia did not move. She should have waited until
evening when she could have approached her cousin
through the shadows. But she was here and must speak.
She begged, "Pray, Lady Stoneyhurst, allow me a word in
private with you."

"Such insolence!" spluttered Lockett. "Shall I send for
a constable, my lady?"

Lady Stoneyhurst raised an imperious hand, frowning
carefully so as not to crack her face paint. "She does not
speak like a scullery wench."

"There's many a one can put on airs and graces. They
go to the play-acting and then ape their betters."

"True," mused Lady Stoneyhurst. "But I still would
like to listen to what the girl has to say. The situation
intrigues me."

"If she's staying, then I am. In my view, it's all very
suspicious. She might attack you."

"I think not. Remain within call, and not a word of this to anyone else, mind you."

The maid sniffed. "I've been with you enough years for you to trust me." She stalked out of the room, giving Sophia a last glance of indignation.

"Dammit, I've overset her," grumbled her ladyship, "and I'll have to talk sweet to bring her around. What do you want with me?" she demanded abruptly. "You dress like a commoner—where in heaven's name did you get that terrible gown?—yet your speech is that of a lady. Explain yourself."

Sophia had considered several approaches, but none were consequent on her having played the scullery maid in Lady Stoneyhurst's own house. She plunged straight in. "I am Lady Sophia Clavering, ma'am, and I've come to you for refuge."

Lady Stoneyhurst sank onto an embroidered stool. "You are who?" she uttered.

"Sophia Clavering, my lady. We are related through my father. I believe we are distant cousins."

"Say you so! I find it difficult to credit. You look very much like a scullery maid. Dammit, Lockett said you are the scullery maid."

"Please allow me to explain, ma'am," begged Sophia. "My plan seemed so perfect at the time, then everything went wrong. And then I was cornered in your kitchen."

"Cornered? You sound as if you were being hunted."

"Sometimes it felt as if I was."

Lady Stoneyhurst, who like many of the *haut ton* was forever seeking new ways to be amused, poured herself a cup of coffee and sipped it thoughtfully. "Speak, girl. You had best be able to prove your claim or I'll follow my maid's advice and have you taken up by a constable."

Sophia talked fast, trying to sound coherent, praying she would not be interrupted, and wondering if the story sounded as incredible to Lady Stoneyhurst as it did to herself. Every word she uttered made it seem worse, but she pressed on and her ladyship listened intently, letting her coffee grow cold.

When Sophia stopped she was asked many searching questions about her family, all of which she was able to satisfy.

Lady Stoneyhurst pondered a while, her darkly-defined brows drawn together, then nodded. "Well, well, you know a great deal about the family. Your tale can so easily be disproved it would hardly be worth your while to lie, and if you had evil designs here you would certainly not have approached me in this way. But, if your story is true, you have behaved extremely foolishly. Thankfully, you appear not to have come to too much grief. I take it as my duty to restore you to your proper sphere." She waved away Sophia's thanks. "I shall provide you with a decent gown and a pelisse and bonnet and procure you a seat on the mail coach. One of my footmen can escort you."

Sophia sat down heavily on a tapestry chair. "Lady Stoneyhurst, please don't send me home. I cannot marry Edwin, I just cannot."

"I doubt if you'll be given the chance after this." Her ladyship's voice was ironic. "It's bad enough that you ran away, but to fall in with Viscount Ramsey! His rakehell reputation could be the ruin of you."

"No, oh, no! How can it? No one will know I was the maid. I'm not really ugly, you know, or plump. I've got myself padded and have used this dark paint and walked with a stoop and—dear Lady Stoneyhurst, I hoped that you would sponsor me into society."

Sophia felt silent at the rise of an imperious hand and an incredulous glare. Then her ladyship appeared to fall into deep thought. Expressions chased across her face —unyielding, pensive, amused, until one remained, a positive leer of anticipation.

"You say you've been maiding Charlotte Ramsey, and fooled that die-away peagoose Lady Ramsey as well as his proud lordship? I'd give a lot to see their faces if they find out."

"But they must never do so, ma'am, if I am to make my mark in society. Never!"

"No, that's true. It's a pity, though. Now, I make no

promises. Lockett shall restore you to rights and I will give
you my decision then. Bringing out a beauty can be a
matter for pleasure; bringing out a plain girl is tedious in
the extreme. You may trust Lockett. She has been with my
family since she was a child and my maid for twenty-five
years. I do not wish to set eyes on you again until you
appear in your proper state.''

Lockett smuggled Sophia upstairs with many sidelong
glances of mingled mistrust and disgust. But her mistress
had issued an order and carry it out she would, whatever
the consequences.

The Chinese influence was prominent in her ladyship's
bed drapes, curtains, rugs, and wallpaper. Lockett led the
way through into a dressing room.

"Stay here. I'll ring down for hot water." Sophia
suspected she had had to bite back an exhortation not to
touch her mistress's goods. Gowns were draped around the
room like brilliant wall hangings, shoes marched beneath
them in rows like soldiers. There was a large chest of
drawers no doubt containing all the requisites necessary
for a society lady. At the thought of the glitter of the *ton*
world, Sophia's heart gave a little jump. After her escapade involving Lord Ramsey, her future lay in her
cousin's hands. Pray heaven those hands would guide her
into the polite world, for now she was reasonably certain
that Edwin's mother would refuse to accept her as a
daughter-in-law.

She undressed and as Lockett wrapped up the gown,
petticoats, and pads in old newspapers and placed them
ready for disposal, Sophia stepped into a fragrant,
steaming bath. She lay back, breathing in the scent of
jasmine, reveling in the sensuous feel of the water against
her skin. She lathered a ball of best soap and massaged her
sore hands. When she stood up and Lockett finally
wrapped her in a large, warm towel, she sighed with
pleasure. More water was brought to wash her hair.
She sat still before Lady Stoneyhurst's dressing table,
watching in the mirror as Lockett brushed her rich
chestnut curls until they shone. As the maid's strokes

lengthened and deepened, her face relaxed its grimness.

"You bear a strong resemblance to your late mama. The sweet countess was a beauty."

Sophia turned her head so sharply the brush tangled in her hair. "Oh, did you know her?"

Locket clucked as she untangled the brush. "You're as lively as her too—though," she continued severely, "I doubt that her ladyship would have behaved as you have."

"But she married Papa, whom she loved," pleaded Sophia. "I was being forced to wed a man I care for only as a brother."

"*She* would have followed her duty."

"Oh, please, Lockett, don't be cross with me. I've had a wretched time. You have no need to tell me I have been dreadfully stupid."

Lockett unbent a little further. She smiled, an odd, secret smile. "When my lady claps eyes on you, I reckon you'll be set for the Season. And, to tell truth, I'm not really certain sure that your mother, the countess, would have allowed herself to be pushed into an unwelcome attachment."

She brought out a silk dressing robe of green, peacock blue, and gold and helped Sophia into it. "Yes, you truly resemble your mama," she said with as much satisfaction as if she had arranged the likeness herself.

Sophia looked at herself in the cheval glass and gasped with pleasure. The colors in the robe made her eyes look as blue-green as the sea. Her skin seemed creamier than ever after the days of the brown *pomade à baton*. Her hair fell in silken waves that clustered into curls on her shoulders. The relief at seeing herself again, at being herself again, was tremendous and she laughed half tearfully and prayed that Lady Stoneyhurst would find what she was looking for in her.

Lockett went downstairs and returned shortly afterward with her mistress. Lady Stoneyhurst stared. "Turn around, child. Pull in the robe so that I may see your figure. Excellent! Excellent! I couldn't have imagined better. How fortuitous this is, Lockett."

Sophia said pleadingly, "Does that mean you'll help me make my come-out, Lady Stoneyhurst?"

"Most decidedly, child. And from now on, you are to address me as Cousin Pamela. Familiarity between us will help us in our war with the gossips."

Sophia blinked. "War?"

"Your debut may turn into a series of skirmishes during which we must keep your reprehensible adventures a secret. You were well disguised, but—your eyes—they could not easily be forgotten. They are the danger. You must endeavor to keep them down for a while, until folk become used to you. Tonight we shall encounter the first test. You will appear at my dinner party."

"Yes, Lady—Cousin Pamela. Only I have no gown."

"A difficulty that can soon be overcome. Most fashion houses have gowns that someone has ordered and then failed to purchase. I daresay there is something in your size. Are you good with your needle?"

"Yes, ma'am."

"Splendid. You and Lockett between you will rig an outfit. Tomorrow I shall arrange for a mantua-maker to call. Meanwhile, I must begin work. I must write to the Duchess of Chiddingley, a *dear* friend of mine whose town house is much larger and more suited to grand occasions. She is bringing out her great-niece, Miss Annabel Willis. D'you know her? No? A *sweet* child, but—well, I have no time for chit-chat. Remain here."

Lady Stoneyhurst swept out, followed by Lockett, both talking, and Sophia was left alone, feeling so nervous she could not keep still and paced the floor, the robe flying out behind her.

There was a knock on the door and she almost cowered. It was an automatic reaction that she sincerely hoped would not persist. She stood straight and called, "Come in," in a voice brimming with false confidence.

Her first encounter as the newly restored Lady Sophia was with Mrs. King, the housekeeper, but a transformed Mrs. King. The pale eyes reflected the smile on her thin lips. "Good morning, Lady Sophia," she said.

"Good morning, er—?"

Mrs. King supplied her name. "I was surprised to hear
you had arrived, your ladyship, and so was Wheadon, our
butler. In fact, I cannot ascertain who let you in. Perhaps
you can enlighten me."

Sophia did her best to produce a look that would silence
the housekeeper. "Should I have noticed who opened the
door?" she asked, haughtily.

"No, no, of course not, my lady." Mrs. King walked
further into the room. "How unfortunate that your
luggage should have been stolen from the back of the
coach. However, you will have much pleasure in
purchasing more. I daresay your coachman will inform a
magistrate of the crime."

While Sophia was attempting to come to terms with the
fresh set of untruths her cousin Pamela had obviously
perpetrated, Mrs. King peered into her face. "How like
your dear mother you are. I came to inform your ladyship
that the hairdresser has been sent for. He's a foolish little
man, but a positive miracleworker with hair."

A small man with tiny, plump hands appeared in the
doorway. "Ah, come in, Mr. Frederick. Here is your
customer. Now, Lady Sophia, if you would be so good as
to seat yourself."

Sophia hesitated, suddenly recalling how short
Charlotte's hair was. "How much will he take?"

"A good deal, a great deal," said Mr. Frederick in a
somewhat squeaky voice.

"But my hair . . ." Sophia touched it defensively.

"*Must* come off," said the little man severely. "It is
vital that your ladyship should be up to all the fashions for
your come-out. I cannot recall the names of the many
young ladies whose hair I have cropped lately. Country
hairdressers!" he said in tones of infinite scorn. "Pray be
seated, ma'am."

He would not permit her to watch in the looking glass,
so Sophia sat and listened as the big scissors snipped and
snipped and worryingly long tresses of rich reddish-brown
fell to the floor. When she was permitted to view herself,
she gasped, "I'm practically hairless!"

Mr. Frederick and Mrs. King laughed. "You'll become used to it," said the housekeeper. "See how the curls cluster around your ears and over your forehead. Do you not think it pretty?"

Sophia looked again. One became used to things quickly. Her new hair style showed her face to better advantage and her eyes looked bigger and more glowing than ever. "Yes," she said softly, "I think it pretty."

She had no money to give the man, but Mrs. King took care of it and once more Sophia was alone. The excitements and alarums of the past days took their toll, the hot bath had relaxed her, and she felt secure for the first time for an age. She lay on her cousin's bed and drifted into sleep and a dream in which Mr. Frederick was chasing her with a garden scythe before he was abruptly turned into Lord Ramsey, who caught her and held her in his arms, making her a willing prisoner.

Sophia was given her own room, hastily prepared by the housemaids. How wonderful it felt to be occupying her proper station in life once more. Her bed was a half tester with drapes of pink and green flowers on a pale beige background, a pattern repeated in the curtains. Pale flowered rugs lay on the polished floor and the bed was furnished with a deliciously soft feather mattress. Soon she would have clothes in plenty to put in the large wardrobe and dressing chest.

Lockett was fully occupied with her mistress, but Mrs. King maided her willingly. Not a trace of suspicion had she shown and Sophia was breathing easier. Her cousin's messengers had returned with a carriage dress and an evening gown that needed few alterations.

Dressed, she took a last look at herself in the cheval glass. The gown of white muslin beneath a pale yellow open robe suited her. Lace sleeves reached her slender wrists and lace garlanded her breasts at the low-cut neck. Tiny bunches of silk ribbons fashioned into flowers were scattered over the muslin. Her hair was adorned by a filmy lace headdress from which fell dainty trails of lace that brushed her ears and a pale yellow ostrich feather curved backward. Cousin Pamela had sent her a string of jade green beads, a white shawl with green spangles, and a lace fan, and Sophia felt ready to face anyone in such an elegant outfit.

She was alone now, waiting to be called. In all the diversions of sewing her gown she had not thought to ask questions about the expected guests. Consequently the shock she received was almost numbing.

The call came, and she seated herself in the drawing room beside her cousin, who was magnificently garbed in red and blue stripes. A headdress of blue feathers, ribbons, and tiny red beads rested upon an auburn wig. Rubies encircled her neck and glowed in a brooch on her bosom. She eyed Sophia approvingly, nodding and smiling.

"Splendid, my dear. I knew those colors would suit you."

Several guests had already arrived when the door opened and Wheadon announced in somber tones, "Lady Ramsey, Miss Charlotte Ramsey, Viscount Ramsey." And Sophia was faced with the biggest ordeal of her life.

Nine

Sophia glanced over at her cousin, who was watching her with sharp eyes just tinged with malicious enjoyment. There was no time to escape, no opportunity to protest. Lady Stoneyhurst was deliberately exposing her to an exceedingly awkward situation, one over which Sophia feared she might lose control. Her heart had leapt and now settled to a thudding beat that made her hands shake. She rose in deference to Lady Ramsey's seniority and curtsied to her and then to Charlotte, who was staring at her in openly frank admiration.

Then it was Ramsey's turn. He bowed and Sophia had to overcome a wanton desire to run her fingers through his thick, dark curls. As he straightened from his bow, she curtsied lower than she need have done, keeping her eyes firmly fixed on the floor.

The viscount said, "Delighted to meet you, Lady Sophia. One has heard of your beauty."

Oh, has one? thought Sophia, angrily recognizing the bored note beneath the flattery. He moved from her and seated himself beside Cousin Pamela, engaging her in a conversation that appeared to afford them both great amusement. Probably exchanging all the latest scurrilous gossip. The other guests were mingling and a young man, obviously as new to society as she, his skin red to his ears with shyness, begged the privilege of sitting by her.

Sophia only half listened to his clumsy compliments and efforts at social niceties; her eyes and her thoughts were riveted to Lord Ramsey as she wondered how it was possible to suspect the motives of someone so much, yet feel an overpowering ache to be close to him. She sighed. That was a dream unlikely to be fulfilled. It was not even a dream she could be proud of; he was a rakehell and, as such, to be avoided. She felt a surge of intense fury that she need take no pains to avoid him; he was making it very clear that he would pay no heed to her. Her only consolation was that he was just as chillingly polite to the other young women present.

Dinner was announced and the guests moved to the dining room. Sophia sat on one side of the shy man, Charlotte on the other. Charlotte leaned forward several times as dinner progressed, trying to engage Sophia in conversation, but Sophia was suffering beneath a drawback. Viscount Ramsey was seated almost opposite her and although he chattered as much as the rest, several times she became aware he was studying her with almost insolent intensity. In the end, Charlotte gave up, looking aggrieved, as she had every right to do.

Sophia, bewildered by conflicting emotions, chose her food at random, then had to force down chicken in savory jelly, a dish she had never cared for, followed by fried trout. She finished with an orange cake that might have been sawdust for all she could taste it. The dinner seemed to go on forever, with dish after dish brought to the table. The viscount enjoyed his food, but with an abstracted air that made Sophia even more nervous. She feared he had the appearance of a man who was trying to remember something.

When the ladies removed to the drawing room, she breathed more easily, though she wished there had been an opportunity to say a few choice words to her cousin for deliberately landing her in such a situation. Then the gentlemen joined them and Lady Stoneyhurst dispensed tea and coffee, handing the cups to a bewigged footman who delivered them as though they were potions of the gods.

Ramsey waved the brews away and came straight to where Sophia was seated. She had deliberately chosen a narrow chair to make certain no one could sit beside her. He circumvented this by dragging over a tapestry chair and seating himself on it, almost knee to knee with her.

"Lady Sophia, I am persuaded that we have met before." He sounded genuinely puzzled, but after a lightning look Sophia saw that his eyes held something else. Amusement? Mockery? Dawning comprehension? She dared not search his face for a clue, recalling Cousin Pamela's stricture to keep her eyes down.

She shook her head, making the curls which peeped from beneath her headdress bounce engagingly. He looked at them for a long minute. "It seems a pity to cover such pretty hair, delectable though your adornment is."

He had seen Susan's hair, recalled Sophia, and although it had been long and cut in a country fashion, its rich, rare color was unaltered. She ventured another swift glance at him and gasped, feeling she could drown in the depths of his teasing, wicked dark eyes. She said flirtatiously, "My lord, you are fulsome for one who has only just met me."

"Ah, yes, but I feel we have been friends for an age. Have you ever come upon anyone with whom you have instant rapport? It is such a desirable sensation. It makes all the difference to our meeting.

"Not to me!" Sophia simpered and fluttered her fan

vigorously, a mistake for she wafted tendrils of her hair and brought them again to the viscount's notice.

"Alas." Lord Ramsey gave a gusty theatrical sigh that almost wrung a laugh from Sophia. "Am I to wait until the Season is well advanced before I am permitted to pay you compliments? Such reticence goes against the grain."

"I don't doubt it, sir," said Sophia. "You waste no time as a rule. Or so I have been warned."

"Warned, Lady Sophia?" Ramsey laughed, revealing his strong, gleaming teeth. Long white fingers slid down a black ribbon and produced a quizzing glass, and he leaned forward to stare through it into her face. He was so near that Sophia caught his scent of sandalwood and her flesh betrayed her into a sudden yearning. She recalled the strength of his arms, the feel of his body close to hers. "Waste no time, ma'am? I think you have been reading the gossip sheets? No, perhaps not. I believe Lady Stoneyhurst has been at you with her list of gentlemen to be avoided by innocent young maidens. She has, has she not?"

"No!" snapped Sophia, "she did not mention your name." She stopped abruptly. Her irritation with her cousin must not push her into further indiscretion. "No, sir," she said more gently, "my cousin did not speak of you. I must have heard your name somewhere else—I do not recall where."

"What a set-down for me. And such a convenient vagueness for you," murmured Ramsey.

"What do you mean?" asked Sophia, then bit her lip for giving him yet another opening.

"Why, only that if you acquire the reputation for absentmindedness it will not signify what you remember or forget. A useful talent in a society so riddled with gossip as ours. You can always plead forgetfulness if something you dislike is attributed to you."

Sophia clenched her hand into a fist in the folds of her gown, but she managed a false trill of laughter, "I declare, sir, you have guessed aright." She fluttered her fan, remembering just in time to keep her lids lowered, peeping as teasingly as she could manage through her long lashes. "How clever of you to extract my secret. Now I remember! I think that you have some repute with ladies, though I do not recall what it is."

Ramsey frowned as he slid his quizzing glass back into a small waistcoat pocket. She had irritated him and she was glad. He rose. "I wish you a happy Season, my lady." He bowed and strolled across the room with athletic grace, joining a girl with blond tresses who welcomed him with girlish laughter and a flattering deference, leaving Sophia consumed with unreasoning rage and regret.

Her ordeal was not over. Charlotte, seeing her brother leave Sophia, walked across and took his vacant chair. She looked exquisite in a gown of cerulean blue with a filmy pink overdress that picked up the blue of her eyes and the rose of her complexion. Her hair was dressed high in the Grecian fashion and pinned with a jeweled butterfly.

"Lady Sophia, pray permit me to talk to you a while. At dinner you did not speak to me or return my smiles. I fear I have done something to overset you, though I cannot think what it is. If I have, I hope you will forgive me."

"Oh, Miss Ch— Ramsey." Sophia felt perspiration dew her upper lip. "You have done nothing, I assure you. If I have appeared uncivil to you, I apologize. I confess, I was somewhat preoccupied at dinner. I think I must have been nervous. This is my first Season, you know."

Charlotte smiled her brilliant smile, her teeth sparkling between dainty pink lips. "Mine also. I thought you had a sudden attack of the blue devils." Her soft white hand covered her mouth and her face became alight with mirth. "I should not use such language. Mama would be very cross with me if she heard. Making a come-out is exciting, is it not?" Charlotte paused and gave Sophia a close look. "Do you know, Lady Sophia, I have the oddest notion that we have met before, yet it cannot be, for we have been introduced only this evening. Do you have any sense of previously having met me?" Fortunately for Sophia's rapidly disintegrating composure, Charlotte could easily hold a quite lengthy conversation with herself. "I am being foolish. Of course, I could not have met you and forgotten you. Pray allow me to compliment you on your appearance."

Charlotte paused for breath and Sophia said, "Thank you for the compliment, Miss Ramsey. I think I should need far more looks than I possess to outshine you."

Charlotte laughed in delight, but protested, "Pray do not address me as Miss. May I be Charlotte to you? And would you permit me to call you Sophia? I am sure we are going to be friends." She continued pensively, "I must not be a bore on the subject, but—are you absolutely positive we are not already acquainted? Maybe we met in some country house, as children. Where do you live? Our principal seat is in Norfolk, but I have other estates. A distant cousin made me her heir—no one ever knew why. Some of my relatives are decidedly eccentric. Are yours? I think everybody has peculiar connections. I don't recall you in Scotland. Have you ever been there? No? I was at a house party in the country recently—" She stopped abruptly, the pink in her cheeks deepening. "No, you were not there. Mama," she called across the room, "do you have the feeling you have met Lady Sophia before?"

Sophia almost ground her teeth. Charlotte reminded her of a dog with a bone, chewing and biting at it until it had extracted every last piece of meat. Lady Ramsey halted her conversation about the latest hat being advertised by the renowned fashion inventress, Mrs. Bell. "Have I previously met Lady Sophia? No, indeed, I should scarcely have forgotten her. Charlotte, my love, tomorrow we must each purchase a Chapeau Bras. It is a hooped affair designed to wear over a headdress without damaging it and can be carried in a reticule. Such a clever notion."

"Delightful, Mama," agreed Charlotte. "Do please look properly at her ladyship. Are you positive?"

But, thankfully for Sophia, Lady Ramsey had returned to her discussion of fashion, a subject she regarded as of first importance.

The shy young man approached and bowed. He flushed and tripped over his words as he endeavored to tell Lady Sophia that had he ever met her before, nothing would erase her from his memory.

Sophia had almost wilted before the barrage of attention, then she snapped back to awareness as she realized
that Viscount Ramsey had stopped talking and was seated
at his ease on a Chinese brocade-upholstered sofa within
earshot. She looked at him, startled, wondering how much
he had heard of Charlotte's ramblings. He got to his feet
and sauntered over, bringing another chair, seating himself
beside his sister, and fixing his gaze upon Sophia. The shy
one scuttled away.

"This is most odd," said Lord Ramsey in silky tones
that sent shivers up her spine. "My sister also thinks she
has met you previously. Yet you are so sure we were
strangers to you before tonight."

"Have you the same sensation, Hugo?" cried Charlotte.
"Why, this is positively Gothic. Do you read Gothic tales,
Lady Sophia? I am devoted to them. Mama's magazines
are filled with them. The best and most engagingly shivery
are set in the Black Forest or the Rhine. This kind of
situation often occurs in such novels. Yes, there is
definitely a delightful mystery here."

Lady Stoneyhurst's deep voice cut across the room.
"Young folk of today read too many novels. When I was
young we were kept too busy *doing* to be forever reading.
Gothic, indeed! Ramsey, don't encourage the young ladies
in such nonsense!"

Ramsey acknowledged her reproof with a lifted hand,
but he stayed where he was. Sophia was sure he was about
to ask yet another searching question when she was saved
by the entry of Wheadon, the butler, who announced,
"Mr. Barnaby Chatteris, my lady."

The gentleman who entered was of medium height, of a
pleasant though undistinguished countenance, and
inclined to be portly. He was dressed for evening in sage-
green breeches, somewhat stretched to encompass his
stomach, and a bottle-green coat. His cravat almost
touched his rounded cheeks. Some young ladies sat a little
straighter and became more vivacious, while their
chaperones watched Mr. Chatteris with a calculating stare.

"Mr. Chatteris," intoned Lady Stoneyhurst, "you were
to be a guest at dinner. You sent no apology. Now you

walk into my drawing room as if nothing had happened."

Mr. Chatteris smiled, not in the least put out by his hostess's reproaches. He bowed, his several fobs and watches making a tinkling sound. "Nothing would have kept me from your side, your ladyship, had I been at home to receive your invitation. I returned but two hours since from a visit to Hampstead. It has taken that long to dress for the evening. The arrangement of my cravat proved somewhat trying." He smiled at the viscount. "I was attempting to follow your new style, Ramsey."

The viscount raised his quizzing glass and stared for an interminable minute. "Alas, my dear Barnaby," he said.

Mr. Chatteris sighed theatrically and grinned, in no way abashed. "I must just keep trying."

Lady Stoneyhurst's frown deepened. "Pay attention to me, Mr. Chatteris. What in heaven's name can a man find to do in Hampstead at the beginning of the Season?"

Mr. Chatteris said, "A relative of mine who lived there passed suddenly from this earth and—"

"I was unaware that you had a relative residing in Hampstead and certainly did not know that he—or she—had died." Lady Stoneyhurst spoke as if her ignorance was a personal affront.

"I was scarce aware of him myself, ma'am. He was something of a recluse and I never set eyes on him, but since he was good enough to leave me his estate, I felt it incumbent upon me to pay my final respects."

Lady Stoneyhurst's eyes gleamed and all the chaperones in the room leaned forward attentively. "An estate! Congratulations! I trust it makes a nice addition to your fortune."

"Certainly one not to cavil at, your ladyship."

A concerted sigh floated through the large drawing room. Talking broke out afresh while Mr. Chatteris walked about greeting his friends and gaining introductions to the young ladies new to the Season. His brown eyes sparkled appreciatively and his face grew pinker. When he reached Sophia and Charlotte, he positively beamed with pleasure.

He bowed reverently. "Such beauty gathered in only

two ladies,'' he murmured. He shook hands with the
viscount. ''Ramsey, you dog, you shall not lay all the claim
to Lady Sophia while I am here.'' He settled himself
between the two girls, who moved apart to accommodate
him. He smelled pleasantly of patchouli scent and in spite
of the way he had insinuated himself between two ladies,
his manners gave no offense. ''And you never told me,'' he
chided, ''that your sister was such a beauty.''

Charlotte preened herself and smiled, and Ramsey
drawled, ''I make no claim at all to Lady Sophia. As for
my sister . . .'' He paused and there was a flicker at the
back of his eyes and he held a white hand before his
mouth, stifling a yawn that Sophia was sure was assumed.
Charlotte flushed and Sophia stopped breathing in secret
sympathy with her as he continued, ''I preferred to keep
her under wraps until the proper time, when her looks
could astonish the world.''

Sophia's heart beat faster. She was beginning to get a
very good notion of how deeply reprehensible her recent
conduct would appear in the eyes of society. Briefly, but
unmistakably to one who was watching for his reaction,
the viscount had pondered his sister's escapade and had
packed his response with care. Charlotte would have his
guardianship throughout the Season and somehow he
would circumvent any nasty suspicions or rumors about
her. He was an eminent swordsman and a crack shot—she
had learned as much from the society pages—and only a
very foolhardy man would risk being called out by him.
But who would defend her if her adventure were
discovered? She wished she had a brother like Lord
Ramsey.

Lord Ramsey as a brother? No, she could not visualize
him in such a role in her life. Nor did she want to. Her
doubts for her future grew as she comprehended that her
attraction to this man, which had blossomed so early in
their acquaintance, was growing stronger. Her dream that
she could meet him in her proper sphere had materialized
and threatened to turn to a nightmare as she understood all
that Miss Sheffield, Mr. Plerivale, and Edwin's mother
had sought to teach her. The way in which a gentleman

could be as big a rakehell as he chose and still be acceptable
to society contrasted with vicious sharpness to the recep-
tion of the news that a young lady had been even mildly
indecorous. The magnitude of her behavior was now
frighteningly clear and she could only pray that her
identity as Susan, the vagrant maidservant, would never be
discovered by the polite world.

Mr. Chatteris said, "When did you arrive in town, Lady
Sophia?"

Lady Stoneyhurst, apparently as watchful as Lord
Ramsey, intervened. "Only a short while ago. She was
exhausted by such a long journey in this dreadful cold. Do
you think it will break soon? I am told that last month a
Frost Fair was held on the frozen waters of the Thames.
Such foolishness. One does so long for the thaw so that
one may walk beneath the trees in the Park."

Her ladyship was known never to walk when she could
ride and had been heard declaiming against those who
bothered to compete in the Grand Strut.

Ramsey grinned wolfishly, "My sympathies, Lady
Stoneyhurst. I too long for the day when we meet walking
in the Park."

Her ladyship fluttered her fan crossly. "As you never
come down off one of your resty animals except to drive
that ridiculous and dangerous high-perch phaeton, I think
the possibility is remote."

"How right you are, ma'am."

"However," said Lady Stoneyhurst, ignoring his
frivolity, "I shall undoubtedly walk with Lady Sophia and
her dear Grace of Chiddingley, who is bringing out a great-
niece this Season, and I trust that if you should chance
upon us when you are driving your fanciful equippage, you
will halt to pass the time of day."

"Do not tell me that the duchess is going to produce yet
another beautiful young lady to astonish us?" said Mr.
Chatteris.

"I was not going to," replied her ladyship carefully.
"The duchess and I are to share between us the somewhat
enervating pursuits of the Season. I daresay there may be
times when her Grace of Chiddingley does not feel up to a

full social round—she is older than I, you know—and I shall chaperone her protégée with Lady Sophia.''

Ramsey said softly, ''You and the duchess have been bosom friends these many years, have you not, Lady Stoneyhurst? Which of her female relatives is she introducing?''

''Miss Annabel Willis.'' Lady Stoneyhurst's voice was a shade too casual. ''Have you met her?''

''I have indeed. At least, when I say met, I saw her once or twice peeping from behind a tree at me during my visit to her home to inspect a fine piece of bloodstock which is now in my stables. She is a—comely girl.''

''A *sweet* child,'' said her ladyship firmly, ''with *sweet* looks. Her poor dear mama is sadly afflicted—quite an invalid—and her papa is kept exceedingly busy in his parish, as well as watching over his wife's health.''

''Has the duchess met Lady Sophia?'' asked Ramsey, his voice shaking slightly with mirth.

''No, no, she has not.''

''Is Miss Willis an acquaintance of yours, Lady Sophia?''

''No, sir.''

''You will like them both,'' said Lady Stoneyhurst firmly. She now had the fascinated attention of the whole room. ''The arrangements for your come-out will be considerably helped by our having the use of the Chiddingley town house in Picadilly. The rooms there are large enough for parties of all kinds—balls, musical evenings, and the like.''

Sophia gave Lady Stoneyhurst a long look and wondered how many more surprises her new chaperone was going to spring on her. Life with her up to now had proved most disconcerting.

She realized that Lord Ramsey was addressing her. ''I beg your pardon, I was deep in thought,'' she said. As she spoke she glanced up at the viscount, whose heavy brows suddenly met over his dark eyes.

''We *have* met previously,'' he said abruptly.

Sophia took a deep breath, raised her head, and stuck

out her chin, adopting the haughtiest pose a lady could achieve while seated. She looked him full in the face. "Lord Ramsey, I wish you would not tease me so. I daresay you are playing some kind of society game with me. I do not appreciate it."

"I don't play games with chits of girls," said Ramsey.

Mr. Chatteris broke off his talk with Charlotte. "That's doing it a bit brown, ain't it, Ramsey? Any man would be glad to play a game with Lady Sophia." There was a general laugh, and he blushed.

Ramsey rose to his feet, bowed to the young ladies, and wandered off, seating himself eventually beside a pretty girl with brown curls who blushed and stammered with gratification.

Peagoose, decided Sophia. She does not see he is making sport of her, just as he did with me. No, it's not the same. She has nothing to hide, while I— She sighed. What a mish-mash she had landed herself in.

Mr. Chatteris gave her a reassuring smile. "Pay no heed to him, Lady Sophia. He has not singled you out for a tease. He is the same with all young ladies."

"Is he so? Well, I see nothing to boast of in that!"

"No, indeed, I do not praise it."

Charlotte said, a flirtatious glint in her blue eyes, "You are far more gallant than my brother."

Mr. Chatteris took up the bait and they bandied nonsense between them. Sophia saw that although Ramsey appeared to be engrossed with his latest simpering victim, his eyes scarcely left his sister. If Mr. Chatteris did not watch his behavior, he might find himself walking up the aisle to marry Charlotte. Perhaps that would please him. Perhaps it would please Ramsey. It might even please Charlotte.

She must hope that Charlotte would soon become betrothed, at the very least; then the viscount would be free to leave his sister in the care of her future husband and be free to follow the pursuits that best suited a gentleman without obligations. Then he would be seen very infrequently at fashionable gatherings. He might even go to visit his estates overseas. He had property in Jamaica. They might not meet again, or meet only when she was married to someone else. She was deeply troubled by the piercing needle of pain the notion gave her.

Ten

When Sophia awoke next morning, her first thought was of Lord Ramsey. She lay still, only half hearing the cacophony of noise in the streets that told lie-abed rich folk that the workers were well into a new day. She recalled his tall, athletic form, his grace, his long white fingers which only a fool would think were soft. Most of all, she remembered his eyes, tormenting, laughing, penetrating. Had he seen through her into the cavity of secrets beyond? Had he recognized Susan, the maid? How could she tell? He was a sophisticated member of the *ton* and as such knew how to dissemble.

Someone was moving in her room and she pulled aside the half-drapes and saw a young housemaid placing a tray of tea and bread and butter on the pretty occasional table by the bed.

"Good mornin', Lady Sophia. You surely slept well. I came earlier, but you was sound asleep and Lady Stoneyhurst said to let you rest, only now she's in a fret to get to the shops an' warehouses, an' says will you please make haste, an' I'm to maid you till your own woman can get here."

Lady Stoneyhurst, thought Sophia a little grimly, was not going to be at all easy to live with. She appeared to be a creature of whimsical, even cruel expectations.

Last night, as soon as the final guest—the blushing young man smitten by Sophia's charms—had left, Sophia had demanded angrily to be told what purpose there could be in exposing her to a situation so fraught with disaster.

Her ladyship merely yawned. "Come down out of the

boughs, child. I had to give you a test. I needed to know how you would behave when presented with a difficult social meeting." Her taffeta gown swished as she walked across the drawing room. "I congratulate you! You did prodigious well." She paused in the doorway. "We must hope that you will behave as calmly under all circumstances. Good night," she tossed over her shoulder.

"Good night, Cousin Pamela," Sophia had responded politely, wondering how much of the explanation was strictly true. She suspected that her ladyship had taken a mischievous delight in watching her discomfiture.

Sophia ate a couple of slices of bread and butter and drank a cup of tea while the maid brought out the new carriage dress of pale orange velvet. At least her cousin was merciful where dress was concerned. Many women had worn their muslins throughout the dreadful winter and some had succumbed to lung fevers and died. A fur-trimmed dark blue velvet spencer and a blue velvet bonnet tied with pale orange ribbons went with the gown. It was difficult, Sophia reflected, as she looked at her reflection, to remain cross with a woman whose taste in clothes for her protégée extended to such flattering shapes and colors.

It was almost her last coherent thought of the day. She was whirled from place to place like dust caught up in a storm wind. First a bootmaker, where Sophia's feet were measured and a quantity of footwear ordered. There were velvet and satin slippers embroidered in gold and silver for party wear and in colored silks for daywear, white and black kid pumps with ribbon laces, dainty boots to keep out the cold and sturdier ones for riding in Hyde Park.

Cousin Pamela said, "You are possessed of a handsome fortune, my dear Sophia, and can well afford the best of everything."

To Sophia's profound relief, the bootmaker produced a pair of jean half-boots, new and uncollected, which were only a little too large for her and she gladly fell in with her cousin's command to wear them immediately and donate her strong country shoes to some deserving soul.

Lady Stoneyhurst seemed intent on visiting every shop in Oxford Street, until Sophia had seen so many colors and materials for such a variety of occasions that they began to blend in her mind into one huge, harmonious whole. It proved to be only the beginning. At three o'clock her cousin, who seemed impervious to fatigue, was hurrying her into an emporium where fans and reticules were on display in vast profusion, then it was on to the milliner for hats, to an Indian muslin warehouse, to button-makers, fancy trimming and fringe manufactories, and an umbrella seller for parasols.

"We do not need umbrellas," pronounced her ladyship. "We have no call to be walking out of doors when it's wet, but every lady must protect her complexion from the sun."

They visited a Bond Street perfumery for violet powder and soap and a flask of lavender water, and Lady Stoney-hurst insisted on purchasing for Sophia a dainty phial with a silver top containing hartshorn.

When Sophia pointed out that she had not fainted in her life or had a single attack of the spasms or hysterics, her ladyship said, "Ah, my dear Sophia, you are so innocent. In high-bred society it is often desirable, sometimes necessary, for a lady to have recourse to a swoon or an attack of the hysterics. Nothing brings a gentleman to heel so quickly."

Their last shopping call was to Bloomsbury Square. Until now, Sophia had only read of Mrs. Bell, the famous Inventress, and her Fashionable Millinery and Dress Rooms, and she entered its precincts with awe. Mrs. Bell herself attended them, surrounded by a bevy of fitters and seamstresses, and Sophia acquired lengths of emerald green silk, pale lavender and turquoise blue muslin, to be made into evening gowns.

To her relief, a young apprentice appeared with a tray of coffee and small sweet cakes, which took the edge from her sharp hunger.

Her cousin accepted only tea and warned, "You may need to curb your appetite, Sophia. It does not do for a young female to put on overmuch weight until she has secured her husband. After that, she may please herself."

"I never have yet, ma'am, and I eat well." Except when I am nervous under the quizzing gaze of a sardonic man like Lord Ramsey. The thought was so trenchant that she feared she had spoken aloud and was relieved when she drew no one's interest.

Back in the closed town carriage, Lady Stoneyhurst announced that they simply must make one more visit. Sophia almost groaned, until she discovered she was on her way to Leadenhall Street to patronize Mr. Lane's circulating library and was delighted.

Lady Stoneyhurst waved a hand at the shelves of books. "I shall pay your subscription, Sophia, while you find a novel or two."

"Novels, ma'am? I thought you did not approve—"

"Good gracious! Will you throw my words back at me? You must pick some well-known, frivolous book which you probably will never read and will mention in society only if the subject is raised and then with a display of ignorance."

"But I love to read!"

Her ladyship looked around hastily at the folk thronging the library. "Good God, Sophia, do not permit the gentlemen to hear you speak so. You will acquire a reputation as a bluestocking and no man of fashion will look twice at you. Now go and do as I bid. Sometimes your gaucherie astounds me. What on earth can your guardian have been thinking of?"

She swept away without waiting for an answer, leaving Sophia feeling exposed and indignant as she recalled the happy, peaceful days of her growing up, when reading was encouraged by Mr. Plerivale and Miss Sheffield. She had written giving them her address and awaited an answer with trepidation.

"How pensive you look, Lady Sophia," said a soft voice in her ear.

She whirled to see Lord Ramsey laughing down at her. Why was it that his appearance always rendered her a trifle out of breath, made her heart beat a little faster? He could not be called handsome, his face was far too strong, his features too pronounced for mere good looks, and his glossy dark curls sprang aggressively from his head. He emanated masculine strength, which must attract any

woman who needed support. He was the sort of man a
woman could depend on. No, that was nonsense. He had
never in his life committed himself to a genuine love. She
stole a quick glance at him. He looked magnificent in a
brown cloth cutaway coat with a darker, velvet collar and a
white piqué waistcoat. His muscular legs were encased
without a wrinkle in white knee breeches, and he was shod
in gleaming black boots. He carried a fawn beaver hat
which he swept before him in a low and, Sophia suspected,
ironical bow. Why did he persist in treating her as if she
were a toy or a joke?

She could not risk another look and kept her eyes
modestly lowered, wondering if she were destined to pass
the entire Season staring at people's feet. She turned to the
crowded bookshelves and said in as flirtatious a tone as she
could manage, "I was wondering which of the volumes to
try, my lord." She held up her kid-gloved hand before her
mouth in a dainty, simulated yawn. "I doubt I shall give
time to reading, though. There will be so many far more
exciting things to do now the Season is begun."

"And all young ladies prefer frivolity to learning,"
responded Lord Ramsey.

Sophia trilled a laugh. "But naturally we do. The
diversions offered by society must take their place before
book-reading. Only horrid bluestockings would say otherwise."

She could not resist another glance and saw that
although his lordship still smiled, his smile did not match
the expression in his eyes, which she could almost have
sworn held extreme dissatisfaction.

"I will be glad to help you, your ladyship," he said. "I
believe I can guide you in your reading."

"Can you, indeed?" Sophia curtsied. "You astonish
me."

"I am delighted to hear it. A gentleman who can
astonish a lady in such decorous circumstances must be
thought clever."

Sophia stopped walking. "You lose no opportunity to
flatter yourself, my lord."

The viscount obligingly stopped too. "I must continue to do so until you begin to flatter me instead," he said blandly.

Sophia moved on slowly. "That day will never dawn."

"Alas, that you should make so cruel a remark."

"You make sport of me, I think. I am capable of choosing my own books, thank you. There must be many other females here who would welcome your attentions, as I do not."

"Upon my word, Lady Sophia, you blow hot and cold. One minute you are all charm and light conversation; the next you talk like an offended dowager."

Sophia gritted her teeth for an instant, then said lightly, "I have discovered that such behavior holds your interest, my lord."

Ramsey laughed with genuine amusement. "Lady Sophia, you are a vast improvement on the usual young lady making her come-out."

Sophia was almost overcome by an urge to step out of the role of idiotic young female and try to amuse and interest her companion by being herself. She overcame it.

"I was under the impression that you rarely grace society with your presence, sir—to society's detriment, of course."

"That is true," he said, his brows climbing a little. "However, I can only be happy that my sister's come-out has arrived at the same time as yours, otherwise we might never have met. What a loss that would have been."

"For whom, my lord?"

"Why, for you, naturally."

Sophia laughed irresistibly. "Now you are teasing me."

"You are so rewarding to tease."

Lord Ramsey reached up and handed her a book. "*The Children of the Abbey*, by Regina Maria Roche, and here is *Rosina; or the Village Maid*, by Louisa Jones. Neither are new, but they sound prodigious Gothic. Do you favor the Gothic novel, Lady Sophia? Do you enjoy situations that make the flesh creep on your bones?"

"Sometimes I find such volumes amusing, my lord. I'll

take these. I may have time to glance through them.''

The viscount had not finished. "Why not try this? It is written by a cleric and edited by a botanist. You might find it useful." He handed her a volume entitled *A Treatise on Human Happiness*.

Sophia stared, forgetting in her surprise to be on her guard. "Why in heaven's name should you suppose I might want this?''

The viscount said softly, "Sometimes, my lady, you have a sad, rather lost look in your eyes.''

"Fustian!" she exclaimed with more vigor than grace, then flushed. He was altogether too discerning for her comfort.

"I must return to my cousin," she said.

"Lady Stoneyhurst does not need you. Indeed, she does not even want you at the moment. She has met one of her chief rivals and is enjoying her first verbal skirmish of the Season.''

Sophia turned to see her chaperone sitting in one of the easy chairs provided for patrons, the feathers in her headdress almost intermingling with those of a woman as imposing as herself who sat close beside her as the two great ladies tried to outdo one another.

In an irresistible spasm of mirth, Sophia laughed and her large hazel eyes sparked with humor as she stared straight at the viscount. For an instant she reveled in his answering humor before she recalled her role, stopped laughing, and turned away from him, delicate color flooding her cheeks. She thanked him prettily for his help and hurried to her cousin's side.

"Finished, child?" Lady Stoneyhurst rose to her feet. "Make your curtsy to Lady Robinson. We will return home. What books have you got? Ah, yes, two novels. Nothing there to worry your mind. La, what an exhausting day, but a most gratifying one. You are a pleasure to dress, my dear, with your great good looks, your splendid coloring, and handsome figure.''

Her voice rose as she got further away from Lady Robinson and she was scarce out of earshot of her protagonist when she hissed in Sophia's ear, "That'll annoy her. This Season she's bringing out her latest daughter in a long line of wishy-washy girls, as well as chaperoning two others who did not take in their years. She has, by some miracle, achieved marriage for three, but with no distinction. Mere clerics and squireens. Ramsey spent a good long time with you. That is most unlike him. What was he saying? He does not suspect, does he?" she finished with sudden urgency.

Sophia sighed. "I don't know why he singles me out and I don't know if he guesses anything. He seems to take a delight in teasing me."

"Does he? That's most gratifying."

"I do not find it so, ma'am."

"Well, you should," snapped Lady Stoneyhurst. "A chit just up from the country can gain a deal of consequence if she is singled out by one of society's wealthiest and most influential men. It could make the difference to our getting vouchers from Almack's, provided your reckless behavior remains a secret. Without them, we had as well give up. He has the ear of several of the patronesses. I hope you did not put him off."

"I behaved like a feminine chuckle-head," said Sophia in glum tones.

"Splendid, my dear. Positively splendid!"

The two ladies were driven home through the crowded, noisy streets. Lady Stoneyhurst closed her eyes, but Sophia stared unseeingly through the carriage window, wondering if the viscount had connected her with Susan, the maid. If he had, then he was toying with her cruelly. If he had not, she must keep up a pretense with him that was taxing her sorely. In spite of his reputation, in spite of the obstacles she had forged, she was becoming increasingly aware of Lord Ramsey as a very attractive male. She castigated herself for such unladylike feelings, but they would not go away.

Two shopping-filled days later, after many fittings for her new gowns, Sophia was called to the drawing room by her cousin. A footman opened the door and she stopped

dead on the threshold. Rising to greet her was the slender
form of her governess-companion, Miss Sheffield.

Sophia paused, walked a few steps, hesitated. Miss
Sheffield held out her hands and she ran and took them
firmly, then embraced her half tearfully, "My dear, dear
friend, I am so sorry. I must have given you and Mr.
Plerivale such a worrying time."

Miss Sheffield nodded. "That's understating what we
felt, Sophia."

The two seated themselves on a sofa. Sophia said, "I
soon realized that I was behaving in a dreadful manner, yet
even then I was afraid to return if it meant I had to marry
Edwin. Please understand."

Miss Sheffield patted Sophia's clasped hands. "We were
somewhat at fault, my dear. Not one of us had realized
how badly you felt about the marriage."

"You do now?"

Miss Sheffield smiled ruefully, "Yes, I can truthfully say
we do now."

"Does my guardian still want to promote the match?"

"Not at all. He was most agitated at oversetting you so
badly. And even if he did, it would make no odds. Lady
Fothergill no longer approves. She is very shocked at your
behavior and even more mortified at your treatment of her
beloved son."

"Oh, poor Lady Fothergill!"

"And poor Edwin, too?"

"Have I made him very unhappy?"

An encouraging twinkle appeared in Miss Sheffield's
eyes. "I have to report that his anger was mostly bluster. I
believe he must have secretly been as appalled as you by the
idea of your marrying."

Sophia stared. In spite of the circumstances, it was a
blow to learn that her foremost beau was relieved to get
out of marrying her. Then she laughed. "That's not
exactly flattering, but I'm truly relieved. I wish I had made
more of a protest and not run away. You will scarce credit
the imbroglio I've had to get out of. In fact, I am still
struggling in it."

Sophia explained what had occurred to her on the road. Miss Sheffield looked horrified and amused by turns. At the end of the sorry recital, she slid an arm around Sophia's waist. "You have been well and truly punished, my love."

Sophia leaned thankfully against her companion's shoulder. Miss Anne Sheffield was gently bred. Her father had lost his money in an unwise speculation, then died when his creditors made him bankrupt, leaving his widow and small daughter living for some years on the charity of a domineering aunt whose only grace, so far as the sorrowing girl could see, was that she had kept intact the extensive library owned by her late husband. Anne spent most of her waking hours there; the French chef (quite unknown to her relatives) encouraged her to become proficient in his native tongue, and Mrs. Sheffield had been a fine musician and water colorist and was a good teacher. When at the age of twenty Anne lost her mother, she felt justified in taking her freedom, and was sufficiently educated to look for a post of governess, and obtained a situation as Sophia's governess-companion without references because Mr. Plerivale knew her aunt. At twenty-nine, she had resigned herself to the state of old maid, in spite of her excellent figure and fine complexion.

"You appear to have weathered your first social event without disaster," she said.

" 'Appear to have,' " sighed Sophia. "It may be no more than that. Lord Ramsey is so unusual a man. I can't tell if he has recognized the former Susan or not. He would find amusement in it." She sighed again and said after a pause. "Viscount Ramsey looks only for amusement."

"He was a precocious boy," said Miss Sheffield.

"Are you acquainted with him?"

"I was once. He lived near my aunt for some years and we met at children's parties and played together sometimes. But I do not remember him as unkind. The reverse, in fact; and he was gentle with all animals."

Miss Sheffield studied Sophia's face. "Have you developed a tendre for him? It would be most unwise and could lead only to disappointment. I think he is not a marrying man.''

"A tendre! Good heavens, what a notion! I should not dream of becoming even remotely fond of him.''

"I am glad to know it,'' said Miss Sheffield, but a slight frown disturbed the smoothness of her white brow. "Mr. Plerivale sends his love, Sophia, and has entrusted me with sufficient money to repay your cousin for any expenditure, and given me a note on your bank. Try to forget what happened and enjoy yourself as a young woman should in her first Season.''

Sophia kissed Anne's cheek. "What a perfect friend you are. I feared you might be so disgusted by me that you would not want to stay with me.''

Miss Sheffield laughed. "How could you believe any such thing? I love you like a mother.''

"A sister would be more like,'' said a well remembered voice from the doorway and Sophia looked up with a start to see Lord Ramsey. Sophia prayed that he'd not overheard what they had been saying.

"You were not announced, my lord,'' protested Miss Sheffield.

The viscount strolled across the room. "I have seen her ladyship, who told me you were here, Anne. The butler is somewhat put out by such informality.''

"As he should be,'' said Miss Sheffield. "I have the keenest objection to folk appearing so suddenly. How are you, Hugo?''

She held out her hand and Ramsey bent and kissed it, bowing from the waist. "It is wonderful to meet you again, Anne. Where have you been hiding your beauty all these years?''

"Do not try to gammon me, my lord. I prefer honesty.''

Ramsey smiled. "You always did.'' His eyes moved quickly to Sophia and back to Anne. "I was not gammoning you when I spoke of beauty. Yours is the quiet, enduring sort. It has not diminished with the years.''

Miss Sheffield gave the viscount an ironic smile. "Quiet and enduring? That is not exactly flattering! I fear the same cannot be said for you, sir. Your—rackety life has changed your expression. You are not the winsome boy I once knew.''

"Winsome boy! Good God, ma'am, I pray you will not use that term about me to anyone else.''

"Well, that is how I recall you. It's a description that cannot be applied now.''

"Thank heavens!'' The viscount seated himself in a chair upholstered in Chinese dragons with fiery breath. "Has no one claimed you in all these years?''

"No one,'' said Anne.

"I can scarce credit it. You were always outspoken; have you frightened your many admirers away?''

"I had no need. They faded away like icicles in the sun as soon as they discovered my poverty,'' said Miss Sheffield, the irony of her tone deepening.

"Such shocking bad form!'' exclaimed Ramsey. He gave an exaggerated sigh. "But I'd wager that not all of your suitors disappeared. Confess! You would have none of them.''

Miss Sheffield warned, "Lady Sophia, if this man offers you flattery, paid no heed. He prides himself on not being a marrying man. Your beauty and fortune will be won by someone vastly different.''

"What a reputation you give me,'' the viscount said, softly. "Your tongue is no more merciful today than it ever was. And Lady Sophia is so exquisite a creature. How can I resist her charms?''

"You must do so as best you can,'' said Miss Sheffield. Lord Ramsey deliberately allowed his dark eyes to wander from Sophia's silk-shod feet, over her orange gown, pausing at the swell of her thighs, the delicate roundness of her breasts beneath the velvet, lingering longest on her face and chestnut curls. She could scarcely sit still beneath such a scrutiny. Her flesh tingled alarmingly and she had to suppress an ache to stare back at him, to assess his masculine beauty, to give him look for look.

Then Ramsey switched all his attention to Miss Sheffield

and the two of them spoke with a great deal of vivacity and humor of past days. Sophia had never seen her companion in such *tonnish* company and was torn between enjoyment and an odd sensation she did not at first understand. When she did, she was shocked. Jealousy! She was jealous of Ramsey's easy camaraderie with Miss Sheffield. What a traitorous response to her dearest friend's lively enjoyment of the viscount's company. What right had she to be jealous? What if Ramsey and Miss Sheffield made a match of it? They certainly seemed to like one another a great deal, and it would be a splendid triumph for her.

Sophia sat on, watching silently, smiling sometimes at a shared memory, a shaft of humor, all the while trying to cope with the unfamiliar, ugly sensations that were taking her over and which she could not argue away.

Eleven

Lord Ramsey was looking forward to the evening's entertainment with a keener expectation of enjoyment than he had known since his early manhood. He was amused by his own eagerness to discover more of Lady Sophia Clavering. He had accepted the duty of overseeing his sister through her first Season, but had looked upon it as a tedious chore until Sophia had entered his life.

He realized that Dunlop, his valet, had appeared noiselessly in front of him. Dunlop coughed behind his hand, a sure indication that he knew that his master was about to be irritated. "Excuse me, my lord, but Miss Price, Lady Ramsey's maid, says that Lady Ramsey and Miss Charlotte cannot agree about Miss Charlotte's gown."

The viscount stared at him. "Good God! Am I now the arbiter of ladies' fashions?"

"It would seem so, sir."

"What's the problem?"

Again the valet coughed delicately. "Her ladyship went to Miss Charlotte's room expecting to see her in a white silk gown with a white gauze overdress and Miss Charlotte wishes to appear in a dark rose gown and a raspberry colored overdress and—"

"Dark rose? Raspberry? Dammit, everybody knows that a girl wears white and pale shades for her appearance at her debut ball! She has a white gown and all the trimmings."

Dunlop hid a smile. His master spoke of Miss Charlotte as if she had been a chicken ready for the table. In a way she was, he supposed. "Yes, sir," he said.

The viscount strode to his sister's bedchamber and Dunlop was hard pressed later fending off the comments from the servants concerning the altercation that had erupted above stairs. He was as discreet as Nell Price. No one ever obtained any secrets from either of them.

The viscount had returned to his contemplation after giving his sister a set-down which left her furious, but obedient.

The principal drawing rooms and ballroom were positive bowers of flowers, brilliant to the eye and delightful to the nose. Refreshments were set out on the large dining table, and the room filled with small tables and chairs for supper. The card tables were ready in other rooms for those who wanted to play. The musicians had arrived and were eating a meal in the servants' hall before taking their places on the raised stand at one end of the large, elegant room. Guests were due to arrive within the hour.

The young Duke of Chiddingley had accepted and so had his great-aunt, the duchess. The title had passed to a brother's line as she was childless, but she enjoyed the cut and thrust of the Marriage Mart and was always prepared to bring out a young relative.

This year Ramsey guessed that her protégée filled her with misgivings. Miss Annabel Willis was an insipid, colorless female unlikely to attract notice.

He had said as much to the trusted Dunlop, who had replied, "Young ladies have an astonishing way of becoming suddenly attractive when they make their come-out. I have observed it often.''

Ramsey grinned. He hoped Miss Willis had bloomed or the duchess would be uncomfortable to live with, especially when she clapped eyes on the lovely Lady Sophia Clavering.

Lady Stoneyhurst had gone to great lengths to make an arrangement with the duchess to share the come-out of their respective charges. Her grace had long been a mix of foe and friend. She was exceedingly wealthy, but disliked spending her money, and she had agreed that parties were to be held for both girls in the ducal town house, the cost to be shared. Ramsey wanted to be present when tonight the duchess caught sight of Lady Sophia's looks and realized that her old protagonist, Lady Stoneyhurst, was sure to score heavily in the marriage stakes.

Above all, Ramsey relished the prospect of further encounters with Sophia. He had soon recognized her as Susan, the woman who had entered his sister's service as a maid, and whom he had first met wandering the roads like a beggar. The memory of her struggles in the embrace of a footman in his employ was sharp. He wished it had not happened. He wished he had not handled her so roughly, yet the physical contact had revealed the full beauty of her unforgettable eyes and it would take an age for the memory of the richness of her chestnut hair to fade. Her mouth was delicately formed, yet so sensual. No maquillage could entirely disguise her from a discerning man who had known many women, and his experienced hands had felt the disfiguring pads beneath her gown. No one and nothing had absorbed and amused him so much for years. He had delved into Lady Sophia Clavering's background and discovered the extreme respectability of her antecedents and the reason for her hasty flight. He could not condone such rackety behavior in a woman, yet her spirit fascinated him and each time he met her he was struck afresh by her looks. He also felt the weight of her well-trained mind behind the idiotic banter she always used in his presence. The fact that Anne Sheffield had been her companion and instructor for years, and that she had

flown to her charge at the first possible moment spoke of
affection and a careful upbringing. It seemed that Sophia
had yielded to an uncharacteristic impulse when she feld
her home. Yet, it was a fact that she had been wandering
the roads alone. Anything might have happened to her.
She had been set upon by a company of thieves. What if
they had stolen more than some of her possessions? What
if they had sampled her body? But surely if she had been
ravaged she would have been far more distressed when she
arrived at the inn. Then again, she would be loth to bruit
her shame abroad and women had a tremendous capacity
for dissembling.

The guests began to arrive, first in twos and threes, then
all in a rush, so that the apartments were alive with
laughter and talk and their scents vied with the perfume of
the flowers.

Ramsey, his sister Charlotte, and their mother waited in
the receiving line on this first ball of the Season, and those
who were bringing out young, marriageable females
wondered if their particular darling would be the one
fortunate enough to break down Ramsey's defenses at last.

Lady Sophia was approaching, accompanied by her
cousin, and his heart beat faster, as if he were a calfling
interested in his first girl. It was absurd, but God, she was
beautiful. Her hair had been cut in a fashionable mode and
was drawn into a loose knot on top of her head, a fine
chain of gold and tiny pearls woven through it, leaving
small, wanton curls to caress her ears and cover the scar.
The soft curves of her figure were suited to perfection by a
shift of white silk with a lavender gauze overdress. Her
ankles, which peeped from beneath her gown, were clothed
in white silk and on her feet were embroidered silk pumps.
An amethyst pendant on a narrow lavender ribbon
encircled her throat. He greeted her with a small bow and a
determinedly placid smile, while his unruly mind dwelled
rampantly for a few seconds on the charms that were
hidden from him.

Ramsey greeted the subsequent arrivals with a slightly
distrait air. Sophia was so damned intriguing. She
appeared to have no awareness of the strong sexuality that

emanated from her. Here was no wishy-washy miss on the hunt for just any husband. She would want a man who knew how to awaken her body to pulsating life. Who would be the one to penetrate that devastating blend of passion and innocence? Surely she was innocent. Her eyes, when he could see them, for the absurd girl still kept them lowered as much as possible in his presence, were as clear as crystal. She would have many suitors and some man would undoubtedly grab such a prize in her first Season. He had to force back a sudden envy for the man who would share her future.

Sophia was overawed by her return to the Ramsey town house. Pray God none of the servants connected her with the runaway maid. Everything was on a grand and lavish scale and in excellent good taste, and the furniture was a clever mix of old and new. The Ramseys had resisted the temptation to gild and decorate everything in the popular *Chinoise* style.

Hundreds of candles twinkled from the crystal chandeliers above their heads, from the wall sconces, and from every shelf and alcove that would hold them. They gave off a heat that would later turn carefully dressed hair limp and play havoc with the maquillage of those who still retained such an old-fashioned practice.

She curtsied to Lady Ramsey and Charlotte and tried to control the sudden wild beating of her heart when she stood before the viscount. One glance at him told her that he was in a teasing mood. God forbid he would try to dig out her secret, yet she longed to be in his company.

He held her kid-gloved hand for a slighter longer time than propriety permitted and she was disconcerted to discover that she wished that she was not gloved and could feel the touch of his skin.

"Good evening, Lady Sophia," he said, raising her from her curtsy. "You will always be welcome in my home."

"I am so happy to be here," replied Sophia carefully, and as primly as any miss out of the schoolroom, exactly as she had been instructed.

She knew she was blushing and her voice was a trifle shaky, but that was surely to be expected in a girl embarking on her first grand ball. She raised her eyes briefly, irresistibly, in a kind of challenge. Even if she sank without trace during the Season, she would go down fighting.

Lady Stoneyhurst nodded affably to the viscount. She had not missed the slight stress he had placed on the word "always." Had the man recognized her charge? He was too damned familiar with the ways of women for her peace of mind.

"Miss Sheffield is not with you?"

"No, she is not," declared Lady Stoneyhurst, "and I must say I wonder at your sending an invitation to a governess."

"But Miss Sheffield is no ordinary governess, is she, Lady Sophia?"

"No, not at all ordinary," replied Sophia, suddenly calm. If Ramsey meant to be unpleasant about her beloved companion, he would feel the weight of her tongue, come what may.

Ramsey stared at her for a moment, then turned to Lady Stoneyhurst. "I knew Anne Sheffield when we were both younger. She lived on an estate near one of mine. We were playmates, great friends. I could never regard her as a servant."

Sophia felt a stab of jealousy which instantly shamed her. "She would not accept your invitation, my lord. She said it was not fitting in her present circumstances."

"What nonsense! I shall fetch her to my next party. You had best warn her to be dressed."

The viscount laughed as he spoke and Sophia showed her teeth in a smile regrettably lacking in humor as she passed on into the ballroom. Lord Ramsey was much of an age with Anne, who was still very pretty, however much she tried to hide behind governessy gowns with high collars, and caps.

The musicians tuned their instruments and struck up a lively country dance. Immediately, it seemed, Ramsey appeared at Sophia's side. He bowed to Lady Stoneyhurst, who gave her smiling permission for him to lead Sophia into a set.

"I did not know you danced, my lord," Sophia said.

"Why should I not? Do I appear so staid?" His dark eyes teased her and he laughed at her blush. "How very pretty you are, my lady."

"For heaven's sake! People will hear you!"

"I have said nothing untoward, though I give no guarantee that I will remain so discreet."

"That does not surprise me!"

"Indeed? Why so?"

"I think you take pleasure in provoking women," she said flatly, relishing the way his jaw tightened in annoyance.

The dance began and Ramsey and Sophia encircled one another, clasping hands above their heads. Then the movements carried them apart. Sophia loved to dance and had graced many a country evening party, but this was different. She had dreamed of London balls, but had never envisaged so many people dressed in the highest of *ton* fashion, so much glittering jewelry, so heady a mixture of scent and pleasure, and so many men of all ages. Some were dancing and watched her admiringly as she tripped through the intricate patterns; others lounged around the walls and stared at the women through quizzing glasses, murmuring to one another and laughing. Their manners made Sophia uneasy and as she approached Lord Ramsey again, she half lost her balance. His arm caught her in an instant, then released her, but the contact set her quivering again.

"Th-thank you, sir," she managed breathlessly.

"It was a pleasure." His tone was urbane. "Any time you would like me to—catch you—I shall be delighted."

"I do not doubt it," flashed Sophia, executing a dainty foot movement, "but I seldom fall."

"How thankful I am." The viscount's voice was no longer flippant. Did his words hold some double meaning? How could they? She felt sure that Susan had been lost forever and that her perilous adventures could be put behind her and forgotten.

The half hour of the dance ended and Ramsey returned her to Lady Stoneyhurst. A lady on the next rout chair held up an eyeglass and stared through it at Sophia, who almost wilted at the malevolence sent her way.

Her cousin turned to the lady. "Allow me to present my little cousin, Lady Sophia Clavering," she said. "Child, make your curtsy to her grace, the Duchess of Chiddingley. And here is the young lady who will be your companion during your come-out, Miss Annabel Willis."

Sophia had scarcely noticed a girl sitting by the duchess's side. In fact, Miss Willis was easy to overlook, with her pallid complexion enlivened only by a touch of pink over her cheekbones, her light brown hair, and pale blue eyes fringed with sandy lashes. Her eyebrows were all but invisible.

She nodded to Sophia, blushing deeply. "I'm so happy to make your acquaintance, Lady Sophia."

The duchess showed no similar sign of happiness and Sophia was uneasy. Ramsey greeted the duchess, his eyes alight with mirth. She tapped him sharply on the back of his hand with her fan. "Don't be making sport of me, Ramsey!"

"As if I would, your grace."

The duchess stared at him for a long moment, then turned away to scrutinize Sophia once more, and the viscount laughed and walked away, joining a group of mamas and simpering girls. Sophia felt a stab of hatred for every one of them.

She continued to watch the viscount with mesmerized eyes. His curling hair was almost black, cut in the newest short style that showed to advantage his well-shaped head. His black coat fitted over his broad shoulders as if it had been fashioned on him and his black silk breeches were worn above white silk stockings that emphasized the muscles in his legs. His white marcella waistcoat was crossed only by his watch chain and the ribbon of his quizzing glass, and his shoes bore small silver buckles. He made many of the other men look overdressed and over-adorned.

The musicians struck up for the second country dance

and Ramsey moved in Sophia's direction. Her nerves
jumped, half in pleasure, half in panic, as she wondered
how she could sustain a further half hour of the conflicting
emotions he stirred in her, until she realized he was asking
for the company of Miss Willis, who almost tripped over
her feet in her agitation. Sophia was immediately disappointed, yet glad that he was a man who showed marked
courtesy to a forgotten girl. She wondered how Annabel
would cope and watched him lead her into the dance,
deliberating on what shafts of wit he would loose upon
her, then saw with surprise that he was looking with a
kindly expression on the embarrassed girl and doing his
utmost to put her at her ease.

She sighed. He was a man of such contradictions, and so
vastly interesting. "Sophia, pay heed," chided Lady
Stoneyhurst. "Here is his grace, the Duke of Chiddingley,
asking you to dance."

Sophia expected to see an elderly man, but found herself
confronted by a very tall, thin, gangling blond youth who
blushed as readily as Miss Willis. She guessed he had been
ordered to approach her by his— "What relation are you
to the duchess?" she inquired as he led her out.

"She's my great-aunt. The duke died without issue, as
the saying goes, and the title came to my father, then to
me." He had spoken straightforwardly so far, then he
gulped and stammered, "Y-you look ch-charmin', Lady
Sophia."

She thanked him prettily and waited, surmising that his
great-aunt had commanded him to pay her pretty
compliments, but he appeared to have come to the end of
his conversational repertoire.

Sophia danced down the set and almost out of it as, with
a heart-stopping shock, she caught sight of someone she
knew, staring at her from the wide doorway. Edwin, her
spurned bridegroom, was watching her every move. She
made a conscious effort not to stumble. If she fell into
another pair of masculine arms, she would gain a
reputation that would blister the ears of the gossips.

In her determination to avoid Edwin she danced tirelessly, eagerly accepting the many partners who enthusiastically offered. Two Scottish reels followed the country dances and Edwin seemed to have vanished. She began to feel unreasonably tired. Usually she could ride, walk, and dance without the least fatigue, but the first grand ball of her life was being spoilt by her apprehensions. Well, it was all her own doing. She could not blame others.

Supper was announced and suddenly there was Edwin, bowing and asking for the pleasure of escorting her to the supper room, his face more grave than she had seen it in all the years of their acquaintance.

Lady Stoneyhurst viewed him suspiciously. "Cousin Pamela, may I present a neighbor of mine, Sir Edwin Fothergill. We are—friends—of long standing. His estate marches with mine. Edwin, my cousin, Lady Stoneyhurst."

Her ladyship held out her hand. "How d'ye do, Sir Edwin. Fothergill? Fothergill? My God!"

"Something troubles you, your ladyship?" suggested Edwin smoothly.

Lady Stoneyhurst, who had been caught off guard, coughed. "Not at all. I suddenly remembered your papa. A charming man. I was sorry to learn of his death."

"Thank you, ma'am." Edwin lost some of his aggressiveness. "So may I take Lady Sophia to supper?"

Sophia's wordless appeal was ignored by her cousin, who nodded. When it became clear that no one would offer for Annabel, the duchess rose with a sigh. "Come, my dear, time to take refreshment. And do try to look more animated."

Annabel blushed, then paled, and Sophia stopped and took her arm in hers. "Miss Annabel, if we are to share the Season we must be friends. Meet Sir Edwin. Edwin this is Miss Willis's first Season too."

Edwin seemed unimpressed, but Annabel's smile rewarded Sophia, who whispered, "Are you terrified of your grand relative? I should be. She is far more daunting even than mine."

Annabel giggled nervously. "They are both such

grandes dames, are they not? I keep wishing I was at home, or that my mama could have brought me to London.''

"Is your mother . . .'' Sophia paused delicately.

"Mama is a sad invalid and Papa is a parson. We are not wealthy, not wealthy at all. Even if we were, Papa would continue to give his substance to the poor. There are so many sadly in want of charity.'' Sophia gave her arm a sympathetic squeeze. "To tell the truth, Lady Sophia, I feel I would be better at home taking around baskets of food and clothing to the parishioners. It is more congenial to me than this.''

"Well, perhaps you will marry a rich man and then you can dispense far more charity.''

Annabel sighed. "I fear I am destined to remain on the shelf. I am not beautiful like you.''

"Fiddlesticks!'' The duchess's voice burst like a bomb behind them. "A girl does not have to be pretty to get a suitable husband. I was not a beauty, but I landed a duke. One needs to be clever''

"But I am not clever either.''

The duchess tutted loudly and the party moved on toward the supper room.

The two elders found places at a table with other chaperones and Edwin pulled out a chair for Sophia, who sank into it. He performed the same office for Annabel, and then to the astonishment of all three Lord Ramsey approached. "May I join you?''

Edwin said, "But of course, sir. You do not need my permission. That is to say . . .''

Ramsey waved him amicably to silence and brought up a subject that had been puzzling Sophia. "I should expect you to be at Oxford at this time, Sir Edwin.''

"Normally I would be, my lord. My tutor gave permission for my absence. I have suffered a disappointment. Mama thought that a taste of the Season would do me good.''

"Wise mother,'' commented Ramsey. "May we know the nature of your disappointment, or is it secret?''

"My apologies, my lord, but I would prefer not to divulge it.''

Sophia was surprised by Edwin's firmness. She knew him so well, she had no doubt that a man as great as Ramsey made him quiver inside like one of the jellies being carried around by servants. She expected Ramsey to frown, but he smiled indulgently at Edwin, whose face had gone red.

"No apologies are necessary, Sir Edwin. I am the one who should express regret."

"Not at all, my lord."

The atmosphere at the table was vibrant with tension, which was increased dramatically when Annabel saw her formidable relative staring at her with a smile of approval that showed her yellowing teeth.

Sophia realized that someone was speaking to her. The viscount's brows were raised and a slightly mocking smile played about his lips. "You are far away, Lady Sophia. This is no place for dreaming." He looked thoughtful. "Or perhaps it is. A lady at her first big ball. I suppose I must once have behaved just the same."

"I should not think so," said Edwin feelingly. "You were surely accustomed to high-toned company long before you entered it properly."

"No, you are wrong. I was a bookish boy and enjoyed school, and especially Oxford."

Sophia stared at the viscount, quite forgetting to be a ladylike miss with lowered lashes. "You! Bookish?"

Ramsey smiled lazily at her. "Astonishing, isn't it? And you may find it even more odd of me to enjoy reading and studying to this day."

"No, sir, I find it commendable," she said. "At home I have a fine library collected over the years by my forebears and I have spent many happy hours there reading. I like novels and also informative books. Dr. Johnson's Lexicon held a particular fascination—" Sophia stopped abruptly.

Annabel's eyes were round with amazement. "How clever you are. Good heavens! You are quite a blue-stocking."

"Oh, no, indeed," trilled Sophia, "I have passed that stage ever so long ago. Books are not as interesting as life. No, not nearly as interesting." She stopped again. Lord

Ramsey had leaned back in his chair the better to watch
her, and his eyes were aglow with amusement. Damn him,
she thought. He led me to forget myself. Had he done so
purposely? She wondered if he believed her last statement.
Pray God he did. According to Cousin Pamela, any
woman who showed overmuch intelligence was spurned
utterly by gentlemen because they always liked to appear
cleverer than their wives.

Supper proceeded. The subjects were kept strictly to the
level of their expectations of fun to be had in the coming
weeks. The sound of music from the ballroom began to
pull the guests back to the dancing, and Sophia rose.
Ramsey and Edwin stood up too and Sophia stood
waiting, dreading them almost equally.

Edwin spoke. "Pray, Lady Sophia, will you honor me
with a turn about the corridor? I noticed some very nice
paintings as we passed. You are so accomplished with your
water color box, I'm sure you would find them most
diverting."

Ramsey almost laughed. The young cub had just consigned his treasured collection of Girtin, Cozens, and
Thomas Gainsborough paintings into a communal bucket
labeled "diverting." He wondered if Edwin's absolute
determination to speak alone to Sophia troubled her. One
glance at her expression told him that it did.

"You must show me some of your work," said Ramsey.
"Are you accomplished in other aspects of art, Lady
Sophia?"

Sophia did not dare to speak for fear her voice would
emerge as a strangled moan. At that moment a life of
retirement similar to Annabel's ideal held strong attrac-
tions.

Twelve

As soon as Sophia and Edwin were out of the supper room, Edwin took her arm in a painful grip and hurried her along the corridor.

"Edwin, you're hurting me!"

"You deserve it," he said through gritted teeth. "I wish you were younger and I could spank you."

"If I were younger," Sophia pointed out, "we should scarce have been ordered to marry."

"Which would have been a mercy for everybody," Edwin almost snarled.

Sophia threw him an indignant look, which he ignored. They arrived at a door and Edwin threw it open. He entered a side room, pushing Sophia before him. Once inside he released her and she rubbed her arm. "It's fortunate I'm wearing gloves," she said. "I am sure I shall have bruises."

"Poor *you*! We must hope they do not hurt as much as the spiritual ones you inflicted upon my mother."

Sophia stared into Edwin's furious light brown eyes. She was shocked. "Spiritual hurt! Your mother! I would not have done so for worlds. How is that possible?"

"If you reflect for a few moments, instead of following your own selfish whims and fancies, you would understand more."

"I am not selfish. Just because I didn't want to marry you—"

"Well, I don't want to marry you either!"

"Is that so?" Sophia stormed, "yet you were perfectly prepared to do so. I did not hear one word of protest from you."

"You idiotic girl! How could I spurn you when you apparently accepted the decisions made. You said nothing to me! If you had, you would not have needed to run away."

For a moment Sophia was silent with amazement. She took a step back. "All my suffering was in vain? Would you truly have cried off if I had asked you?"

"Definitely! Don't mistake me, Sophia," Edwin said, more gently, "I like you tremendously. At least—yes, I do still like you. I've been exceedingly angry with you, but now we are together I know I can forgive you. You are too dear to me to lose as a friend. The problem is, I feel only a brotherly affection for you."

"Exactly!" cried Sophia. "And I feel like a sister to you!"

Edwin sounded calmer. "What a mish-mash we have made of things."

"I behaved the worst." Sophia walked across the small room and seated herself on a tapestry bench, remembering the desperate days on the road, contemplating the problems that surrounded her. "All because I was a coward," she murmured, half to herself.

"We are equally to blame," said Edwin.

"I don't think so. It is up to a woman to make her feelings clear."

"If a man is a gentleman, he should not permit such a situation to arise."

"I wish we had been more candid," said Sophia. Edwin was behaving like her dear friend again and she longed to gain his sympathy by relating the dreadful account of her journey to London. She decided against it. The fewer who knew the truth, the better, and she was apprehensive of Edwin's strong streak of conventionality. She could not know quite what his reaction would be.

She knew she had been right to be cautious when he said, "We must hope that no one learns of your unseemly behavior. For a young girl of your age and upbringing to travel to London alone on a common stage—it does not bear thinking of. One or two folk have told me that Charlotte Ramsey is unconventional, but I cannot credit it."

"No, indeed not! She is sweet, though rather hen-witted."

"I do not see her as such!" declared Edwin. "And if she ever was, it is because she needs a man to guide her. Lord Ramsey, I collect, was used to spend much time away from his home."

Sophia bit her lip. She hated to hear Ramsey villified. "You like Miss Ramsey, Edwin."

"I most certainly do, though she is far above my touch."

"I think not," said Sophia gently. "At least you can try to win her."

Edwin nodded somewhat gloomily. "Do you think Ramsey knows about your adventures on the road?"

"He—he gives no indication of it."

Edwin paced the room once. "Pray God he remains in ignorance. He can make or break a reputation with a few words."

Sophia asked, a miserable catch in her throat, "Edwin, is your mama so overset? And is it true that you came to London to get over your unhappiness?"

"It is true of Mama. I confess I came to London more with the intent of seeking you out and telling you what I thought of you."

"Oh! How unkind! I didn't mean to hurt anyone."

" 'Didn't meant to hurt'! Famous! That's how thoughtless, unkind people often excuse their behavior."

"I am not thoughtless, or unkind. Just because I didn't want to spend my life shackled to you. It's your vanity that's hurt, Edwin Fothergill, not your feelings."

"I haven't a vain bone in my body!"

"Oh, is that so! What about the day you brought home a pair of primrose yellow pantaloons and your mama gave them to a poor box? She said you were vain. I heard her."

"A boy can make a mistake, can't he? At least I didn't run away and inflict misery on every one just because I was sulky."

"Do you equate marrying the wrong man with buying a pair of pantaloons?"

"For God's sake, keep your voice down, Sophia. Not everybody would understand our discussing my pantaloons. Some *might* think it indelicate."

"Fustian! We have known one another for an age."

"Society does not know that, and if it did, it would not care. You would be branded as—as a—barque of frailty!"

"What?" Sophia's voice rose in fury. "How dare you compare me with a loose woman!"

Edwin's color rose also. "I didn't—that is, I did not mean—in any case, a young girl should not know the meaning of the term."

"Oh that's what a boy *would* think! Girls know far more than you realize."

"Indeed! Well, I'm amazed to learn it!"

They glared at one another, both pink and incoherent with renewed rage.

Edwin said in a grimly calm tone, "Mama was looking forward to sponsoring you in your first Season.'

"As a married woman, probably pregnant—"

"Sophia!"

"Oh, don't act so outraged. We've watched the birth of lambs and calves and rabbits together when we were children, and when your favorite pony was in trouble having her foal, we assisted the farrier."

"That's different! Those are animals and we were too young to know better."

"Growing older doesn't change us. Well, not much."

"It does not appear to have matured you! And you never told me you had a cousin in London."

"What's that to do with anything? Have you told me about all your relatives?"

"Probably not, but I'm a man. You're a woman!"

"Have I ever denied it? And why is it different?"

"It just is!"

Sophia sprang to her feet. "I refuse to listen to any more of your ridiculous statements. Pray, Sir Edwin, escort me back to the ballroom."

Edwin bowed and held out his amber velvet-coated arm. Sophia felt swift regret when she looked into his eyes. They were troubled as she had never seen them. She wished they had not quarreled. She wished she could tell him that his coat color flattered him and made his light brown eyes glow. Or was that fury? She stopped at the door. He had every right to be angry.

She drew a deep breath to apologize, but Edwin threw open the door and moved into the corridor. They walked together in an artificial stateliness, their color high, silent partners returning to the ballroom. Sophia was dismayed to see Lord Ramsey standing outside the wide double doors. His eyes were fixed on them and she knew that her cheeks flared as red as Edwin's. Ramsey's heavy brows were drawn together. No wonder. She and Edwin must both look guilty. What interpretation would he put upon their appearance? She wished she could give a hearty, full-bodied curse. Servants were luckier in some ways, not the least being their greater freedom of speech. No lady cursed unless she was elderly, or grotesquely unconventional. She removed her hand from Edwin's arm. "Pray excuse me, sir. I need a little cooling water on my wrists."

She fled before Edwin could reply, but not before she had caught the cynical gleam in his lordship's eyes. That was to be expected, but what puzzled her most was the strong impression that he was disappointed in her. Why should he be? And why should she care? She hurried along the corridor, causing more than one gentleman to take out a quizzing glass the better to view and admire this tempestuous looking beauty.

Sophia entered the bedchamber set aside for the ladies. The dancing had not yet restarted and there were several occupants. One or two lay on the couches provided by the thoughtful hostess, girls were whispering secrets and giggling, one held up her face for a maid to dab a little discreet powder on her shiny nose. Sophia tottered to a chair before a mirror and sank into it. As she did so a maid who was mending a bit of torn lace at someone's hem, cut off the thread and rose to her feet. Sophia met her eyes in the mirror and was devastated to realize that she was face to face with Kitty.

She felt completely at outs with fate. Had ever a woman been so harried by the results of a foolish adventure? It was all very well for Edwin to tell her she needn't have run away. Long years of obedience to their elders had endowed them with a strong sense of the inevitable, a powerful reluctance to rebel openly, and she was sure they would be married by now had she not acted. Her eyes refocused and she realized with a horror that seemed to dissolve her muscles into shaky blancmange that she had been staring at the maid's reflection without seeing her and that Kitty was puzzling over something.

She swung around and said as distinctly and as unlike Susan as possible, "Pray, my good woman, will you fetch me a glass of water? I vow the ballroom is vastly over-heated." She fluttered her fan.

Kitty stammered. "Y-yes, ma'am. At once, ma'am."

Sophia watched Kitty overtly as she poured some water, thoughtfully adding a piece of lemon. Sophia drank and the cool water helped to calm her.

" 'Twas a good idea to add the lemon," she heard herself say in a falsetto. "It is most refreshing."

"Yes. Ma'am. Thank you, ma'am."

"Are you one of the lady's maids?"

Kitty shook her head and dark curls escaping from her cap danced. "No, ma'am, but I would like to be. My friend, Tindal, 'e's a footman, would likely marry me if I could better myself. It's awful 'ard to get to be an upper servant, an' I've upset my Septimus 'cos I be'aved bad. That's what 'e says, but I couldn't 'elp bein' jealous. I caught 'er kissin' *my* man. It was dreadful."

Two ladies within earshot looked around in amazement at this burst of confidences from a serving wench. Sophia was genuinely sorry for her.

Kitty sensed her sympathy and said, "Oh, miss—"

One of the other maids muttered, "She's a 'ladyship,' you nodcock!"

Kitty's rosy face took on a pinker glow. "Beg, pardon, your ladyship."

"It does not matter," said Sophia. Servants could be as

cruel to one another as members of the *haut ton*. She shivered.

"Are you cold, your ladyship? Shall I bring a shawl?"

"No, thank you. I am merely tired." She simulated a yawn.

"I shouldn't be chatterin'," said Kitty. She looked into Sophia's eyes and a half-puzzled expression filled her own, as if she was struggling to recollect something. Her wide eyes were as dark as her hair and Sophia almost flinched at their sharp curiosity. "Excuse me, your ladyship, but 'aven't we met before? No, that ain't possible. I suppose you 'aven't got a relative what's come down in the world."

Sophia laughed and fluttered her fan. "Good heavens, woman, of course I have not. What a question!"

Kitty's remark had been overheard and was being repeated all through the room, and Kitty and Sophia became a focus for all eyes, some scandalized, some amused. Sophia bit her full underlip.

Kitty apologized. "Cats!" she muttered. "Pay no 'eed, my lady."

There was no doubt that Sophia should give a severe set down to a servant who assumed such intimacy, but unexpectedly she found she liked Kitty very much. In an odd way she seemed a kindred spirit. Kitty said quietly, "If you should 'ear of a lady wantin' a maid, I'd be right grateful to you. Then my Septimus wouldn't scorn me nor go for other maids. An' she was so *ugly*. Would you remember me, ma'am? I'd be grateful forever."

"I'll remember," said Sophia. Weariness and strain hoarsened her voice and again Kitty stared at her. "Are you sure you don't know of a relative—no, o' course, it's impossible. She truly was *awful* ugly, except for 'er eyes. They was lovely. I 'ave to admit that, though I denied it when Septimus said the same thing."

Sophia rose, handed Kitty a silver sixpence, and left. The orchestra was tuning up for a Scottish reel and she wondered if her overstretched nerves would hold out until the end of the ball.

She returned to her chaperone as the sets were being

formed. "There you are!" declared her cousin. "Mr. Chatteris wishes you to dance with him."

Mr. Chatteris bowed and led his partner into the set and they danced together almost without speech. Sophia was abstracted; Mr. Chatteris, short of breath.

When the dance finished, she sat at the end of a chaperones' bench and folded her hands in her lap. She longed for a little peace to collect her thoughts, but Ramsey appeared before her. "I have your cousin's permission to lead you into the next set, Lady Sophia."

"I do not care to dance, my lord."

Sophia caught Lady Stoneyhurst's outraged expression and heard the snort she had been unable to contain. She had best resign herself to the fact that everything she did angered someone.

Lord Ramsey had spoken equably, but she realized that his eyes betrayed anger which he was managing to contain. Why should he be angry with her? What right had he?

"Are you weary, your ladyship?" he asked. His voice was soft, but subtly hostile.

She almost glared at him. "Certainly not!" She softened her tone. "Well, maybe. All the shopping, the engagements, you know. By the time one reaches one's first ball, one does grow a trifle enervated."

The dark eyebrows rose, his eyes suddenly alight with a kind of mischievous fury. "Nonsense, Lady Sophia, I dare swear you could weather events far more strenuous than the Season." He led her out. "You are the picture of health. And beauty," he added, as the dance began.

Sophia, hands on hips, completed the foot movements before skipping down to meet Mr. Chatteris.

His cheeks were almost as vivid with heat as his deep crimson velvet coat. His yellow breeches and white silk socks clung to slightly plump legs. His sandy hair, which had been cut, combed, and pomaded in a short, fashionable style, was wilting. He was not a romantic figure, but he beamed at her with such pleasure that Sophia felt a surge of welcome for his friendly face. She returned his smile with a dazzling one that made him blink before they tripped away from one another.

Sophia half expected the viscount to quiz her over Edwin. He did not. He returned her to her chaperone and before she had time to analyze whether she felt relief or an odd disappointment, he surprised Sophia and gratified Lady Stoneyhurst by asking, "May Lady Sophia take a turn about the corridors with me? It will be refreshingly cool there."

Sophia wanted her cousin to refuse. Ramsey scared her with his percipience, his dominating presence, the essence of maleness he exuded, even as he attracted her dangerously.

She was being watched by, among others, the duchess, Lady Ramsey, and her cousin, whose smile was turning into a glare as Sophia hesitated. It would be far easier to accept than to refuse. She rose, "Thank you, sir."

This sortie must be kept on a trivial footing, the conversation frothy; she would flirt with him a little. One glance into the viscount's face half took her breath away. He had what she could only describe as a meaning look. He held out his arm and she placed her fingertips upon it and allowed him to lead her around the edge of the ballroom, knowing that she was the cynosure of many calculating eyes.

She said, scarcely moving her lips, "You have singled me out, my lord. We are causing speculation."

"Do you know, Lady Sophia, I believe you are right. But surely no one can take exception to the host's offering a little extra hospitality to a lady."

"It depends on his intentions." She fluttered her fan. "It's easy for a man to flout society's rules. A woman must take great care."

"I do so agree. Yet, I would have sworn you are a woman of spirit who would dare to challenge the dowagers."

"I cannot think what gave you that idea!" Sophia forced the words out flippantly, but her heart had begun to race. He could not recognize Susan in her, surely. She took another quick glance to find he was watching her closely, an expression of wicked amusement lighting the dark depths of his eyes.

She was not one to fade in the face of problems, especially ones she had created. She gritted her teeth and decided upon attack. "You look at me so strangely, sir, so very strangely. I cannot think why."

"I apologize, my lady" he said effusively. "I do not mean to disturb you. I believed that a creature as lovely as you would be used to admirers."

Sophia swallowed. If she agreed she would sound vain; if she disagreed she would sound flirtatious, as if she were fishing for further compliments.

"It's know as the horns of a dilemma," whispered Ramsey, bending to her ear, so close she felt his warm breath on her skin.

She was surprised into a laugh. Ramsey laughed too and for a moment there was complete rapport between them. It was not until they passed through a room, empty save for an inebriated papa asleep with his mouth slack, and into a smaller one with a window open to the night that she realized they were to be alone. There were few candles here and the room had dark corners. She should draw back. Was she imagining the threads of feeling between them? She held on to her panic, taking in gulps of fresh air, scrabbling in her mind for words to deflect him.

"Sophia . . ."

She whirled around. "I did not give you permission to address me by my forename, sir."

"No, and I think it very unfriendly of you. Surely you can sense the way I am attracted to you."

"What way? No, don't answer that! Please return me to my cousin. She will be getting anxious."

"Indeed, she will not. In fact, she will be very annoyed if you return in under half an hour."

"She's supposed to watch over me."

"She is doing so, Sophia. As I never make young girls the object of my attention she, and the polite world, will assume that I am smitten by you. They will be waiting for me to make you an offer. Your consequence will rise tremendously."

"Of all the vain, conceited—upstart—"

She was stopped in midsentence by his lordship's hands which suddenly encircled her waist. "Good God, sir, what are you doing?"

"Only what you want me to do."

"I don't!"

"You have been flashing messages at me ever since we met in—where was it?"

Sophia held her breath. Was this a threat? Was he promising her to keep her secret if she gave him what he wanted? And what exactly did he want?

". . . in your cousin's drawing room, was it not?"

Sophia expelled her breath in a long, relieved sigh. Her nerves were rendering her oversensitive, but she was not imagining the firm grip about her waist. She caught his wrists and tried to prise away his hands. She had as well try to remove an iron band.

"Sir, I appeal to you! This is unseemly."

A candle flame flared in the breeze, then died, but not before Sophia had caught fervid gleams in Lord Ramsey's eyes. "This is more so," he said.

She read his intention and put her hands against his broad chest and pushed. "No! No, you could not! You will not!"

"Oh, but I could and I will."

"Sir, I entreat you—this is not the behavior of a gentleman!"

He laughed softly and shivers rippled down her back. "Is your way always that of a lady?"

"I don't know what you mean."

"Oh, I am sure that you do."

His tone frightened her. "Let—me—*go!*"

"Don't you want me to kiss you?"

"No, of course I do not."

"Liar," he said softly. He moved swiftly backward, pulling her deeper into the shadows.

Sophia's nerves were quivering. Her body trembled, her knees shook. She stood quite still. He was right. She did want him to kiss her. An unfamiliar sensation had taken possession of her. She ached to touch him, to have him touch her, to hold her as close as he could, to—

His lips touched hers and moved on them lightly. "Your mouth is sweet, Sophia, and so cool."

"So is yours," she murmured. Surely that could not be her voice, soft, welcoming, beguiling. His mouth was on hers again, touching, tormenting, until she wanted to beg him to kiss her properly. It was on her forehead, her ears, her shapely nose, and returned to her lips. His kiss deepened and any remaining idea of discretion was routed as she drowned in sensation, until her lips moved under his, then opened, savoring the taste of him, and her arms crept around his neck, her hands twisted in his hair, pulling his head closer.

When they broke apart he looked deep into her eyes. "Not a girl in ten thousand would have responded like that. I dare swear you have been kissed before. Perhaps even tonight."

Shock rendered Sophia speechless for a moment. "I am not one of your easy flirts," she raged, wounded cruelly by his accusation. "Why should you think it?"

"Sir Edwin?" he intoned gently.

"Yes, you saw us emerge from one of the parlors. I must suppose that you think I was flirting with him."

"You both had an amazingly guilty appearance. For your sake, I hope that only I noticed it."

"If you had not, would you treat me so lightly?"

"That is speculation. I never speculate, except at gaming."

"And is your favorite form of gaming making love to girls to test their innocence?"

"No, it damn well is not! But I see no reason why I should not kiss a woman when she encourages me. I used no force. If you had been really frightened, I would have let you go."

His words brought her to the full realization of what she had done. Her hands went to her burning cheeks and she stared at him, knowing he told the truth. "Edwin and I have always been friends."

"Do you kiss all your friends?"

"No! I am *not* experienced, my lord."

"Your lips said otherwise."

"I was betrayed by—"

"Do go on. I am fascinated."

"I cannot." How did a woman explain to the first man who had really kissed her that she was innocent when she had responded in a way that must seem exceedingly worldly, perhaps wanton? She had been betrayed by her body, but how could she say so without making matters worse? She stared at him, and suddenly wanted to weep, though she could not explain why.

Ramsey caught his breath. "Sophia—"

"I wish to return to my cousin. Do you hear? I am not interested in your excuses."

He frowned, his black brows heavy above his eyes. "I make no excuses!"

"Take me back," she said again.

He paused in the brighter inner parlor to see if she was disheveled. "Try to look as if you have not just been kissed," he advised in a sardonic voice that made her long to slap him. Her hand moved convulsively. "Gently, my lady. If you do strike me, I shall kiss you again." His amusement had returned, though his words were a threat.

Lady Stoneyhurst greeted the arrival of her protégée with a smile. "Did you enjoy your turn about the corridors, my dear? Are you feeling cooler?"

Sophia dredged up an answering smile. "Much improved, your ladyship." She sat beside her chaperone. She was sure Anne would not have permitted her to be taken out and kissed by Lord Ramsey. And think what you would have missed, said an insistent voice inside her. And maybe if Anne had been present he would have preferred to kiss her. She turned aside from the thought.

How unfair society was. A man, especially one who was rich and titled, could please himself what he did and then expect to marry any woman he fancied. A girl could not take a single chance with her reputation.

She stood. "I shall go the ladies' retiring room, ma'am."

"Hurry back, my dear." Lady Stoneyhurst clearly approved of her. "The duke has engaged you for another dance." She bent forward and said conspiratorially, "An old title, my dear, and very rich. I believe he likes you. A good match there."

Sophia stifled the retort that came to her lips and left the ballroom. In the passage she saw a liveried footman trimming the candles. Her heart almost stopped as she recognized him. As if she had not been dealt enough blows in one night, she had to walk past Septimus Tindal as if nothing had happened. She swept by, flickering the candles with her speed, and almost staggered into the ladies' retiring room. She leaned back on the door, fanning herself. Knowing she was watched she said lightly, "Lord, what a crush. I am so hot."

There were not many present. One lady had fallen asleep on a daybed. The maids were tidying dressing tables and dusting away spilled powder. Thank God, there was no sign of Kitty. She sighed. She would have a few minutes' respite. Then a lady half hidden by a painted screen gave a small gasp and Miss Hill, Charlotte's companion, emerged to stare at her, a disbelieving expression in her pale blue eyes. There was no mistaking the look. Miss Hill recognized her.

Thirteen

Sophia walked shakily to a chair in front of a mirror and pretended to be tidying her hair. In her nervousness, she was clumsy and her glove became entangled in her gold and pearl chain so that it became loose and fell partly over one ear.

Miss Hill hurried to her, waving away a maid. "Pray allow me, ma'am," she said, her small hands fluttering above Sophia's head. She secured the hair ornament, not meeting Sophia's eyes.

A red-haired girl in a green gown tottered into the room and announced that the heat would kill her, or at the very least give her a dreadful headache. Maids escorted her to a daybed and brought hartshorn and a restorative.

Beneath the chatter, Miss Hill bent low to Sophia's ear. "Susan, it is you, is it not? You cannot hide yourself from me. You forget, I saw you without that foolish maquillage!"

Sophia shook her head, her voice suspended by dread, and Miss Hill whispered, "It is of no use to shake your head at me. What in heaven's name are you doing here? When Lord Ramsey discovers you to be a fraud, he will probably send for a constable. In fact, he should! Your deception cannot be for any good purpose."

Sophia managed to speak. She made an attempt at flippancy. "Good heavens, ma'am, have your wits forsaken you, or are you foxed?"

Miss Hill looked outraged. "I have never been—foxed, as you so vulgarly put it, in my life."

"Then why do you address me as Susan? I am Lady Sophia Clavering."

Miss Hill gasped. "What effrontery! It is certainly my duty to report this matter to his lordship. The family could all be murdered in their beds."

"Not by me, I assure you," said Sophia, trying to hang on to her disintegrating composure. "Remove your hand from my shoulder, if you please. I wish to return to Lady Stoneyhurst. She is my chaperone."

"Good heavens, how many other decent folk have you imposed yourself upon? And you may as well stop denying your identity. I *know* who you are."

Sophia sighed. "I truly am Lady Sophia."

"Nonsense! I have heard of the Claverings. A gentlewoman of substance would never, in any circumstances, travel a country road alone and offer herself as a lady's maid! It is utterly impossible! I liked you, Susan, I truly did, even though you abused the Ramseys' trust by running away. At least you did not steal his lordship's money, or the clothes Miss Ramsey so generously provided you with, but everything else points to your being engaged in some very questionable activity. I shall tell Lord Ramsey. I must!''

"Pray, hush, ma'am. You are beginning to attract attention.''

"Not as much as you will when you are discovered."

"Betrayed more like," snapped the goaded Sophia. "Oh, I'm sorry, but really!''

"It is a good thing that Lord Ramsey gave me leave to appear at the ball tonight. People call him harsh, but he has been kind to me. I was too nervous to go near the dancing, much as I cared for it in my youth, and came in here to bathe my wrists. I feel the heat, you know. I was on my way to partake of some of the delicious supper dishes that I saw carried in, that is, if my shocking discovery has not destroyed my appetite.''

Sophia stared at the twittering companion with sympathy. "Miss Hill, I see it is useless to prevaricate. I admit to having acted as a maidservant, but I can only assure you that I *am* Sophia Clavering. I had a mishap on the road and my purse was stolen. I was forced to hide beneath that awful disguise to protect my honor." Sophia paused. Miss Hill looked unconvinced. "I swear, I am telling the truth. Pray, do not make a scene tonight. Tomorrow, you may call on me at my cousin's house in Upper Brook Street and my dear governess-companion will vouch for me. She recently arrived from the country. She was a friend of Lord Ramsey's in their younger days. So please, Miss Hill, forget all about Susan, the maid, forever. I have proved you to be good-hearted."

Miss Hill sank upon a chair next to Sophia. She rubbed her forehead with a small hand, her papery skin rasping a little."I—I do not know—your speech—your appearance —you seem to be telling the truth. I want to believe you. I liked you even when you were Susan.''

"And I am fond of you, Miss Hill."

"You brought succor to my room when I felt indisposed. I will always remember that.''

"And you were good to me when I felt friendless. I remember that.''

Miss Hill stared at Sophia from watery blue eyes. "Are you truly Lady Sophia Clavering? But what peril you have been in! Anything could happen to a lady on the road or in a public inn."

"Exactly. Nothing terrible did, but it *could* have, and I do not want the *ton* to get even a suspicion of an idea that I have behaved in so unconventional a manner. My good name would vanish."

Miss Hill shuddered, "Dear me, no, my lady. It must be our secret." She looked suddenly pleased. "This is so exciting, Lady Sophia! Just fancy, my becoming your ally. I shall not fail you," she added with a touch of melodrama.

Sophia breathed deeply, then rose and said, "Come, then, and I'll walk with you to the supper room."

Sophia seated herself at a small table with Miss Hill and ordered a cup of coffee for herself. Hearing giggling from a table near a large plant, she looked around and saw the heads of two young people held close together. Miss Annabel Willis was being entertained by the young Duke of Chiddingley and clearly at home to a peg with him. Who would have thought it of her? She was so eminently biddable and gentle. It was impossible to judge folk by their outward appearance, as she knew only too well.

When Miss Hill had eaten she declared she would, after all, sit a while in the ballroom and watch the dancers.

"You should know, dear Lady Sophia," she said, her tongue tripping over her words as the third glass of wine took its toll, "I was considered to be quite a beauty in my youth. Ah, youth!" She fell silent for a while. "Ah, youth . . ." she said again when they reached the crowded ballroom.

Lord Ramsey came to meet them. "I was wondering where you were, Miss Hill."

"You thought of me in the midst of your gaiety." Miss Hill's voice wobbled and Ramsey leaned close, his eyes mirthful. "They are forming a set for a country dance, ma'am. May I lead you into it?"

The companion was so astonished she lost her tongue

completely and put up no resistance, and Sophia was left to ponder on a man who was benevolent to a dowdy little woman whom most of the world had forgotten and who frequently irritated him.

Sophia joined her cousin and was instantly accosted by the duchess. "Have you seen my nephew, or Miss Willis? She did not ask my permission to absent herself, and the duke should be doing his duty and asking you for a dance. You have stood up together only once."

Sophia smiled. "I believe I did see Miss Willis. She was drinking lemonade."

"Indeed!" The duchess's tone revealed that she was not interested in Annabel's type of refreshment. Then she frowned. "Is she in the supper room alone?"

"Oh, no, ma'am, there are several others present."

"Infuriating girl! I mean, is she with a gentleman?"

"Um, yes," said Sophia cautiously.

"Ah," her grace's eyes brightened. "With whom is she drinking lemonade?"

"With the Duke of Chiddingley, ma'am."

"What! Be so good as to tell her I command her presence beside me. Whatever next! And you may tell my idiot nephew to return as well."

Lady Stoneyhurst placed a small pair of spectacles on the end of her imposing nose and stared. "Really, duchess, Lady Sophia is not a serving wench to run errands."

"Would you prefer me to send a footman and cause whispers among the lower orders? Or perhaps I should go myself. How well *that* would look to inquisitive people ever ready to scratch away at a reputation."

Sophia ended the spat of discord before it could become too acidic. "I shall go at once to the supper room and come straight back."

She delivered the duchess's orders to Chiddingley and Annabel. They stared at her as if she were a being from another planet. "Why must we go back?" demanded the duke plaintively.

Annabel recovered her wits. "We may be causing unwelcome speculation, duke."

"What? Ah! Ah, yes, but I like you and I don't care who knows it."

Annabel's fair skin was bright with blushes when she and her escort followed Sophia back to the ballroom to receive a whispered castigation from the duchess.

Lord Ramsey was thoughtful as he partnered Miss Hill through the intricacies of the dance. She had been on the road with Sophia and just now the two had been sitting, absorbed, their heads close together, in the supper room. What had they been discussing? Could they possibly be accomplices on some proposed villainy? The possession of a title did not necessarily point to lawfulness. No, he could not conceive such a thing of Sophia—or indeed of the nervous little companion. Especially not of the diffident Miss Hill.

He followed the rhythms and smiled upon her whenever they met, yet his thoughts were with Sophia. More and more she dwelt in his mind—and his emotions. He wanted her as he had never wanted any other woman. For the first time in his life he had met a female who attracted him in every way, who even turned his thoughts to matrimony.

He could have laughed at himself. Here he was, taking a full part in the dancing, when he had expected to amuse himself playing cards while his sister was displayed as a matrimonial prize. He was aware that he was causing much cogitation among the chaperones, many of whom had long since given him up as a candidate for a wedding. He bowed and thanked Miss Hill, whose eyes were excessively bright. It could be the wine and the dancing, but he was not convinced. Why did she, usually so timorous, suddenly resemble a cat who had just swallowed a bowl of cream? She had a knowing look.

The ball ended with the dawn. Lady Ramsey and Charlotte were full of delight.

"A triumph," stated his mother.

"Utterly delightful," said his sister enthusiastically.

Ramsey looked at Charlotte's flushed face and shining eyes. Her favors had been sought by numerous gentlemen, including Sir Edwin Fothergill, Sophia's discarded lover. His mother had the young Duke of Chiddingley in mind for her only daughter, but he liked Edwin and might have considered him a desirable suitor had he not seen him emerge from a private parlor with Lady Sophia, both of them in a flushed, excited state. The memory angered him. Fothergill need not think to come courting his sister while he was dallying with another girl. The viscount almost convinced himself that his entire concern was for Charlotte and not at all for himself.

The ladies retired and he left Lorimer and his small army of footmen to see the musicians off, to put out the candles, and to check that there were no incipient fires. He passed a pretty maid in close and agitated conversation with a footman as he went upstairs and pretended not to notice.

He had long ago stopped trying to make his valet go to bed early, and Dunlop was waiting for him.

"Did you enjoy the ball, sir?"

"I can answer that in three words. Yes and no. Society has not changed since I was a green member of it. Many of the girls are beautiful, but brainless. Some show more intelligence. Others are clever in their conversation but not brainy enough to know they would do better to hide their cleverness from men."

Dunlop grinned as he laid his master's coat reverently on the bed, before brushing it and hanging it up.

"Why the grin, Dunlop?"

"I have heard your lordship insist that his bride must be beautiful *and* clever."

"Ah, yes, I did say so in the days of my youth."

He fell silent as Dunlop removed his shoes and later lay in bed wakeful for an age, his mind returning constantly to Sophia Clavering. Not for worlds would he have missed her unusual debut into society. The fact that only he outside of her family was aware of her shocking behavior gave piquancy to the situation. But *was* he the only one? Miss Hill, the closest to her during the journey, had such a strange air about her. And there was young Fothergill. How much did he know? His mind slid from the puzzle and back to Sophia, and he forgot everything else. How lovely she was. How fascinating her unconventionality and her keen mind. What courage she had! If he were a marrying man, she was just the kind of girl who would capture him.

The days were crammed with excitement and Sophia relaxed and began to enjoy herself. No one had recognized her except Miss Hill, and she had vowed silence. Charlotte and her mother were too bound up in themselves to think any more of a rather ugly maid who had absconded.

Her maid had declared herself promised to a farmer and refused to leave the country and Sophia was sharing with Lady Pamela until a substitute could be engaged. Cousin Pamela had sent Mrs. King to a trusted agency to look for a suitable girl.

One morning Sophia descended the stairs to be greeted by Wheadon. "If you please, your ladyship, there are two persons waiting for you in the small parlor." His tone made it clear that the visitors were members of a lower order. She hoped a suitable new maid had been found. Her wardrobe was growing considerably and she had not the time to look after her clothes. Probably the girl's mother was with her. That boded well for her respectability.

She pushed open the door of the small parlor and stopped dead on the threshold as a man turned from the window to greet her and a woman rose from a chair. Tindal! And Kitty Jenkins. Sophia advanced into the room striving for calm, and seated herself.

"Good morning," she said.

"Good mornin', my lady," said Tindal. "I was at the Servants' Registry this mornin' and saw that you needed a maid, so I fetched Miss Jenkins here to apply for the position."

"Good mornin', your ladyship," said Kitty in a quavering voice.

Sophia controlled the quake in her own voice and asked, "What experience have you had?"

"N-none as lady's maid, but my mother was an upper servant with a duke an' taught me all manner of things. I know my speech ain't—isn't—proper, but I'm a quick learner. Could you give me a trial, my lady? I can sew and dress hair, an' I'm strong an' very willin'.''

"An' I can vouch she's quick to learn," broke in Tindal.

"In what relationship do you stand to Miss Jenkins?" asked Sophia, as coolly as possible.

"I'm her man. We're gettin' married one day if Kitty can improve herself."

"I see. Your ambitions are commendable and I am sorry to disappoint you, but I have not the time to teach. I need a properly trained woman. I regret I cannot offer you the job, Miss Jenkins."

"Is that so?" demanded Tindal in an abrupt change of manner, ignoring a remonstrance from Kitty. "I'm sure once your ladyship has thought the matter out, you'll be more than willin' to take her on."

Sophia stared at the footman indignantly. "I have already told you, I have not the time."

"Well, maybe you will when you can see the full picture. It's like this, your ladyship. Kitty told me you reminded her in a peculiar way of a certain runaway maid, name of Susan, a vagabond creature what was picked up on the road. So I watched you, an' I know you're that same maid. Your eyes give you away, and your hair, too, and don't forget, I cuddled you." Kitty clenched her hands convulsively and drew a sharp breath. "A man can learn a lot from holdin' a woman. And what will your grand friends say when I tell 'em that you're not a lady at all, but a beggar wench what tricks herself into folks' lives?"

Sophia stared at the arrogant footman. He had stumbled on a travesty of the truth, but if he went around spreading such rumors there would be inevitable complications. Someone would sense a delicious scandal and pry deeper and discover the whole truth. Or they would make up what they did not know. Either way, she would be humiliated and ruined.

Kitty wrung her hands nervously. "Septimus, go easy. I don't like this at all. Let's forget it and go 'ome."

"Shut your noise, clunch-head. You'll never get on." He turned to Sophia, "You see, Susan, the world's a hard place for folks like us. We want to improve ourselves and you can help.''

"And if I refuse?"

Tindal stared insolently at her. "Oh, then I'm afraid that there'll be some nasty stories. No one will know how they began, but they'll all know where they're goin'. A little bird tells me you ain't got vouchers for Almack's yet. Just let the top-lofty patronesses hear of your jauntin' about the countryside an' you'll never get them, an' I expect you know that a society lady that doesn't get into Almack's can't make much of a go of her Season.''

Sophia was angrier than she had ever been in her life. She rose so abruptly that Kitty jumped and Tindal took a step back. She said in measured tones, "I *am* Lady Sophia Clavering and you can go to hell, both of you. Even if what you say were to be true, I would never submit to outrageous extortion. I would sooner rusticate forever. Now get out, the pair of you, before I send for a magistrate.''

Tindal's mouth fell open and Kitty began to weep. "I wish we 'adn't come 'ere!"

Tindal glared at her. "You'll do what I tell you unless you want to lose me. There'll be no marriage between us unless you obey me. Love, honor, an' *obey*, that's what I expect.''

"It ain't honorable to 'urt a lady what's never done you no 'arm.''

"Lady! She's no lady!"

Sophia turned from him and said gently, "Kitty, how can you endure the way he behaves?''

"I love 'im, Susan—your ladyship, I mean. Always 'ave an' always will. An' now I'm carryin' 'is baby and I got to marry 'im.''

Sophia made no further attempt to speak. She rang for a footman, who showed Tindal and the still tearful Kitty out. Sophia watched them go. She had been poised on a tightrope between servants and masters and was on the verge of unbalancing and falling to ignominy.

The evening brought an assembly given by Lady Stoneyhurst and the duchess in the large ducal residence. Sophia was so worried she could take small pleasure in her appearance. Her gown was of white satin with a white, spangled overdress of gauze. Mr. Plerivale had replied to her letter in a forgiving way and had dispatched her jewel case with Anne Sheffield. Her hair was cleverly dressed, in an ordered disorder of gleaming chestnut curls, with silk lilies-of-the-valley, pearls, and tiny diamonds. She turned from the cheval glass with a sigh. What use would handsome looks, money, or anything be without reputation?

Sophia stood with Lady Stoneyhurst, the duchess, the gangling figure of the duke, and the shy Annabel to receive guests. The many faces and compliments had begun to blur one into the other when her mind became searingly sharp at the appearance of Viscount Ramsey. In spite of her effort at control, her heart thudded harder. She could not forget the intensity of his kiss, the sensation of strong masculine arms around her, the unfamiliar craving he aroused in her. She flushed now at the memory as he took her proferred hand and kissed it, lingering a shade too long for propriety.

"How enchanting you look, Sophia."

She frowned. She could not reprimand him here, but she certainly would if he cornered her again. A wave of hungry longing swept over her at the thought and she was angry and dismayed to realize that she wanted very much to be trapped by the viscount and thoroughly kissed. His wicked eyes seemed to tell her that he could read her thoughts.

The duchess greeted him effusively, but Miss Willis blushed and stammered in a way that brought frustrated anger to her chaperone's eyes.

Miss Sheffield had consented to attend and stood a little apart. She was greeted with enthusiasm by Lord Ramsey and a thrill of jealousy frightened Sophia. Her emotions were getting out of control. She must not allow herself to fall in love with a man who showed no inclination to esteem her.

Musicians had been engaged and the orchestra was throwing itself into a sparkling composition of Mozart's.

Annabel was escorted from the receiving line by the duke, who totally disregarded his formidable great-aunt's signals. Annabel was also in white, as became a young woman making a debut in her own home. She was pale and looked more insipid than ever.

Lady Stoneyhurst hissed, "What a pair. They resemble a couple of pet rabbits. Pink and white with pale eyelashes."

"Ma'am!" protested Sophia as the duchess moved away. "Her grace will hear."

"No, she won't. She's too cross to listen, because they've gone off together. She has hopes of you for the duke and of Ramsey for Annabel."

Sophia was shaken. The proposed alliances seemed remote, but the chaperones were well versed in matchmaking. Many a girl was manipulated into a wedding with a husband who got her with child as often as possible and spent between times in town with his mistresses.

The heat was building up and the music almost lost in the clamor of the many voices when supper was announced. Lord Ramsey appeared like magic at Sophia's side.

"May I take you to the supper room?"

"You are singling me out, my lord."

"Is that wrong?" The expressive brows were raised.

"No, not wrong."

"What then?"

"How persistent you are, sir. You must know that folk will talk if you pay me more attention than is proper."

"Proper? You amaze me! I had not thought you proper."

Sophia was disturbed. Once more the viscount's words seemed to hold too much meaning.

"I assure you, sir, I am correct in my behavior."

"Of course she is," insisted the Duke of Chiddingley who had, once more, just offered his arm to Annabel, driving the duchess into a near spasm.

"Hold hard," she boomed in a voice incongruously deep, coming as it did from a stout woman of five feet one inch. "Why do not you, Ramsey, escort Annabel?

Chiddingley can take in Lady Sophia. The duke and
Annabel can see one another any time.''

"Can't," said the duke. "Always busy. Shopping and
so forth, don't you know," he explained.

In spite of her anxiety, Sophia giggled.

"Hush," remonstrated Ramsey. "It's no laughing
matter.''

Sophia glanced up at him to find him grinning at her and
she dissolved into further giggles, while the duke and
Annabel wandered off, oblivious to the varying emotions
they were engendering.

Annabel and Sophia arrived in the supper room with
their escorts and seated themselves, beneath the gaze of
many interested eyes. A central table was laden with
savories and sweetmeats and a footman filled Sophia's
plate with cold capon and beef, pickled artichokes and
mushrooms. A dish of forced strawberries, a syllabub, and
a plate of macaroons and lemon cakes was placed on their
table. All was to be washed down with fine champagne.
Miss Sheffield appeared in the doorway, looking perfectly
at ease. Ramsey rose and escorted her to Sophia's side
while she protested laughingly at being press-ganged.

"Sir, I prefer to be left quietly to myself. It is not seemly
to pay me such attention. My position—my age—''

Ramsey gave a shout of mirth. "Your age! It is the same
as mine. You are not a day over twenty-eight.''

"Twenty-nine!''

"Well, you don't look it. Now, pray give your order for
food.''

Miss Sheffield shrugged, smilingly, and obeyed. Sophia
ate steadily, trying to keep her mind from the possibility
that Ramsey might like an older woman to share his life.
Indeed, they were on such easy terms she wondered if
Ramsey could be part of her companion's past.

A latecomer arrived in the supper room. Mr. Chatteris,
resplendent in claret velvet, hurried to greet his friends,
proffering a low bow and an apology for his late arrival.
"I threw out at least a dozen cravats. I could not appear at
so important a function without perfection in my cravat.''

"Fop," murmured Ramsey.

Mr. Chatteris laughed and took the chair brought by a footman. "I have learned what I know from you, my dear fellow."

Ramsey's long fingers slid down the ribbon of his quizzing glass through which he beheld his friend's cravat.

"What's the verdict?" asked Mr. Chatteris, his expression as grave as such a matter deserved.

Ramsey smiled. "Mr. Brummell is here. Ask his opinion."

"I would not dare," said Mr. Chatteris.

Ramsey inspected his friend's cravat again. "Perhaps you are right."

The banter was going over Sophia's head. She was tinglingly aware of the way Ramsey's hand brushed hers when he handed a dish, the way his dark eyes frequently rested on her with an inexplicable emotion in their depths, the way her senses betrayed her when he was near.

She could have groaned aloud. At times it seemed to her that Ramsey was attracted to her, but it was all of no consequence. Tindal had left seething with rage. The rumors would begin. How would she know when? How long would they take to circulate? Would folk begin to ostracize her? The London Season had been her dream for years, and with it a pattern of a man who would fall in love with her and offer for her. She had found the man, but what of the rest of her dream?

The hours wore on, filled with the hustle and bustle of folk leaving for, or arriving from, other parties. The atmosphere was hot, scent-filled, and noisy with endless chatter, and Sophia grew almost dizzy. Charlotte reveled in it, her beauty untouched by heat and fatigue. She appeared to take a positive delight in oversetting Edwin, who had eyes for no other girl, and flirted outrageously, and all the head-shaking directed at her by her brother and mother failed to prevent her from joining a set with Sir Walter Crawley, a notorious fortune-hunter. Lord Ramsey watched the couple dancing, his face grim.

Sophia felt half suffocated and, hurrying toward a seat near the door, almost tripped over a pair of black shiny shoes. They were surmounted by exquisitely cut

pantaloons and she looked up apologetically to find herself
regarded by a pleasant looking man impeccably tailored,
with a snowy, starched cravat that fell properly just short
of an excess of perfection. In her agitation, she dropped
her fan.

He picked it up and gave it to her. "Madam, you have
left dust on my shoes. I may need to return home to change
them."

Fancy a man caring so much for his shoes! Yet, there
had been humor in his voice and Sophia had a sudden
desire to giggle as she considered offering to dust them
with her handkerchief. She tendered apologies, dropping a
curtsy.

"I forgive you. I could not remain angry for long with
such a fair member of your sex." He handed her fan to
her. "Pleased to have been of service."

"Thank you, sir. Fatigue has made me a trifle clumsy."

"Fatigued? So early in the Season?"

Sophia remembered that she was supposed to appear
vivacious at all times. "Well, only a little. I am not
accustomed to town hours."

"You reside in the country? I could not endure to do so.
I tried soldiering, you know, but my regiment was once
ordered north—a dreadful place—I should have been
forever splashed with mud. Naturally, I resigned my com-
mission."

"But of course, sir," said Sophia, not quite suppressing
a laugh.

The man favored her with a singularly sweet smile.
"You are evidently a woman of discernment. May I know
your name?" Sophia gave it, and he bowed again and
strolled to a lady who had watched his encounter. He
talked earnestly to her, occasionally glancing Sophia's
way, before he called for his carriage and left.

"My dear child," greeted her cousin later in tones of
gratification. "How clever of you. Our vouchers for
Almack's are assured."

"Clever? Almack's?"

"You cannot pretend to me that you did not know you

were speaking to Mr. Brummell. By all accounts, he is most impressed by you. He went at once to Lady Jersey, one of the patronesses, and soon afterward I was given the splendid news.''

"But I vow—"

"Come now, Sophia, take credit where it is due. Almack's! The rules there are strict above anything. Only a half dozen of the Guard's officers and a quarter of the nobility have gained entrance. The patronesses are ruthless.''

Sophia yielded. Her cousin was adamant in believing what she wanted and, after all, getting the vouchers was the important thing.

Fourteen

Sophia slept badly, her mind unbearably active with nightmares of being turned out of polite society. She had seen little of the *haut ton*, but enough to know that the claws and jaws of the tabbies were merciless toward those who transgressed its laws.

The next day she felt tired. Her cousin was scandalized. "You are not permitted to be tired during the Season. Afterward, you may rusticate in the country as languidly as you please. Make yourself ready. The weather is somewhat better at last and we shall walk.''

Sophia, accustomed to striding around the extensive grounds belonging to herself and Edwin, looked forward to the exercise. She was disappointed. Hyde Park was large enough for vigorous walking, but it was used by most gentlefolk to perambulate at a stately stroll to show off their clothes and greet friends and opponents; for young ladies to impress suitors with their graceful riding; for eligible men to cause their horses to skitter and dance, then bring them skillfully under control beneath the gaze of admiring girls. The well-dressed people under the mostly bare trees whose growth was held back by the late spring looked as if the Park had thrust promenading flowers of every hue through the hard earth.

Sophia was satisfied to know that she held her own in a dark green merino gown, a lighter green spencer, and a high-crowned poke bonnet trimmed with pale blue flowers and a green velvet bow. Her feet were shod in fur-trimmed half-boots. Annabel strolled beside her, silent for the most part.

A voice hailed them from behind and the duke appeared, a redingote flowing almost to his ankles, his head crowned by a high beaver hat that increased his height.

Lady Stoneyhurst muttered, "Faith, what a beanpole!" She smiled graciously as he bowed to her and to his great-aunt, the duchess, before he made his way to the young ladies and offered his arm to Annabel.

"Pray, take Lady Sophia'a arm," ordered the duchess stridently.

Annabel went a deep shade of crimson, but the duke seemed unperturbed. "I've had small opportunity to talk to Miss Willis. You've either got her at a crush somewhere, or closeted with the mantua-maker, or—"

"Enough! Here is Sir Edwin Fothergill. He can escort Annabel while you accompany her ladyship." The duchess's voice continued with perfect clarity as she said to Lady Stoneyhurst, "Two acceptable matches there, ma'am, if we can pull 'em off."

Sophia squirmed inwardly and the look directed at her by Edwin showed his frustration. "You've got no call to stare at me like that," she hissed. "I am not responsible for what her grace says."

"Did I say you were?"

"No, but you looked it."

"I did no such thing. How could I look something I don't feel?"

"I cannot answer that. I only know it's true."

"Poppycock! I'm going to find Charlotte. She said she'd be here." He bowed and stalked off.

"He has gone," pointed out the duke unnecessarily.

The duchess almost stamped her foot. "I can see that for myself, nodcock. You must escort both ladies."

"Trouble with Edwin again?" The voice made Sophia jump. Lord Ramsey appeared from a side path and attached himself to her side. The duke took the opportunity to move apart with Annabel.

Ramsey watched Edwin disappearing. "He'll not find my sister that way," he said blandly.

"Well, I daresay he'll discover her in the end. I think he is in love."

"With Charlotte?" His voice was severe.

"Should you object to a match? Edwin is well born and rich."

He avoided the question. "I gather you are to wed Chiddingley."

"I most certainly am not! I don't want a numbskull for a husband."

Ramsey laughed, but his eyes were unsmiling and watchful. "You would be a duchess, very wealthy, high in society."

"No, thank you, not with his grace." Sophia shuddered.

"What kind of husband do you look for, Sophia?" Ramsey's voice held more than curiosity.

A man like yourself, rushed into Sophia's mind. She breathed deeply. "I have told you before, you are not to use my first name. It is unseemly. And I am not on the catch for any husband. If I fall in love, well, that's something different."

"Do you believe in love? I thought you had too much sense to give credence to illusions."

"Is love an illusion? If so, it must have fooled many thousands."

"I believe it has and will go on doing so." Ramsey's voice was unexpectedly sad.

"That's a cynical attitude, my lord. Is there no lady you could love?"

Ramsey hesitated. "Sometimes I think—perhaps I just hope for my perfect woman."

"There is no perfection in any woman. How tedious she would be."

"I said *my* perfect woman. She would have flaws of the right kind."

"That sounds dreadfully arrogant. I can only pray that you may discover her before you are too old to enjoy her."

"How kind of you, Sophia."

The sardonic voice grated on her nerves and she turned and walked back to Lady Stoneyhurst and remained by her side for the rest of the walk.

When Sophia learned the next day that a visit to the theater was planned, nothing could prevent a thrill of anticipation.

"Oh, ma'am," she said, clasping her hands in delight. "How wonderful."

"Have you never seen acting before?" demanded Lady Stoneyhurst.

"Yes, but not in London. I was used to playing parts myself when we got up charades and theatricals and I once dreamed of becoming an actress."

"Good God! I trust you will keep such an ambition to yourself. Whatever next? Sometimes I think the younger generation has lost all sense of decorum. They think nothing of taking part in that new dance introduced from Germany—the waltz—during which the man actually places his arm around his partner's waist. In public!"

"Indeed, ma'am," said Sophia. "I did not see it performed in the country." She wondered how it would be to have Ramsey's arm about her while they danced.

A maid had been engaged by Miss Sheffield for Sophia —Tabitha Carter, a pleasant, experienced woman nearing her middle years. She enthused over her new mistress's extensive wardrobe and gave her whole attention to the correct attire to be worn on a first visit to the London stage. They settled on a opera dress of turquoise satin that turned Sophia's luminous hazel eyes to sparkling blue. It had long sleeves and a low, lace-trimmed neckline. Sophia smoothed her hands down its gleaming surface with delight.

"My first satin gown," she breathed.

"An' very handsome you look in it, ma'am," said Tabitha, hovering with a frothy headdress of tulle and lace. She pinned it on Sophia's gleaming chestnut curls with a tiny butterfly of gold and sapphire. Matching eardrops swung from her small ears.

Lady Stoneyhurst regarded her with satisfaction. "You must take a warm shawl with you. The weather continues cold and some of these theater boxes are prodigious draughty. I suggest the white cashmere embroidered with forget-me-nots."

They arrived at Drury Lane a trifle early. "I find as much pleasure from watching other folk as from what one sees on the stage," announced Lady Stoneyhurst, "especially in the pit where the lower orders meet the young society dogs. Such wrangles and brangles they have! Reminds me of my youth."

Sophia scarcely heard her. She was drinking in the smells and sights and sounds. This was it. This was real romance, the world she had dreamed of.

The duchess and Annabel arrived. Sophia wondered who had dressed Annabel in a pale lemon gown that made her fine skin appear sallow, and a cap of yellow ribbons and tulle that was insecurely attached to her light, fine-textured hair. She clutched at a yellow shawl and Sophia felt sorry for the shy girl who scarce lifted her eyes. It must be dreadful to make a come-out when money was insufficient and to be so bashful that every public appearance was an agony of embarrassment.

Then Sophia was totally absorbed by the drama of *The Merchant of Venice*. During the interval, callers began invading the duchess's box. One gentleman was dispatched for wine, another for tea. The duke was commanded by his aunt to "take Lady Sophia for a turn about the corridors."

Sophia scarcely knew who was most to be pitied—the duke, herself, or Annabel.

After a few moments of silent pacing, Sophia asked, "Are you enjoying the play, your grace?"

"No!" he said, then feeling a little more was needed, "Read it at Eton, you know, and couldn't understand much of it. Something about a pound of flesh and no blood. Stands to reason that's impossible. Fell asleep at school. Fell asleep here, too, but no one beat me for it as they did at Eton." He returned Sophia to her chaperone and they parted with mutual relief.

After the play came a farce, *High Life Below Stairs*, at which the audience laughed immoderately. Sophia, her recent experiences still sharp, could not enjoy it so well. In the next interval Chiddingley rose instantly and offered his arm to Annabel.

The duchess fumed. "Why am I cursed with a numbskull for a nephew? He is the hope of the family and should be paying his addresses to a woman of equal rank and fortune. If I had known what would ensue, I never would have offered to sponsor Miss Willis. She is becoming a viper in my bosom. I am half inclined to send her home."

Sophia was shocked. She was wondering if a word in Annabel's defense would moderate or increase her grace's anger when her cousin intervened. "Best not, my dear duchess. 'Tis my experience that to forbid an acquaintance merely makes young people more stubborn. He is sure to get tired of such a namby-pamby girl."

Immediately the duchess bridled indignantly. "I see no reason for you to malign Miss Willis, ma'am. She is a respectable girl from a distant branch of my family."

Lady Stoneyhurst shrugged exaggeratedly and raised her blackened brows. To Sophia's relief, she was prevented from replying by the entry of Viscount Ramsey.

The duchess smiled. "Ah, my lord, you will find Miss Willis taking a turn with Chiddingley."

Ramsey bowed. "How pleasant for them. Lady Sophia, will you favor me with a walk before the next act?"

Sophia rose and took his arm. They strolled slowly along the corridor. The duke and Annabel were nowhere to be seen.

"The duchess has selected you as first choice for her great-niece," she said.

"Miss Willis is a mouse," said Ramsey. He threw up his hand. "All right, don't attack me. I defer to you, she is a sweet little mouse, but still—a mouse. In the end, the duchess will accept willingly any suitor with breeding and an income. You, of course, are marked down for Chiddingley. Shall you like being wedded to him?"

"That is something I shall not discover, since it will never happen."

"I wish I might hear you tell her grace so."

"She will not have to be told, since I shall not permit him to propose."

"Indeed! And how do you intend to prevent it? Chiddingley follows orders, and he would be impervious to gentle hints."

"A woman has her ways of discouragement," said Sophia lightly, then flushed crimson.

Ramsey looked down at her and laughed softly. "Am I to understand then that you were willing for me to kiss you?"

"No, sir, you are not. I did my utmost to resist you."

Ramsey stopped and rubbed his head reflectively, disordering the dark curls. "I do not recall a great deal of protest."

"Your memory is at fault. I protested strongly."

Ramsey sighed gustily. "I recall only your delightful response."

"I am inexperienced. You imagined my response."

"If I believed that, it would wound me, Sophia. Now we know one another better, will you kiss me again?"

"That I will not."

Another couple strolled by and the gentlemen exchanged bows. "You are right. This place is altogether too public. At our next meeting I shall discover a secret corner. Then I shall hold you for the, er, third time, is it not?"

"You have an unflatteringly poor memory, sir. You have held me once and you shall not again," flashed Sophia, her nerves scratched raw by his words. The first time he had tried to embrace her was in his own home when she had been heavily disguised. Was his memory truly at fault or was he hinting that he had seen through her machinations? Perhaps Tindal had already begun to spread his poison and the viscount considered her fair game. She felt a little giddy.

"Are you ill?" Ramsey's flippancy left him. "Pray be seated." He guided her to a small chair and snapped his fingers at a passing attendant. "Bring wine at once."

In a gentle voice, Ramsey urged her to drink. She sipped and felt better.

"Is your health poor?" Sophia was astonished at the tenderness he displayed. She felt almost like confessing to some indisposition to keep him in so sweet a mood.

"I am perfectly well, sir. I think I am overcome with excitement. To attend a London theater has long been my goal. At home we got up theatricals and I always played a part and—" She stopped abruptly. She was touching on a hazardous subject.

She left the glass on a side table, rose, and resumed the walk. "I collect that Mr. Huddart is new to the part of Shylock," she said. "His performance is powerful. Is he better than others you have seen?"

Ramsey said, "You have unerring judgment, Lady Sophia. He has recently come to this theater and is astonishingly proficient, especially as he must overcome the handicap of following in the footsteps of Mr. Kemble and Mr. Cook."

Sophia sighed in pleasure. "How wonderful that I should have seen his debut."

"You truly do care about the theater, don't you, Sophia? Tell me about your play-acting at home. What parts did you take?"

She kept her tone even. "You cannot wish to hear about a group of amateurs, however enthusiastic we all were."

"I assure you I do. I swashbuckled with the best when I was a boy, swinging a cloak and wielding a mock sword."

Sophia glanced into Ramsey's face. It displayed only a friendly interest. "I never felt happier than when I was play-acting," she said. "It seems odd now I am grown, but once I dreamed of being a real actress. I daresay I should not say so, but I found it pleasant above all things. Of course, I gave up such pretentions long ago."

"Naturally. It must be years since you thought of acting. You are so great an age. Fortunately you carry your years well."

Sophia laughed irresistibly. In this mood Ramsey was such a joy to be with. She lifted shining eyes, brimming with mirth, to him and he caught his breath. "God, you're beautiful, Sophia."

She should reprimand him, she should dismiss him and stalk away. She did neither. She was mesmerized by him, by the closeness of his body, by his dark, burning eyes.

They fell silent, strolling on a few paces, Ramsey guiding her with a gentle touch on her elbow.

"Are you enjoying the farce?" asked Ramsey.

Sophia's nerves jumped. "It is trivial," she replied lightly.

"It is meant to be. The tendency of some servants to ape their betters has always been a subject for mirth. Do you not find it so? Perhaps your sympathies lie with those below stairs. Do you know much about the lives led by our servants?"

Sophia dared not look at him. Did his voice hold an ominous meaning? Was her imagination, already stimulated by this visit to the theater, lending his words too much weight? "I know a little. Do not you?"

"Not a great deal," he said cheerfully. "Are you skillful in the use of disguise, Lady Sophia?"

"What?"

"During your amateur theatricals, were you clever with maquillage?"

She wished profoundly she had not raised the subject. "Yes, in an amateur way." Her reply was abrupt.

"I daresay you could make yourself look entirely different."

"Perhaps."

"Fascinating. You have probably fooled many with your clever make-up."

Sophia swallowed hard. "It is not difficult to appear different on a stage," she breathed. "And now, sir, pray, return me to my cousin."

Ramsey obeyed her without another word.

* * *

Wednesday was the night for Almack's. Sophia was feverishly excited. She took no chances on displeasing the patronesses and wore an unexceptionable pale blue satin slip with a round neckline. A white lace overdress fell from beneath her breasts, and the blue satin bodice was edged with blond lace scallops. Her kid gloves met her tiny sleeves and her hair was drawn up in a Grecian style with a circlet of silver leaves and pearls which were matched by the single strand around her throat. When the carriage took its place in the line leading to the door, Sophia found it difficult to remain still. The duchess sat beside Lady Stoneyhurst, their gowns vying for space, and Annabel and Sophia faced them. Sophia had given up expecting Miss Willis to wear anything distinguished or even very pretty, and was not surprised to see that she had on a pale tan slip with a pale yellow overdress.

Two of the most formidable patronesses, Mrs. Drummond Burrell and the Countess Lieven, were present and Sophia sank low in her curtsies to them. While she waited for the dancing to begin, she was able to look around her. The famous room was not especially grand. It had its complement of wall mirrors and benches and there was a balcony where those who preferred to watch could sit and gossip. Sets were formed for country dances and reels in which Sophia took part with a number of partners, and later she ate the refreshments of thin, rather stale bread and butter with tea.

She ventured to whisper to Annabel, "Why do people care so much about this place? It is a dead bore!"

Miss Willis looked shocked. "You had best not let anyone else hear you say that."

Sophia subsided. She continued to take the floor with gentlemen introduced to her, received their compliments, behaved with outward vivacity, and felt surprisingly weary.

Then, just before eleven o'clock, when the doors were implacably closed to latecomers, Viscount Ramsey arrived. Her spirits leapt and her heart beat faster. She tried not to stare at him, tried to deny that she ached to have him approach her and lead her into a dance. He saw her and strolled across the room. He was, as always, impeccably dressed. His bottle-green coat fitted over his broad shoulders without even a suspicion of a wrinkle, his white piqué waistcoat was crossed by a modest watch chain, and he wore black knee breeches and black shoes with small buckles. He bowed to the duchess, Lady Stoneyhurst, and Annabel, and requested permission to lead Sophia onto the floor.

Sophia placed her fingertips on Ramsey's left sleeve and for an instant his right hand was laid over hers. She glanced up at him in surprise, their eyes met, and there was a moment of harmonious rapport between them, then it passed, his customary ironical look returned. She had not imagined it, she told herself firmly, and a feeling of warm happiness spread through her. They were parted by the movement of the dance and she wished with all her heart that she could remain by his side, singled out by him not merely for the dance but for always. Her chaotic thoughts made her stumble and only the intervention of a stout gentleman with a face as pink as his coat saved her from falling. She made a desperate effort to gather her wits, but it was difficult to concentrate when she was trying to cope with the undeniable knowledge that she had fallen helplessly in love with Lord Ramsey. She had always supposed that love would fill her with delight and contentment. How wrong she had been. This love was harrowing. There could be no future for her with a man who was so cynical about women, whose name was a byword for dalliance. All she could anticipate was heartbreak.

The danced ended and Ramsey led her back to her chaperone. He paused before they reached her. "Sophia, my dear, you look positively gloomy. What ails you? Can you tell me?"

Sophia could have wept. The consideration in his voice unnerved her, but at all costs she must hide her love from him.

"I am quite well, my lord," she responded, her voice icily sharp in her effort to hide her sudden self-knowledge.

Ramsey looked angry. "I rejoice to know it," he rasped. He led her to a seat next to Lady Stoneyhurst, bowed, and walked away to solicit the hand of a young girl for a reel.

Lady Stoneyhurst hissed, "Sophia, what have you done to send Ramsey flying into the boughs? What did you say to him? I know the world says he ain't the marrying sort, but you can never be sure with men, and in any event, you'd do well to stay on his good side. He knows everybody and could do damage to your reputation."

"Indeed, ma'am. And should I toady to him out of fear?"

The duchess, who had bent forward, the better to listen, tutted. "My dear Lady Stoneyhurst, you would do well to teach your protégée the conduct expected of her."

Lady Stoneyhurst laughed and replied in a voice like the clash of metal on ice, "Dear duchess, my cousin is perfectly well aware what is expected of her, are you not, Sophia?" She did not wait for an answer. "I think it my duty to remind you, duchess, that your protégée, the amiable Miss Annabel Willis, and your young relative, the Duke of Chiddingley, have been scarce apart this evening."

The duchess ground her teeth, smiled, and said sweetly, "Maybe we should pool our power. The duke would be an excellent match for Lady Sophia, and if Ramsey don't come up to scratch with Annabel, and I don't hold out hopes that he will, young Fothergill would be an excellent husband for her."

Sophia wondered how many society marriages came about through love, and how many through the machinations of the dowagers and chaperones. She decided not to tell the two conspiring ladies that she had seen Edwin and Charlotte wandering off together to the refreshment room with no thought for anyone else.

It was her last coherent thought of the evening. The band struck up for the German waltz, still regarded as shocking by many. The music was lilting and gay and

Sophia stared at the dancers whirling around and around, the man with a hand on his partner's waist, and her mind ran riot at the thought of such public intimacy with a man of one's choosing. She had to work very hard at not appearing envious when Ramsey whirled by holding Lady Jersey.

Lady Stoneyhurst, noting the tapping of Sophia's foot in time to the music, said, "You must not hope to dance a waltz yet, Sophia. At Almack's, only ladies with the express permission of the patronesses may do so and this is your first visit."

"Indeed, ma'am. I was not considering such a thing. It looks excessively—indecorous."

There was to be another waltz and Ramsey approached Lady Stoneyhurst. "I have Lady Jersey's permission for Lady Sophia to dance the waltz with me. May I lead her out?"

Lady Stoneyhurst was gratified. She looked speculatively at her great-niece, who had just declared her aversion to the dance, wondering if she should give permission. Lady Sophia was regrettably headstrong and might actually decline. But she could not resist the temptation and she nodded. Sophia moved swiftly and a moment later she and Ramsey were among the other couples, the eyes of less fortunate young ladies fixed on Sophia jealously.

She had never learned to waltz, but the steps were simple, then Ramsey's hand slid around her slender waist and the touch seemed to melt her bones to liquid fire. He laughed down into her eyes. "Follow my guidance, Sophia, I shall not let you down." She felt the movement of his muscles as, clasped together, they turned and spun and the music and movement ran into one and filled Sophia with a mixture of bliss and aching longing. Why had she to fall in love with a man who eschewed marriage? Why had he to be the kind of man who dwarfed all others in her eyes? When the dance ended, the viscount bowed his thanks, returned her to her cousin, and strolled away, and for Sophia all pleasure departed with him.

* * *

The days passed swiftly. There was endless shopping. Light sandals quickly wore out with much dancing, gloves grew grubby and holed, lace was torn, more clothes were needed if one was to keep a place in the fashion stakes. In spite of her worries, Sophia enjoyed the expeditions to the warehouses, silk mercers, milliners, and mantua-makers. Never before had she had so many opportunities of buying such magnificent articles and in such profusion. She was expected to spend lavishly and even Miss Sheffield did not advise caution.

"You have but one come-out, my dear. Enjoy it," she said, smiling.

Sophia was presented at court, after she and Annabel had spent a hilarious afternoon learning how to control the out-of-date hoops that were decreed. Annabel, when she forgot to be shy, was pleasant company and Sophia hoped she might be allowed to marry the man she wanted. Chiddingley made no secret of the fact that his choice had fallen upon her, and she was not clever enough to hide her tendre for him.

After more than a week there had been no word from Tindal and she prayed that he had repented his threat to expose her. Ramsey escorted his mother and sister to all the best places and therefore she was bound to meet him. She tried to argue herself out of her tormenting ache for him. It was essential to do so for, although he paid her flattering attention, he gave no particular indication that she meant anything special to him and a lady did not give her heart where it was not wanted.

Lady Ramsey and Charlotte decided to hold a musical evening at which any talented young person would be expected to perform, and Sophia was thankful for Miss Sheffield's stern tuition when her turn came to play and sing. Ramsey turned the pages of the music and she had to try to forget his nearness if her fingers were not to stumble over the keys and her voice to grow hoarse. She was begged for another rendition and this time the viscount joined her, his pleasing baritone blending well with her soprano. He had suggested a love song, but she refused. Glades and heather and pretty cottages were safer subjects.

The entertainment ended, older folk settled themselves around the card tables, others sat and gossiped, while the young element begged to set up dancing and servants were sent for to roll up rugs. Sophia's heart skipped a beat when she saw Tindal among them. He made it evident that he had caught sight of her and his brief, malevolent grin filled her with unease.

There were eight couples for the dancing and Miss Hill obliged by playing the pianoforte. Chiddingley had been persuaded to ask Sophia to dance and Ramsey took a place opposite Annabel. Charlotte and Edwin stayed firmly together. The pleasant occupation drove fear from Sophia's mind for a while. She sat and talked to Charlotte while Miss Hill sorted through the music sheets, but before a second dance was begun, she noticed that an elderly lady in a gray bombazine gown and a large cap was pointing in her direction with her fan while whispering behind her hand. The whispers were being passed on, hands were raised in enjoyable horror, and there were malicious smiles. From that moment, she suspected every covert glance and every laugh. She became convinced that Tindal had set tongues wagging and she was thankful when the party broke up, though she found little respite from her fears and lay awake for an age wondering what hazards the following day would bring.

Fifteen

The next morning Sophia felt disconsolate and heavy-eyed, and her cousin stared at her disapprovingly. "Tired again? If I can keep in good health and spirits at my age, I'm sure I don't know why you cannot. You had better have some nourishing broth."

She rang the bell, ignoring Sophia's protestations that she could not stomach chicken broth at breakfast. Beneath the stern eye of her chaperone she had to drink it.

When Lady Stoneyhurst had gone, Miss Sheffield grew solemn. "Sophia, my dear, I have never known you to flag even after a day in the saddle followed by a long evening of merrymaking. Are you unwell?"

Sophia surprised both of them by bursting into tears, "I am ruined, I know I am. I shall have to return home in disgrace and I'll be scorned by everybody."

Miss Sheffield looked horrified. "Ruined! Good God! What have you done?"

"I told you, Anne. I left the shelter of my home, strayed on the road like a vagabond, and now I'm found out, and by a very unpleasant footman in Ramsey's employ who has threatened to bring my misdemeanors to the notice of influential people."

Miss Sheffield let out a sigh, partly of relief. The situation was alarming, but might have been a good deal worse. "I see. We are in a quandary, to be sure."

Sophia pressed Miss Sheffield's hand gratefully. It was just like her to include herself in the imbroglio.

"Perhaps it isn't so very bad, dear. Who will believe a servant against you?"

"Anyone who resents Ramsey's paying me attention instead of their protégée. Rumors spread like wildfire. And last night I had the strongest feeling that I was being discussed, and not in a nice way at all.''

Anne frowned. ''Maybe you imagined it, Sophia. Your nerves are ragged. Viscount Ramsey is an old friend of mine. Perhaps if I spoke to him he might be able to deal with the situation.''

''Oh, no! Please, don't! He half suspects me already. He saw me first in my disguise looking as if I'd been dragged through a bramble bush. In fact, he—'' She stopped. To no one would she speak of Ramsey's embraces. Her voice would surely betray the way she felt about him. ''He knows I was on the road alone for days. Oh, no, don't speak to him, I implore you.''

''How vehement you are. Too much so, I fear. It would be unwise to develop anything more than friendship for him. No female has interested him in marriage in all the years he has been in society.''

Did her voice contain a little sorrow? Could she possibly care for Ramsey?

Anne was watching Sophia's face closely. ''Are you positive you haven't a tendre for him?''

''I have not,'' said Sophia, too vehemently. ''As if I would care for such a reprobate, and even if I could, I would not allow myself to esteem a man who gave me no encouragement.''

Sophia blushed deeply as she recalled Ramsey's kiss, and Anne asked, ''Are you positive he has given you none?''

Sophia sighed. Miss Sheffield could be ruthlessly determined if she believed it necessary. ''He kissed me. I did not give permission. I was angry, but he did not care.''

''Are you so sure you minded? I fancy you look at him in more than friendship.''

''Do I, indeed! No, you are mistaken. How dreadful. Do you think he notices? I can't believe it!''

Anne kindly ignored the contradictions in Sophia's denial. She was of the opinion that Ramsey missed nothing, but she held her tongue and dried Sophia's tears. She rang for Tabitha, who helped her mistress into her new apple-green velvet redingote and placed a poke bonnet of the

very latest design—with a high crown and a wide brim—on
her head, tying the green satin ribbons in a big bow under
her ear.

Miss Sheffield drew her heavy winter cloak about her
and said, "You look delightful, Sophia. Now put on your
gloves and we'll join the others for a walk in the Park. The
last thing you must do is hide. Face out your fears, my
dear. It will be best in the end."

The air was still icy and Sophia was sorry for the ill-clad
street dwellers. She bought a piece of hot spiced ginger-
bread and dropped coins into the hand of a beggar-woman
and gave the cake to her child. She had been close to them
for only a short time, but she would never view them the
same again.

The ladies entered the Park gates, where they were
joined by Edwin, the Duke of Chiddingley, and, to
everyone's amazement, Lady Ramsey, her body swathed in
furs, an immense velvet and fur bonnet on her head.

"Well, this is an astonishing thing," declared the
duchess. "I don't think I've seen your ladyship walking in
the park for years."

"No, you haven't," said Lady Ramsey in a die-away
voice. "Ramsey insists that I owe it to Charlotte to attend
her, though I can't think why when he could do it."

The duchess tripped along, her small plump feet stuffed
into red shoes, trying, like a dog rounding up sheep, to
control the young people who, to her fury, went where
they chose.

"Chiddingley," she hissed at her nephew, "there is
Lady Sophia looking utterly charming. Won't you walk
with her?"

"No, ma'am," said the duke, who did not believe in
wasting words. "I promised to walk with Miss Willis. I like
her."

"How can you prefer a washed-out creature like
Annabel," demanded the duchess in a whisper that was
clear to all, "when a beauty such as Lady Sophia is without
a partner?"

"Washed-out? What can you mean, ma'am? She is

delicately pale. I do not care for girls of high color. And she don't act the flirt, or talk about stuff I can't understand and make me feel stupid.''

He was gone with Miss Willis before the duchess could express her fury. She had once considered Charlotte for her nephew, but had since set her sights on Lady Sophia, she being a lady with handsome looks, a good fortune, impeccable birth, and, importantly, enough intelligence to control the duke in his haphazard perambulation through life. Also, Sophia was conformable, while the harumscarum Charlotte had always needed all her brother's authority to behave. While the argument took place, Edwin had quietly led Charlotte ahead and they were talking earnestly, their heads together.

"Those two will be betrothed before long," stated Lady Stoneyhurst.

"Do you think so?" asked Lady Ramsey. "For my part, I like Sir Edwin. He shows a pleasing solemnity upon occasion and his birth is impeccable." She sighed. "But Ramsey does not seem much taken with him. I fear that he will never countenance their connection. Such a pity. I long for the day when I can retire to follow my own pursuits. The Season is so fatiguing, is it not? Miss Sheffield, pray be so good as to catch them up. It is not seemly for them to be left alone in such a way."

"Alone!" cried the duchess. "With us not yards away and the world and his wife here!"

"That is the trouble," said Lady Ramsey. "The Park is filled by people who would not hesitate to rend an angel if they thought she had transgressed and heaven knows, Charlotte—" She stopped abruptly and buried her face in her fur collar and hurried on a few steps.

The duchess gave Lady Stoneyhurst a malicious smile and murmured, "That young woman has done some rackety things. I heard tell t'other night that she fled from some man at a house party and was discovered on the road in the most flagrantly suspicious circumstances."

It hurt Lady Stoneyhurst to deny herself the pleasure of gossiping, but this was dangerous ground for Sophia.

She yawned. "I declare I am almost fatigued. So unusual for me. I daresay rumor lied. It does more often than not."

"Where there's smoke, there's fire," said the duchess, touching the side of her nose in what Lady Stoneyhurst considered a vulgar manner worthy only of a stable boy.

The following day, Sophia and Lady Stoneyhurst attended a breakfast party in Park Lane, took part in a musical afternoon, and visited the circulating library before returning home to dress for a soirée in Cavendish Square.

"Depend upon it, Sophia, it will be a grand affair. Lady Weybridge is noted for her lavish hospitality."

Sophia had gone through the day in dread, suspecting every glance, every laugh, sure that beneath the surface of bland smiles and honeyed words lay poison darts of gossip ready to impale her.

As her maid brushed and arranged her chestnut hair, securing it with a fine gold band set with tiny emeralds and pearls, Sophia stared at her reflection in the mirror without the least satisfaction. She knew she was in very good looks, but beauty would not save her from the tabbies; in fact, it would increase their delight in bringing her down.

"You'll surely be the most handsome lady there tonight," said Tabitha enthusiastically. Sophia could barely smile. The thought of the people who could be damaged and hurt by her reckless actions was a constant pain. Everyone who was connected with her would suffer.

She stood obediently while Tabitha tied the wide green sash around her gown of white and yellow tulle, then pulled on a new pair of white kid gloves and took up her silver thread reticule. She had the distinct feeling that she was being decked out for the kill.

The soirée was a crush and Lady Stoneyhurst was pleased. "It's a success. It is always best to be seen at a successful gathering. Somehow the credit rubs off on one."

After what seemed to Sophia an eternity spent exchanging nothings in the usual stifling heat, Lady

Ramsey, Lady Stoneyhurst, and the duchess decided that they needed a trifle more air and led their charges along a corridor to a smaller salon. They were followed faithfully by the duke and Edwin.

Viscount Ramsey had been called out of town and Sophia was doing her utmost to pretend she cared nothing for his absence and was not at all concerned about his reasons for leaving London.

The salon was thankfully less crowded and Sophia breathed in the cooler air gratefully. Mr. Brummell was holding the floor with a witty dissertation on young gentlemen who copied every new style of cravat he introduced. "And of course they do it ill, but they force me to invent yet another style."

Charlotte and Sophia seated themselves near their chaperones and Sophia became lost in thought. Then she was jerked into awareness by a reedy voice.

"One hears such odd tales." The speaker was a man whose dissipations had aged him prematurely. He was dressed in an absurdity of fashion, his cravat so high he could scarce turn his head, his sunken cheeks dusted with rouge. "Only yesterday I was told of a gentlewoman who decamped from a respectable house-party and took to the road like a common vagabond. And, would you credit it, the lady—if one can call her such—is admitted to Almack's."

Heads were turned, eyes stared, lips were licked at the prospect of some juicy tidbit of scandal.

"Really, Mr. Cartwright," trilled a large woman in green and pink stripes, "I vow you exaggerate. No *lady* would behave so."

"I have it on very good authority—"

"Whose?" demanded a dozen voices.

"Why, among others, that of my valet."

Laughter burst out. "The most unimpeachable source," declared a stout gentleman. "I hear all the latest *on dits* from my man. The servants run a regular channel of information."

"I heard something similar from my woman," said

Lady Robinson, who was surrounded as usual by her insignificant daughters. "Pray, continue your story, Mr. Cartwright."

He extracted a snuff box from his pocket with slow deliberation, flicked open the lid, and took a pinch from the back of his hand. Sophia's gaze was riveted upon him. Somehow he had gotten hold of a garbled story in which she was confused with Charlotte. She glanced at the girl and saw that she had lost her color. Pray God no one else would notice it and draw conclusions.

A gentleman in a light blue coat shifted his position to stand nearer to Charlotte, who looked appealingly at him. His thin lips twisted in a smile, his eyes glittered.

Sir Walter Crawley was enjoying the situation. A year ago he had met Charlotte Ramsey in a country house and had been attracted by her looks and enchanted by the size of her fortune. In her customary careless way, she had flirted with him and he was still persuaded that he could have won her, but his vision of marriage with a rich and beautiful girl had been quickly dissipated by Viscount Ramsey, who had sent him off with the harshest of words. Not only had Ramsey forbade him ever to make an offer to his sister, he had declared in the strongest possible terms that he would expect Sir Walter to remain always at a distance from her. The baronet squirmed with humiliated rage whenever he recalled the incident and seethed at the accusations of libertinism and reckless gaming leveled at him by the viscount, as if Ramsey were himself not a fast member of the *ton*. Now he had information that would bring the family low. He was far too clever to declare his interest publicly, and had engaged Cartwright, who was barely tolerated by the *haut ton* and would do anything for money, to perform his unpleasant task for him. This was only a beginning. By the time he was done the proud Ramseys would welcome him as a son-in-law, for who would want her once she was utterly disgraced? He had bided his time until Ramsey was unable to escort his womenfolk, but matters had fallen out far better than he could have anticipated. Not only had he Mr. Brummell as

a witness, but, even better, Mrs. Drummond Burrell and
Lady Castlereagh, the most autocratic of the patronesses
of Almack's were present, their eyes positively bulging.

"Speak up," said a lady whose niece had not been given
a voucher for Almack's and relished the idea of seeing if
the two *grandes dames* could be discomfitted. "Who is this
abandoned creature?"

"She is not far from here," said Cartwright. "It seems
that the young lady in question went against the wishes of
her guardians and refused to wed the man of their choice."

Cries of horror filled the room, only one or two genuine,
the rest simulated in an orgy of delight. "Continue, sir,'
ordered the dowager.

Charlotte was trembling as the sadistic voice went on,
"The young woman ran away from the respectable house-
party—and here I have the assurance of the distracted lady
from whom she ran—and disappeared on the road
somewhere between there and London. It is not certain
how she came to lose the somewhat dubious protection of
her coachman, but she was later seen in a common hedge
tavern dressed in a most odd way, poorly disguised and
totally alone, as she had been for more than one night."

The room was silent now and Sir Walter enjoyed the
moment.

"Who is she?" breathed a dozen voices.

"Ah, a gentleman cannot speak a lady's name in such
circumstances," said Mr. Cartwright.

Charlotte, deeply distressed, tried to rise and was
restrained by her mother's almost cruel grip on her arm.
The movement was small, but it was seen, and those in
doubt as to the identity of the lady in question had such
doubts resolved. Brows were raised and smiles concealed
by fans. Viscount Ramsey had disappointed many by his
disregard for the marriage state and this was a situation
even he could not ride out with impunity since it concerned
his sister's honor.

Sophia sat rigid, her hands clenched. She ached to stand
up and tell Mr. Cartwright and all the grinning people
what she thought of them and their nasty tongues and,

more than that, she wished to give them the truth about
Charlotte, whose misdemeanor had not been so very
dreadful after all. It was she, Sophia, who should bear the
brunt of disapproval, but to speak at this moment would
not help. The mischief was done, the twisted story
accepted, and anything she said would be assimilated,
gossiped over, and regurgitated with further distortion.
Oh, why had Ramsey to be absent tonight? How angry he
would be with her when he discovered that it was she who
had acted the part of Charlotte's maid, become embroiled
with servants, and given evil tongues a perfect opportunity
to wag about his sister. She must tell him everything for
Charlotte's sake, and it grieved her to know that if he felt
even the remotest tendre for her, the knowledge of her
scandalous behavior would ruin all hopes of his love.

The three outraged chaperones remained in the salon for
a while, the center of attention, unwilling to appear to run
away; but eventually they had to move. They walked up
the corridor, followed by Sophia, and Charlotte, and
Annabel and the duke, who were puzzled by the under-
currents. Edwin followed, seething with such rage he had
almost succumbed to his first impulse to call out Mr.
Cartwright. He had wisely resisted the temptation. Any
such move on his part could only make matters worse.
Charlotte was exceedingly pale; conversely, Sophia was red
and her eyes blazed with anger.

The ladies found a private parlor and ordered the
gentlemen to wait outside. "Now what is all this about?"
demanded the duchess of Lady Ramsey. "Here am I with
my nephew and Miss Willis entangled in some heinous
situation that has nothing to do with us at all."

Her ladyship wrung her hands and moaned. "If only
Ramsey had been here. He would have done something,
although I cannot conceive what. Even he would be hard
put to—"

"Is the story true, then?" demanded the duchess. "The
gossips referred to Miss Ramsey, did they not?"

"Yes, oh, yes," moaned Lady Ramsey. "No, of course
it is not true. At least, it is in part, I suppose, and that is

what makes it so damning. One can deny an outright lie, but it is impossible to deal with half-lies.''

"For God's sake, explain, madam,'' insisted the duchess. "Lady Stoneyhurst, what do you know?''

"Nothing,'' said her ladyship firmly. She directed a look at Sophia that would have stripped bark from a tree, daring her to speak. Sophia felt unbearably guilty and troubled. No one could long for Ramsey's return more than she. He would find a way out of the nightmare.

Lady Ramsey said, "During my daughter's recent stay in the country she fancied herself in love, as young girls so often do, as you know.''

"I know nothing of the sort,'' snapped the duchess. "Annabel is the model of decorum.''

Lady Ramsey continued in a faint voice, "The object of her affection proved unsatisfactory and she set off home.''

"Alone!'' The duchess was scandalized. "Wandering the roads and sleeping anywhere?''

"No!'' exclaimed the goaded Charlotte. "I had servants with me and money for proper inns. I do not know why it is suggested I was a vagabond. As if I could be! And my companion, Miss Thomasina Hill, accompanied me.''

"Is she a wispy woman without spirit or wits?'' demanded the duchess.

Lady Ramsey moaned again and held a phial of hartshorn to her nose.

"I take it that she is,'' stated the duchess. "I have known her for an age. Good birth, but useless. And now, Lady Ramsey, you can see the unwisdom of employing her, for no one will believe she could keep any unsuitable person at bay or deal with any unusual situation.''

"She is highly respectable,'' said Charlotte indignantly. "Surely that will count for something.''

"What is to be done?'' groaned Lady Ramsey.

Lady Stoneyhurst spoke. "We must all rise above it. Mr. Cartwright is well known as a tittle-tattle and a liar.''

"That won't stop folk believing him, or at least pretending to,'' said the duchess. "And that cat, Mrs. Boston, whose pimply granddaughter cannot get into

Almack's, was there and trying to hide her nasty grin, and there are others who resent anybody more fortunate than themselves who will be equally spiteful. And, worst of all, Lady Castlereagh and—''

"Oh, my God!" Lady Ramsey put a hand to her head. "How could I have forgotten her? And Mrs. Drummond Burrell, too! They will certainly revoke Charlotte's voucher."

"Oh, no, Mama, they can't," wailed Charlotte, even more deeply shocked by such a threatened catastrophe.

Lady Stoneyhurst said, not looking at Sophia, "We must walk among the guests at once. We must all pretend that nothing has happened."

"It's easy enough for you to say," said Lady Ramsey. "Your charge is not threatened with disgrace."

"And neither is mine," said her grace, "and I have no intention of allowing her to risk social ruin. I shall remain in your company at present, Lady Ramsey, and I daresay Lady Stoneyhurst will do so also, but you cannot expect more after tonight."

Sophia was unequal to keeping up any further pretense and opened her mouth. Before she could speak Lady Stoneyhurst pinched her savagely, rose, threw open the door, and demanded that they all follow her to the great salon. Edwin and Chiddingley were outside. Edwin was ordered by all three great ladies to stop asking stupid questions and they proceeded in a body to face the stares of the *haut ton*, most of whom were happy to have such a delicious piece of gossip to mull over.

Sophia saw out the evening as best she could, returning home in the early hours, her mind a turmoil. Not even in her bleakest moments had she visualized such a situation.

Poor Charlotte was in the direst disgrace and Miss Hill was likely to lose her precarious position. She urged her cousin to allow her to tell the truth and restore Charlotte's good name.

Lady Stoneyhurst stared. "When and where? And what good do you imagine the truth will do, you foolish child? The Ramseys have been plagued by Charlotte's antics for an age. The best thing is to contrive untruths and dissimulations. They will be far more convincing. Society cannot stand hearing the truth.''

Miss Sheffield was asleep. ''The poor lady had a megrim,'' explained Tabitha.

''She gets them severely from time to time,'' said Sophia. ''What has been done for her?''

''Mrs. King put a hot brick to her feet, bathed her forehead with lavender water, an' gave her a draught of laudanum. I peeped at her just a moment ago an' she's sleepin' soundly.''

Sophia was subdued as Tabitha helped her to bed. It was four o'clock and the servants would soon be stirring. She had counted on asking for Miss Sheffield's advice. She lay sleepless. If she had not decided to embark upon her original lunatic scheme, Charlotte's behavior would have stayed hidden. What in heaven's name had Tindal and Kitty been saying? Whatever it was, it must have traveled to Mr. Cartwright via several mouths. She sat up with a jerk. What about Miss Hill? She was so easy to forget, but she knew that Susan, the maid, had been Lady Sophia. She would tell the Ramseys what had really happened.

I will be discredited forever, thought Sophia miserably, but that is the price I must pay for my idiocy, and maybe Charlotte will escape disgrace. She lay back, feeling some relief, but it was so mixed with unhappiness at her conviction that Lord Ramsey would never smile on her again that an hour later she was no nearer sleep.

A light knock on her bedchamber door made her sit up. Pulling a shawl about her shoulders she called, ''Come in.''

Tabitha entered in a long cambric bedgown, curling papers in her hair. She placed her candle on Sophia's bedside table. ''Lady Sophia, I've got some shocking news. It's Miss Charlotte, ma'am.''

''Charlotte? What now?''

''She's run off with one of her beaux. Miss Hill is down in the hall, your ladyship. She keeps moaning of Miss Ramsey's disgrace and that it isn't fair and she's not to blame.''

Sophia swung her legs out of bed, slid her feet into

pumps, and raced downstairs. Miss Hill was seated on the edge of a hard chair, her whole demeanor one of total defeat. When she saw Sophia she began to weep, tears sliding down her face and plopping onto her thin hands. Sophia hated and despised herself in that moment. The repercussions of her unconsidered action seemed endless. She led the weeping woman into the library and poured a glass of sherry. "Pray, drink this. It will steady you."

Miss Hill drank, gulped a few times, wiped her tears with a corner of her shawl, and said, "Charlotte has flown into one of her fits, by far the worst—it is truly dreadful and what Lord Ramsey will say, lord only knows. She is so sure that gossip will force her from society she will never get a husband, which she has always wanted above everything, and I could swear she is in love with Sir Edwin Fothergill, and Lord Ramsey is still away, and I am persuaded that only you can save poor Miss Charlotte because you know exactly what happened on the road to London and that my mistress has not been guilty of all the things she's accused of, and someone must go after her."

Sophia felt a little sick. "Where is she? What has she done?"

Miss Hill wrung her hands. "The poor, foolish, misguided child has eloped with Sir Walter Crawley."

Sixteen

Sophia stared at Miss Hill in horror. "Sir Walter Crawley! That cannot be. You have made a mistake. He is odious. Even Charlotte—"

"There's no mistake, my lady, none whatsoever. Here is her note. It is quite soggy with tears, but she makes it plain that last night Sir Walter offered her an escape from the impending scandal. I do not know what she means, do you?" Sophia nodded speechlessly, and Miss Hill continued, "She says that Sir Walter spoke privately with her and was exceeding kind. She did not intend her note to be discovered until much later, but I had the toothache and was looking for laudanum in her room—the unfortunate child is a martyr to the megrims, just like her mama—and I saw it propped against a bottle of lavender water. It was addressed to Lady Ramsey, but Charlotte's bed was empty and I have to confess that I feared to entertain the idea of sending Lady Ramsey into hysterics, what with my having the toothache, and being Charlotte's companion and supposed to guide her, though how to do it, I do not know, and it wasn't sealed, so I read it, and I have come through the streets very early—it is still almost night—and I was dreadfully frightened—they were crowded with noisy vendors and the most disreputable looking women who made remarks to me that fortunately I could not comprehend, though I am sure they were lewd—and I hope you can think how to restore Charlotte to her family before this shocking business is public knowledge, though we cannot expect to overtake her before her honor is besmirched forever." Miss Hill sniffed and sobbed her way through, then wept copiously.

Sophia read Charlotte's tear-stained note. "Pray forgive me, Mama and Hugo," it began, "but I cannot endure to be disgraced in society and Sir Walter Crawley has confessed his love for me on numerous occasions and was so very kind last night and asked me to marry him with complete disregard for my disgraceful behavior and said he would wait at the corner of the square if I chose to go off with him. I know you do not care for him, but he was so *very* kind to me in my distress. Sir Walter assures me we shall arrive in Gretna Green with no stops on the road, so I shall soon be wed. I remain, your affectionate but miserable daughter and sister, Charlotte Ramsey. P.S. Whatever the gossips say, I did not sleep in a hedge tavern. Nor did I wear an *ugly gown*. As if I would."

The naiveté of the postscript went straight to Sophia's sensibilities. Charlotte was the same age as herself, but little more than a child in her understanding. She must be rescued at any cost.

"Why did you not take this to Lord Ramsey?" she asked Miss Hill.

"He is still out of town. Someone is ill and I have no notion where he is and did not dare to ask a servant."

Sophia thought fast. To try to find Ramsey would not only bring others into the affair, but would use precious time. A moment's thought convinced her that Lady Stoneyhurst would have nothing to do with the problem and would, if necessary, lock her charge in her room to keep her out of it. She must go after Charlotte herself. Miss Hill waited in her bedchamber while she dressed. Then Tabitha was sent to hire a coach. Sophia left a letter with her maid to be handed to Lady Stoneyhurst and gave her Charlotte's letter to return as soon as possible to the Ramsey house, and she and Miss Hill, who said she preferred anything to returning to the Ramsey household while her charge was missing, seated themselves in the coach and Sophia directed the driver to Duke Street.

"Why are we going there?" demanded Miss Hill. When informed that Sophia intended to enlist the help of Sir Edwin Fothergill, she held a phial of hartshorn to her nose. "My dear Lady Sophia, a gentleman's lodgings—a bachelor gentleman—you cannot . . ."

"I can and I must," said Sophia. "Sir Edwin has been like a brother to me, he is fond of Charlotte, and if you think we can overcome Sir Walter Crawley on our own, you sadly mistake the affair."

Miss Hill shuddered and protested no more.

Edwin had only moments ago pinched out his candle after a convivial night spent indulging in modest gaming at White's where he had gone after the Soirée, and to which high-flown club he had easily gained entrance because of his late father's distinguished membership. Hearing the knocker and expecting to find one of his new, spirited friends with some outrageous suggestion for high jinks, he opened the door in his nightshirt and a cap with a tassel. On seeing two pairs of female eyes regarding him, one from a coach and one from his doorstep, he blenched and slammed the door with an echo that resounded through the street. Three drunken revelers approached and Sophia fled

to the safety of the coach, from which Miss Hill stuck out
her elderly head and, in quavering tones, ordered them to
move on. They were arguing noisily with her when Edwin's
door opened again and he stepped to the coach in breeches
and a hastily buttoned shirt.

He gave a swift glance at the inebriates. "Stow it,
Charles, these ladies are not for you."

Charles gave a high-pitched giggle. "Two at a time,
Fothergill. And one of uncertain age. You must tell us
sometime exactly how you go on." He and his companions
laughed immoderately and passed on, leaving Edwin, who
prided himself on being respectable in his dealings with
ladies, fuming with rage and deeply embarrassed.

Edwin listened to Sophia with increasing astonishment
and fury and for a moment she thought that his whole
reaction was shock at Charlotte's behavior.

She had misjudged him. "Poor Charlotte," he
breathed. "She's such a sweet innocent and no match for
that evil libertine, Crawley. Oh, my God, to think of her in
his power!"

He finished dressing within minutes and climbed into the
coach. "Sophia, there is no need for you to be jolted over
the roads. I shall drop you at your home."

"You will do no such thing, Edwin. Charlotte needs a
woman with her."

Edwin accepted the truth of her words and suggested
that Miss Hill might prefer to be left behind.

She looked stubborn. "My place is here. My presence
will give countenance to Lady Sophia and Charlotte is *my*
charge and nothing shall move me."

Edwin looked baffled, but was too worried to waste time
in argument. He leaned back against the squabs and the
coach rattled over the cobbles, and no one saw Mr.
Chatteris as he stood in the shadows and watched it pass,
its interior momentarily lighted by the flambeau of a
linkboy escorting a lady half asleep in a sedan chair. He
quietly whistled his astonishment at the sight of Lady
Sophia Clavering seated beside Sir Edwin Fothergill at
such an hour, both looking prodigious solemn.

Lowering clouds kept back the dawn and the coach set

off intolerably slowly, the only comfort being that Sir
Walter would be equally handicapped. With the advent of
dawn the four horses were urged to greater speed by the
driver and postillion. The horses were changed and
inquiries made at all the post houses, but no one recalled
seeing anyone fitting the description of the runaways.

"That's not to be wondered at," said Edwin. "Post
boys are not employed to look at their customers." He
was pale with fear. "The sweet girl cannot realize how far
it is to Gretna Green," he had said, after hearing the
contents of Charlotte's note. "It is above three hundred
miles and they will be forced to put up at inns along the
way." His voice cracked and he turned to stare from the
window, his jaw working.

Sophia sank deeper and deeper into gloom. By now,
Lady Stoneyhurst had probably read her message in which
she had stated that she and Edwin had left town on an
urgent mission. She had omitted Charlotte's name
deliberately. How angry her cousin would be. Sophia was
resigned now to the fact that she would certainly be sent
home in disgrace. Well, she deserved it.

They partook of refreshments standing in an inn and
resumed the journey with fresh horses. The hours spent
rocking and jolting along icy, potholed roads seemed
endless. At one inn they were lucky to find an ostler who
recalled seeing the fugitives. He had been struck by
Charlotte's beauty. "If that's the young lady you want,
you'd best make 'aste, sir. She didn't look 'appy to me—
not 'appy at all."

Edwin flung him some silver and grimly urged the driver
to greater efforts.

"Sir Walter will be in no hurry to reach Gretna," said
Sophia. "The sooner they stop, the better pleased he will
be. To speak plain, I doubt he will wait for marriage to—
fully compromise Charlotte."

Miss Hill gave a little scream. Edwin flushed, then
paled. "I am well aware of it!"

Miss Hill said excitedly, "I do not believe they will be
able to travel long distances at a time. They will be sure to

use a post chaise and dear Charlotte feels sick in any coach, but in a post chaise, with all the rocking about she will be worse. She needs quite frequent rests."

"Has she traveled north before, do you know?" asked Sophia. "Has she a favorite place to stay?"

The companion's brow creased. "She spoke of a delightful visit she made to St. Neots. There is a fifteenth-century church and she spent a pleasant day on the river."

"St. Neots is not on a direct route to Gretna," snapped Edwin.

"No, but dear Charlotte has no more notion of geography than she has of arithmetic, which is to say none whatsoever, and she clearly thought they would reach Gretna Green in the course of the day. If she wanted to visit St. Neots, she would insist. She can be extremely, er, persuasive, especially if she is feeling not quite the thing, and I am sure she will not be."

Edwin, his teeth clenched, glanced at his watch. "Oh, God! We are about two hours behind them. Plenty of time for that snake, Crawley . . .! Well, we will try St. Neots. It is only a little out of the way." Edwin looked bitterly unhappy.

St. Neots was unusually crowded with men of all description and class. "There's a prize fight on tomorrow morning," explained the landlord of the Cross Keys, "and every bed for miles around is bespoke."

At the Falcon the landlady stuck her big coarse hands on her hips. "Ah, I did see a couple of that description. The gent came in first and asked for a room for hisself and wife. Got very uppity when I told him I'd not a bed to spare. The young lady followed him in and looked fit to drop. She said she felt dreadful ill and wanted some sleep. I would like to have obliged, but I've got gentlemen sleeping everywhere. In any case, a town where there's a fight ain't no place for a lady."

Edwin groaned. "Can you tell me where they went next?"

"I can tell you where I recommended 'em to go, though can't say if they did. I was that sorry for the lady, I sent 'em to my sister's farm a mile along the Brampton road. Mrs. Grey's the name. I should get there fast, if I was you. It ain't my place to say, but I didn't like the looks of the man at all, an' I've got my own ideas of what was up.''

Edwin thanked her and ten minutes later the carriage arrived at a prosperous looking farm. Dogs barked, and hens set up a cacophony as the horses clattered into the yard. Mrs. Grey was pleased and relieved to welcome them. ''Are you friends of the lady, sir? Thank the lord! She's in a shocking state.''

''There was a man with her,'' grated Edwin.

The woman grinned, revealing gaps in her teeth. ''He's sittin' in my parlor gettin' through a bottle of my best black currant wine and not a good word to say about it, as well as 'avin' one of the finest black eyes I've seen in many a day.''

Edwin, Sophia, and Miss Hill were shown to the parlor. Sir Walter was sprawled on a couch, a glass in his hand. He looked murderously angry to see them. His customary dandified attire was sadly crumpled and, if anything, the farmer's wife had been moderate in her description of his eye. It was half closed and the area around it was several shades of black and purple.

Edwin strode up to him with menacingly clenched fists. ''Where is Miss Ramsey? What have you done with her, you vile creature?''

''I've done nothing with her and you can have the termagant any time,'' snarled Sir Walter. ''I meant her no harm. I was going to wed her in spite of her reputation. She's got the very devil of a temper. Smacked her fist right in my eye, then bolted her door.''

''Good!'' rasped Edwin, ''but she must have been fearfully provoked to behave so and if you've harmed a hair of her head, I swear I'll kill you.''

''You can try, I suppose,'' sneered Sir Walter. He slid a hand into his pocket and produced a small, wicked looking pistol.

Sophia and Miss Hill gasped, but Edwin took a step nearer his tormentor. ''You will not shoot me out of hand.

That would be murder before witnesses, but I can challenge you to a duel. You may kill me, but I shall take you with me, I swear."

The baronet looked Edwin up and down and gave a falsetto laugh.

"I don't fight boys, which is as well for you for I'm a dead shot and have killed my man in more than one duel."

"But I fancy you are not quite as skilled as I am," drawled a voice from the door.

Lord Ramsey stepped inside the room, tugging off his driving gloves, and strolled forward with athletic grace.

Sophia half ran to him, forgetting propriety in her relief. "Oh, my lord, how glad I am to see you! How did you get here?"

"In my curricle. It's a sporting model and covered the ground very fast."

"Pray, don't make sport of me," she begged.

Ramsey's look softened. "Mr. Chatteris caught sight of you and Edwin leaving town. He seemed to be laboring under the delusion that you were eloping."

"What an addlepate! As if I would, when I left my home to avoid—" She stopped, her face flooding with color.

"You were saying?" asked Lord Ramsey.

"N-nothing of any import."

Sir Walter rolled off the couch and stood up. "I am leaving. I shall return to London. There is nothing now to hold me here. If you want my advice, Ramsey, you will not touch the black currant wine."

Ramsey closed the door and stood with his back to it. "I shall tell you when you may depart."

"What effrontery! Let me pass! I have done nothing without the full assent of Charlotte."

Ramsey stared at the baronet with glittering eyes. "That is something I shall soon discover. Meanwhile, I would prefer you not to mention my sister's name." His voice was quiet, but Sophia shivered at its menace. The baronet slumped back onto the couch.

"How did you know where to find us?" asked Sophia. Ramsey sighed. "I returned home and was handed

Charlotte's letter by my mother. She was having her third
—or was it her fourth?—attack of the hysterics."

"Oh, poor Lady Ramsey," exclaimed Miss Hill.

"Runaway young ladies leave behind a legacy of
distress," said Ramsey dryly. Sophia wondered if she had
imagined his quick glance at her. The opinion he held of
her now was not significant, she thought miserably. For
Charlotte's sake, for his sake—because to have a dis-
honored sister would reflect horribly on him—she intended
to confess to him her part in the whole sorry business. The
more he knew of the truth, the better placed he would be to
defend his sister. "I left Mama to her maid," continued
Ramsey, "and had fresh horses put to my curricle. I
received the information about the farm from the same
source as you, and here I am. I owe you much gratitude for
your attempt to save Charlotte, Sir Edwin, and you, Lady
Sophia and Miss Hill."

"I wished very much for your help," explained Sophia,
"but you were out of town."

"Yes, indeed. I had been called to the bedside of an old
and valued retainer who asked to see me before he died."

"Oh, I am so sorry. One comes to care for old
servants."

"Yes, that is so. However, I am glad to report that after
drinking the best part of a bottle of brandy I took to cheer
his last hours, this one recovered."

A nervous giggle escaped Sophia. "If he drinks brandy
like that, it will kill him anyway."

"I thought of that, but decided that at the age of eight-
nine it would be a pleasant way to go. However, it was
most unfortunate that I was not in London. I gathered
from my mother's almost incoherent account that you
were sadly discomfited at Lady Weybridge's soirée. I feel
that Mama was a trifle muddled. She appeared to believe
that my sister was accused of wandering like a vagabond
and sleeping alone in taverns."

"She is correct," spluttered Edwin. "No names were
mentioned, but the company was left in no doubt about
the lady being referred to. That unspeakable fop Cartwright brought up the subject."

Ramsey took out a gold snuffbox and took a pinch.

"I see." The viscount replaced his snuffbox and looked at Sir Walter Crawley. "I wonder who put him up to it."

Sir Walter stirred uneasily. "I meant Ch—the lady no harm. I was going to marry her." He waxed indignant. "I think you might be grateful. After all, her reputation must be entirely destroyed by now."

Ramsey stared at the baronet for a long moment and Miss Hill made an incoherent sound.

Ramsey turned to her and said kindly, "Pray, be seated, Miss Hill, and you too, Lady Sophia." He picked up the bottle of wine, inspected it, and sniffed at it. "Good God! Sir Edwin, be so kind as to ask for tea or coffee for the ladies. I will take a glass of home-brewed and then I shall visit my sister."

There was no tea or coffee, but the ale was refreshing and Mrs. Grey brought oil of cloves for Miss Hill's toothache, which eased it. Ramsey rose to leave the parlor.

Edwin jumped to his feet. "Sir, I beg of you to deal gently with Miss Ramsey. She could not possibly know what she was doing. In fact, I daresay the reprobate made off with her against her will."

"I did no such thing," said Sir Walter. "Char—" He spluttered to a close at the icy look shot at him by Ramsey.

The viscount said in kindly tones, "Please, Sir Edwin, stand aside. You may safely leave the situation to me."

"But, I—"

Ramsey thrust out his hand in a commanding gesture. "Not now! She is my sister. Later, you may address me."

As soon as he closed the door, Sir Walter was on his feet. The door reopened and Ramsey said, "It will be useless to try to leave, Crawley. Mrs. Grey and her husband have been splendidly dedicated to the task of bringing fine sons into the world and if you care to look from the window you will see several stalwarts who have orders to keep you here. There is also a daughter, the youngest child, exceeding pretty. I have taken the precaution of suggesting that she is kept well out of your sight."

Sir Walter went crimson with fury and Sophia shivered

when she imagined how they would have fared with him if
Ramsey had not arrived.

After half an hour, which seemed to Sophia like a week,
the door opened and Charlotte preceded her brother into
the room, tottered to a sofa, and sank upon it. She must
have spent many hours weeping, for her face was actually
blotchy. She kept her eyes lowered.

Edwin went straight to her and seated himself beside
her. She glanced up at him and her face flooded with color,
and became even more blotchy. Sophia would not have
credited that Charlotte could look so unappealing, though
Edwin was gazing at her as if she were the most beautiful
creature in the world.

Lord Ramsey seemed to fill the parlor, and not merely
because of his muscular height; Sophia sensed his fierce,
contained anger.

"Sir Edwin, Lady Sophia, and you, Miss Hill, please
remain with Miss Ramsey." His voice grew soft, but made
Sophia shudder. "Sir Walter, I wish to speak to you before
you leave."

He opened the parlor door and gestured to the baronet,
who tried, but failed, to swagger through it. As soon as
they had gone, Edwin took Charlotte's hands in his. "Are
you harmed?"

Charlotte shook her head. "No, but he—he—I had to
fight with him. What a dreadful creature!"

"Why did you go with him? Could you not have turned
to me?"

"No, oh, no, I could not!" burst out Charlotte. "You
are the very last person I could approach."

Edwin dropped Charlotte's hands and walked to the
window. Sophia, who knew him so well, realized that his
whole attitude reflected pain at Charlotte's wounding
words. She wished she could comfort him. She wished
someone could comfort her. What a hideous tangle they
were all in, and she had played a major part in wreaking it.
By now, the story of the elopement would surely be
infiltrating the *ton* and even Ramsey would be incapable of
setting matters to right.

There was the sound of a carriage leaving the farmyard and Ramsey strolled in. "Sir Walter has returned to London," he said smoothly.

"He'll tittle-tattle," said Edwin vehemently. "If he does, no one shall prevent me from calling him out." Charlotte's eyes widened as they rested upon him.

"You will do no such thing, Sir Edwin," said Ramsey. "Such a course of action would simply add to the already virulent gossip. But he will not speak, for if he does, he knows that he will end in a debtor's gaol. My excellent valet, Dunlop, informed me three days ago of the stories that were circulating the servants' halls. He discovered they were being spread as fast as possible by Crawley's unsavory servants, who had learned something discreditable from members of my own household. I have already begun to deal with them. I blame myself in part for this. I should have acted quicker. I should have known that a poltroon like Crawley would take advantage of my absence."

Sophia almost sank with shame. If he had talked to Kitty and Tindal, he would most likely know about her reprehensible behavior. What must he think of her?

Ramsey brushed a speck of dust from his elegant driving coat with its several capes and continued, "Before I was called away from town, I instructed my man of business to buy up every one of Crawley's many debts, including the gaming ones of honor. I hold his future in my hands and he knows it. I have bought his silence."

Edwin spoke stiffly, "That was a clever move, my lord, but I do not see how we are to overcome all the problems. How can Char— Miss Ramsey's reputation be recovered?"

Charlotte said, hiccuping a little, "I want to retire to the country. I will not return to London only to have my voucher for Almack's withdrawn and be an outcast on the fringes of society. And now I've made everything much worse. That horrible man said he would marry me in Gretna Green, and I soon wished I had not listened to him, but when I told him I wanted to go home, he laughed at me. He said we would stop at several inns on the journey. It turned out he meant to—meant to—'' Charlotte's lips trembled.

"We know what he meant, Charlotte," said Lord Ramsey, not unkindly. "I congratulate you on your spirited defense."

"I felt *dreadfully* sick in the post chaise—you know, Hugo, how the swaying affects me—and I wanted above all things to rest. The inns were full and *that man* tried to insist we drive to the next town. But I refused and said I would be sick all over the chaise and we were directed here. And then he—'' Charlotte blushed— "he engaged one room!"

"The villain!" cried Edwin.

Charlotte flung him a desperate look. "I was only aware of it when he followed me into the bedchamber and said he would stay with me and not leave me *all night*. I hit him as hard as I could. Do you remember when I was small, Hugo, you showed me how to make a proper fist with my thumb tucked in? I never thought to find it so useful. He went to find beefsteak to put on his eye and I bolted the door. But that will not help me now," she finished mournfully.

Ramsey surveyed the unhappy company. "Never fear. We shall come about in style. I have devised a way, but you must all do exactly as I say."

Seventeen

Complete silence fell upon the company and Lord Ramsey was regarded by eyes that looked doubtful, hopeful, pleading.

"You have thought of a defense, sir?" asked Edwin.

"Not defense, attack! It is the only way."

Charlotte looked a little less dismal and Edwin and Sophia brightened. "What must we do?"

Ramsey's eyes rested briefly on Charlotte, then he said, "My sister's foolish escapade in running away from a house in which she was a valued guest has offended, and rightly so, her hostess—who is now, quite innocently, confirming a gross exaggeration of the facts put about by some ill-wishing servants. Of course, I do not know exactly what has been said, and to whom, but as usual, truth and falsehood have become garbled and it is being spread about that Charlotte was roaming the country roads and sleeping God knows where."

Charlotte gave a cry of distress. "Yes, and wearing a hideous gown into the bargain."

Sophia put out her hand blindly and opened her mouth.

Ramsey's frown was terrifying. "Do not interrupt me, Lady Sophia!"

He continued, "As if that were not enough, Charlotte has made matters infinitely worse by running off with one of the most disreputable roués in London." He paused and bowed to his sister, and the severity of his expression lifted a little. "I must say, I'm delighted to discover that you defended your person so competently. And Mrs. Grey shall be rewarded for her protection."

Charlotte cried, "But who will believe that nothing bad happened? Society seems to be far more ready to despoil a character than to search for the truth."

"A splendid lesson to discover," said Ramsey, smiling acerbically, "if a trifle late, and one which your guardians have tried, but failed, to instill in you for an age. I trust you will remember it in future."

"What future have I?" moaned Charlotte.

Edwin sprang to his feet. "Pray do not torment her, my lord!" His face was flushed and he looked exceedingly disturbed.

Ramsey waved him back to his chair. "You have my sister's welfare much in mind, Sir Edwin. I cannot thank you enough for what you have done."

Charlotte turned glowing eyes to Edwin. "Indeed, yes. I thank you too, Sir Edwin."

Edwin reseated himself beside her, "A gentleman could do no less. I—" His voice faltered and he stopped.

Ramsey looked at Edwin for a moment before his eyes flickered to Sophia.

"There will be no duels," he said. "Tomorrow night the Prince Regent is holding an Assembly at Carlton House. We are all invited and I have decided that we will face our detractors there. You, Charlotte, must pretend to be betrothed to Edwin who will, I am persuaded, be gallant enough to assume the status of engaged man."

Edwin's flush grew deeper. He glanced at Charlotte, who was staring at him wide-eyed, but he said nothing, only nodded.

"And you, Lady Sophia," continued Ramsey, "will return to society's bosom as my affianced bride."

"No!" Sophia cried. "No! I cannot! I will not!"

Ramsey's brows rose. "I had not thought the prospect would be quite so unappealing."

"You know that has nothing to do with it. I can't pretend because—" Sophia stopped. She had almost said, I love you and the idea of hoaxing the *haut ton* in such a way will be an hourly torture.

"Because?" prompted Ramsey.

Sophia stared into his challenging eyes. "I spoke without thought. I will do as you say."

Miss Hill quavered, "How can that silence the gossips?"

"You have a part to play also, ma'am. In fact, much of our success depends on you."

"You alarm me, sir. I was always a failure at charades and I am no good at telling untruths. My face shows my guilt."

"Even though you will be dissembling to save the reputations of two young ladies?"

"N-no, perhaps not, but it is of no use to make plans for me. Lady Ramsey will dismiss me the instant I return. This is the second time I have failed her daughter."

"Lady Ramsey will do nothing of the sort," stated the viscount with authority. "Please help us? I shall be obliged to you forever."

"Oh, sir, you are too kind. Yes, though I do not yet quite comprehend . . ."

"First I will engage the assistance of two trusted

servants, my valet, Dunlop, and my mother's maid, Nell Price. They will put it about that when Charlotte left the house party it was to meet me. I shall back you up and no one will query it." Ramsey was grim for a moment. "It will also be understood that Sir Edwin Fothergill joined us during the journey, he having been accepted as Charlotte's betrothed but the news kept secret until now. Have either of you any objections?"

Edwin stared first at Charlotte, who had gone a little pale, then at Ramsey. Two heads were shaken in confirmation. "Good! And we shall all assert that Lady Sophia was with us on the journey."

Charlotte asked, "Why must Lady Sophia be implicated? She has done nothing wrong."

Ramsey regarded his sister thoughtfully. "Mr. Chatteris —and maybe others—may be putting it about that she eloped this morning with Sir Edwin. They were seen."

"Oh, how dreadful," cried Charlotte, "when they were intent on saving me."

"That will not signify," assured Ramsey. "We shall present a united front and the fact of our betrothals will silence the gossips."

Edwin said, "I am honored and privileged to help Miss Ramsey, but I still do not see the necessity for Sophia to be implicated. She left her home precipitately for her cousin's, but Lady Stoneyhurst is perfectly respectable. And when my—betrothal to Charlotte is made public, society will know that she did not elope with me."

Sophia held her hands tightly together to try to arrest their trembling. Ramsey turned to her and said gently, "My dear, you may speak now."

Sophia, ready a few moments ago to confess, found she had lost her voice. Lord Ramsey, whom she had thought herself cunning enough to deceive, clearly knew she had seen Susan, the maid. When had he learned it? Why had he done nothing about it? Had he been amusing himself with her, making her an antidote to his boredom?

"Speak up," advised Ramsey in a voice that brought moisture to her eyes. If only she could gain such tenderness truly. He was cossetting her along as if she were a restless filly, gentling her into following his path. How could he know that her love for him would make the masquerade unendurably painful?

In a small, breathless voice she told her story. Miss Hill smiled approvingly at her, but Edwin and Charlotte were astonished.

"You were my maid?" asked Charlotte. "But you are Lady Sophia Clavering. Or are you? Which one of you was the imposter? It must have been the maid, for society has accepted you and you are a lady, or seem to be. Or are you of humble birth playing a part?"

"She's Lady Sophia," hissed Edwin. "I am shocked, Sophia. I would not have believed it of you."

Sophia's eyes flashed, "Would you not? No, I daresay you wouldn't. If you were not so top-lofty, I might have liked you better."

Charlotte cried, "He is *not* top-lofty!"

Ramsey sighed. "Charlotte, my dear, have you any notion of the meaning of the phrase?"

"Of course not! Where would I have heard it?"

"Evidently the first time from the lips of my betrothed. I really must request you, Lady Sophia, not to come out with these cant expressions during our engagement."

"We will not be engaged, my lord. Not properly, that is."

"But the world and his wife will not know that and I shall expect you to conform to my standards of propriety laid down for a lady." Ignoring Sophia's gasp of fury, he explained, "Top-lofty merely means proud, haughty."

"Sir Edwin is nothing of the sort, Lady Sophia. Just because he don't countenance your fly-by-night behavior—"

"That's the pot calling the kettle black, if ever I heard it—"

Ramsey held up his hand, "Ladies, I implore you. If we are to carry this mission through, it would be better for you to be friends."

Both Charlotte and Sophia were red with anger. Sophia

took a deep breath and spoke first. "I was too hasty, Miss Ramsey, and Edwin is not—what I said."

Charlotte said, "That is handsome of you, Lady Sophia. I apologize."

"And so do I, though I still wonder what Edwin would have had me do when my money was stolen."

"You should have returned home in the quickest possible time," said Edwin.

"To marry you!"

"Are you going to marry Edwin?" asked Charlotte, her voice cracking a little.

"No, indeed, I am not," said Sophia. "That is why I ran away in the first place. Our guardians were forcing us into a wedding. They would not listen to anything I said."

Charlotte leaned back. "But Edwin followed you to London. I daresay he has proposed marriage again."

"No, I have not!" declared Edwin.

Ramsey came to sit beside Sophia. "Pray, don't be overset because I guessed your secret. I knew very quickly that the beautiful Lady Sophia was also the ugly maid. Your eyes—and there were the pads—" He stopped and smiled, his eyes dancing. "Your masquerade was clever. If you were not possessed of a fortune, you could make a good living treading the boards."

Sophia put out her hands. "Don't mock me, sir, I beg. Is it truly necessary for me to pretend to be your betrothed?"

"I fear so. Too many people know a little of what happened. Half-truths, guesses, are difficult to deal with. You too need protection from the evil tongues. When the tabbies see all four of us looking so happy—and I shall try to make it easy for you—"

"But the servants—it is Tindal and Kitty, is it not, my lord?—will go on with their gossiping."

"I can engage for it that they will not," said Ramsey. "Believe me when I tell you that the stories will soon die away. And then," he finished, "we can dissolve our connections. We will do so after the Season and by next year folk will have forgotten all about us. There will be other unfortunates to rend."

Charlotte said suddenly, a small sob in her voice, "I don't want to pretend to be engaged to Sir Edwin. I find I do not care at all for the notion."

Edwin turned to her. "You will do as Lord Ramsey tells you," he said in a commanding voice that startled everyone. "Your brother is putting himself out to help you repair your damaged reputation and you should thank him for it. So stop putting on airs like a tragedy queen and prepare yourself."

Ramsey stared as Charlotte rose silently to her feet and allowed Edwin to help her on with her traveling coat, thanking him in a small voice. When the viscount looked back at Sophia, she saw that his eyes held deep amusement. She thought, at least he can never claim that *this* Season bored him.

The journey back to London was almost silent. Edwin traveled in the open curricle with Lord Ramsey, and Sophia had dreaded questions, but Charlotte was too exhausted to say much and Miss Hill preferred not to dwell upon recent events. The hours passed, long and wearisome, with several halts when Charlotte felt unwell. The horses were changed and refreshments offered, but no one felt much inclined for food.

Sophia refused the offer of an escort into her cousin's house, so they delivered her to her front door and waited to see it opened to her. She stood on the top step of the short stone flight and watched the carriages rumbling away, feeling as if they were taking away her security.

It was one o'clock in the morning and she did not expect to find her cousin at home, but she had put only one foot on the stairway when Lady Stoneyhurst's voice boomed at her from the direction of the drawing room.

"Lady Sophia! Come here!"

She walked, chin up, past her ladyship and into the drawing room. Her cousin wasted no time. "What is the meaning of your conduct? I am given a note when I awaken at noon which tells me that you have an urgent journey out of town. Not a word of explanation, simply a request that I wait for further news. Is this the way I am repaid for my goodness to you?"

"No, ma'am. I beg you to forgive me—"

"Forgive you, is it? I have been to a card party this evening and had to listen to a dozen scurrilous tongues speculating on the mysterious lady on the road who slept in hedge taverns. The stories have, as I scarce need tell you, become embellished. 'The lady was a highwayman's discarded mistress, I have it on the best authority!' That was *sweet* Lady Robinson. 'She was turned from her home because of infamous behavior with a coachman and bore a child in a ditch.' That was her *dear* Grace of Devonshire. One wonders how they came by such foul imaginations. Possibly from the Gothic novels they devour. So far, they have not yet mentioned you by name. They believe the strange roaming woman to be Charlotte Ramsey. But *I* know it was you and I had to pretend to an ailment and leave early, for I could not bear any more. Well, it seems you are to escape censure and the Ramseys must get out of their scrape as best they can. It's Charlotte's own fault, for she is noted for her madcap behavior. The duchess wants you and your fortune for her son and you must do all in your power to induce him to declare himself as soon as possible and secure your position in society. Mind you, I think her Grace of Chiddingley will prove a fearful mother-in-law."

"Not to me, ma'am," said Sophia, adding quickly, before she could be interrupted, "Tomorrow at Carlton House the news of my betrothal to Hugo, Viscount Ramsey, is to be released."

Lady Stoneyhurst stared, then her face broke into a broad smile. She clasped Sophia to her bosom, almost impaling her on a diamond star brooch. "My dear child! My dear, dear child! What a triumph! What bliss! Oh, how I shall enjoy tomorrow. How graciously I shall smile on Lady Robinson and the duchess and all of them. But how did it come about? Where have you been?"

Sophia said carefully, "I must tell you, ma'am, that there are almost certain to be rumors regarding my masquerade as a servant girl."

Lady Stoneyhurst gave a small scream. "What if Lord Ramsey believes them? He will withdraw his offer. Just because a man has led a rackety life does not make him any less particular in his choice of a wife—''

"He already knows what happened and appears to find the situation amusing," Sophia interrupted Lady Stoneyhurst's dire prophecy. "I have been on a journey with Sir Edwin Fothergill and Charlotte's companion, Miss Hill, to rescue Charlotte from Sir Walter Crawley, who had made off with her. They were eloping to Gretna Green and Ramsey was out of town and could not be traced. I felt it my duty to save his sister."

"Good God! This is incredible! Does Ramsey know? And how can it be? Sir Walter turned up—late, I grant you—at the card party. I saw him. And he had a badly bruised eye. He had tried to hide it with paint, but everyone could see it."

"It was administered by Charlotte."

"What? Is the world run mad? That idiotic piece of fluff struck Sir Walter such a splendid blow?" She lowered her voice. "Were you in time, my dear? You know what I mean."

"We were, thanks to Charlotte's own efforts. Ramsey followed us and sent Sir Walter packing, and obviously he raced back to London. We were much delayed by Charlotte's inability to travel fast."

Lady Stoneyhurst paced the room. "Will not Sir Walter blacken Charlotte's reputation?"

"He will not dare. Lord Ramsey has bought up all his debts and could put him in a debtors' gaol. And tomorrow Charlotte's betrothal to Sir Edwin Fothergill is also to be announced, and that must close all mouths."

Lady Stoneyhurst clapped her hands. "The gossips will be utterly confounded. The duchess will lose Charlotte, whom she placed second after you for her nephew, and Lady Ramsey will not be exactly joyful. She wanted at least an earl for her daughter." Her tone was regrettably jubilant.

Sophia opened her bedchamber door to find Miss Sheffield and Tabitha awaiting her. As soon as she had been put to bed, her companion sat by her side and Sophia told her almost everything. She could not bear to confess, even to such a beloved friend, her hopeless love. Miss Sheffield looked sad as she contemplated the brangle her charge had made of her life. She suspected that Sophia cared for Ramsey and that her heart was aching. She kissed her forehead, whispered a good night, and pulled the bed curtains, leaving the bed in blessed, quiet darkness, and utter weariness allowed Sophia to drop quickly into sleep.

Eighteen

When Sophia opened her eyes, she was refreshed but bemused. Something was to happen tonight? Was it good or bad? Then she remembered and sank into gloom. If only her betrothal could be genuine. She sat up in bed, hugging her knees, thinking of Ramsey. He was everything she had dreamed of in a man. Strong, clever, resourceful, and, judging by his kisses, a fierce but tender lover. She felt she was flushing to the tips of her toes at the idea. How she loved him! Tonight would be agony, but she must play her part. She owed it to Charlotte, to Lady Stoneyhurst, to Lady Ramsey, and to Ramsey himself.

He had suggested that the two girls dress in white. She remembered his voice, tinged with irony, "So suitable for wedding announcements, and prettily innocent."

Perhaps he did not truly accept her story of her adventures on the road. Did he think of her as despoiled, a wanton even?

Later she smoothed white stockings onto her legs and slid her feet into kid sandals. Tabitha eased her white silk tunic over her head, tied the tapes, and fastened the tiny pearl buttons. Over it came a heavy satin overdress with a train, the edges embroidered with silver thread. Her hair was pulled up into a Clytie knot and a few rich chestnut curls fell over her forehead and ears. Her only jewelry was a modest diamond pendant on a silver chain and eardrops to match, and she carried a white lace fan.

When she saw herself in the cheval glass, she panicked. She looked like a bride. "Surely I need not deck myself out like this, Anne!"

Miss Sheffield nodded. "I believe you must, child. Lord Ramsey is right, you know."

Their carriage joined the long line leading to the Prince's dwelling. Lady Stoneyhurst was magnificent in wine-red corded silk, her headdress of red and green dyed feathers brushing the carriage roof.

At last the carriage reached the pillared entrance and they were able to enter the glory of Carlton House where Lord Ramsey, Lady Ramsey, afflicted with a die-away air, Edwin, and Charlotte awaited them to join the line of guests being received by His Highness. They made their greetings to the now hugely rotund Prince, who yet retained much of his charm, then strolled together, in and out of crowded, very hot rooms lavishly decorated in a variety of styles, and talked, laughed, greeted, and were greeted by, friends and rivals alike. They ended up in the rose satin drawing room, where the ladies seated themselves gratefully on a pair of pink-upholstered gilt sofas.

"The color sits well with your white gowns," said Ramsey. His eyes, holding brief amusement, flickered over Lady Stoneyhurst's ensemble. "His Royal Highness will join us when he has finished welcoming his guests."

Charlotte said, "Why? Have you asked him to?"

"Of course not. What a notion! I merely hinted that my future with a lady was now assured and I would be honored to introduce her. He likes to be first with the news. He was somewhat jocular, but intrigued."

"Must you bring the Regent into all this deception?" Sophia muttered to her facetious betrothed. "As if matters were not already dreadful enough!"

"It will be helpful to our position in society, my dear."

Whatever else Ramsey might have added was cut short. "Heavens!" exclaimed Lady Stoneyhurst loudly, "here comes the duchess with Annabel and the duke. Her grace's face is as red as a farm woman's. She's decided to know us, after all. She's just dying to hear if there is any more gossip about Miss Ramsey. And that snake, Sir Walter Crawley, is with her."

Sir Walter abandoned his companions as soon as he realized the duchess was making for the party grouped around the sofas and attached himself to an elderly maiden lady who welcomed him profusely.

"I'm sure he heard what you called him," said Lady Ramsey breathlessly.

"Good!" Lady Stoneyhurst fluttered an immense fan, painted with a peacock with extended tail feathers.

The duchess bore down on them like a small, fussy boat, her plum-colored draperies flowing behind her.

"So you are here!" she declared.

Ramsey said laconically, "But naturally. One does not refuse an invitation to Carlton House."

"I know that! I meant I have come upon you. I have been looking for you for an age."

Ramsey brought a chair for her grace, who plonked herself on it, sighing a little. "My poor feet. It is so very hot. One longs for some air."

Lady Stoneyhurst stared at the duchess's shoes. "If you did not insist on cramming your feet into shoes too small for them, you would not suffer so."

"My shoes fit perfectly and my feet have been one of my chief beauties. Everyone says so." The duke urged Annabel to seat herself beside Sophia.

"We have momentous news," said Ramsey. Sophia had a distinct impression that everyone but he had stopped breathing. "Two betrothals to announce," continued Ramsey. "One between the lovely Lady Sophia Clavering and myself, and the other between my dearest sister, Charlotte, and Sir Edwin Fothergill."

The duchess's face grew redder. She looked from one to another of the company, clearly aching to give them all a piece of her mind at discovering her matchmaking schemes had been thwarted. But her anger was as nothing compared to the heights it reached when the Duke of Chiddingley spoke up.

"I perceive that tonight is the time for good news," he

said, beaming broadly. "I can tell you all that my dear Miss Annabel Willis has consented to wed me."

The congratulations, especially from Lady Stoneyhurst, were hearty. The duchess looked in danger of an apoplectic seizure. She dredged up a smile that would have curdled cream and bestowed it upon the three couples.

The rest of the evening passed, for Sophia, like a dream. Or a nightmare. They were joined by the Prince Regent who, when he learned of the betrothals, was profuse in his congratulations. He kissed Sophia's hand and said archly, "One day, my dear, you must confide in me just how you attracted Lord Ramsey into the married state—and at the very start of your first Season. You are a beauty—that goes without saying—but Ramsey has resisted all comers before. And Miss Ramsey, you too have scarce had time to cheer us with your handsome appearance before being snatched from us by Sir Edwin." He continued, sportively, "You, Sir Edwin, should be at Oxford. Well, who can blame you for playing truant to be by the side of so lovely a lady?"

The Regent brought his attention to bear on the Duke of Chiddingley and Annabel. "Ah, duke, you too have found a bride." He looked Annabel up and down, as if searching for words. "Charming!" he said at last, still gazing at the pale Annabel. "Charming!" he said again, before suddenly recalling he had promised to meet Lady Alvanley in the Chinese room—"to discuss a new porcelain pagoda I have purchased."

The news of the betrothals circulated around Carlton House as fast as a forest fire, and congratulations and good wishes were many and fulsome. The fact that they were frequently said through stiff lips by frustrated guardians forced to watch no less than three eligible gentlemen fall prey to three ladies barely out of the schoolroom was of no moment, declared Lord Ramsey, who treated everyone with casual grace.

Sophia's smile began to feel as if it had been artificially stretched over her face. Her jaws positively ached. She endured the hours as best she could, while each felicitation began to feel like a knife wound in her nerves. Ramsey's constant nearness, the touch of his hand beneath her elbow, his smiles rendered loving for the benefit of the *haut ton*, sharpened her understanding of how deeply she loved him. And he expected her to keep up such a show of affection until the end of the Season, months away. She had no choice if she and Charlotte were to remain in polite society. She wondered how Edwin was faring.

Sophia and Ramsey walked in the cathedral-like conservatory and he told her that she had nothing more to fear from Tindal and Kitty. "I have seen them and I fancy Tindal wished he had never started the gossip. He is not a bad man, you know, but an ambitious one, and Kitty was much overset by his behavior. They were married today and I have given them the tenancy of a comfortable inn on my Cornish estate."

Sophia stared up into his dark eyes. "Would not sending them away have been sufficient to halt the gossip? Did we have to begin this horrible masquerade?"

Ramsey's heavy brows drew together in a fearsome frown and his face darkened. "Horrible masquerade? Yes, we did. The scurrilous tales have gained ground and would eventually have sunk you without trace. And do not forget, my lady, that your incredible behavior was the trigger for the near disaster in the polite world of my sister."

Sophia shrank inwardly. "I do not forget," she said in low tones. "I never forget. If you could but know the unhappiness I have endured—still endure—" She stopped, her voice suspended by emotion.

"For God's sake, don't weep. Not here." The viscount looked around hastily to see if they were observed. They were, by almost every eye. He paused where they were partly concealed by a pillar. "Control yourself," he said harshly. "This is no time for missish airs. We both know you can be resolute when it suits you."

Sophia's head went up. She blinked away her tears and flashed the viscount an angry look.

"That is much better," he said. "Now, place your

fingers upon my arm and smile. Smile, I said, madam, not show a sick grimace. I do not intend to be a peepshow for the vulgar.''

"Indeed, sir, I have been led to understand you cared nothing for that in the past.''

The muscles in the viscount's arm tightened for an instant. He showed his teeth and bowed, acknowledging the cool greeting of a noble lady who had entertained hopes of gaining him as a son-in-law. "Just what do you mean by that, madam?''

"Even young ladies in the country learn something about your exploits among—a certain sort of creature,'' said Sophia.

"Good gracious! I had no idea that my fame was so widespread!'' Ramsey paused for them to receive congratulations from the Princess Esterhazy. Sophia made her curtsy and smiled and spoke as was expected of her, and they continued on their way.

"Where are you taking me, my lord? I hope it may be somewhere cooler. I believe I have the headache coming on, and is it any wonder?''

"None at all. But permit me to remind you that you brought your problems on yourself.''

Sophia, seething with anger, paced beside her betrothed, her fury making her eyes shine with greater luminosity, and filling her face with delicate color, so that many of the young men present muttered at the unfairness of Ramsey's winning one of the beauties of the Season, and he not needing her fortune at all.

At Ramsey's command, two astonished footmen opened a double door and Sophia found herself in the garden. The air was almost icy, but after the heat of Carlton House it was welcome. Ramsey led her along a path between flower borders and trees. The stars were clear and bright, there was a half-moon, and Sophia could make out various pieces of statuary.

"Last year the Prince held a fete here,'' said Ramsey. "It was during the day but everyone wore their grandest clothes and jewels. Fortunately, it did not rain.''

"How delighted I am to hear it," said Sophia. She had cooled and she shivered.

Ramsey stopped, removed his coat, and placed it around her shoulders. It was warm with his body heat and she pulled it closer, her heart thudding with longing.

"Shall we not return, my lord? I am quite composed now. I shall not fail you again, and you must be cold in your shirt sleeves."

Ramsey put his hands on her shoulders. "No, Sophia, I am not cold. Quite the opposite. I did not like to be so severe with you, just now, but it would have done our reputations no good if you were seen weeping on your betrothal night. Why did you?"

"I—I don't know. I felt suddenly sad."

"You should be happy. You have a splendid Season before you; you will be the envy of many because of your prospects, and His Royal Highness is quite taken with you."

"I fail to understand your reference to a splendid Season," Sophia said, a catch in her voice. "Our false engagement will frighten off sincere suitors. Lord, what an idiotic world society lives in."

"Doesn't it!" agreed Ramsey cordially. "Yet we must follow its dictates if we wish to be part of it. Some folk say they despise it, but they are the people kept out for one reason or another. I did not want that to happen to you."

"Nor to Charlotte!"

"Nor to Charlotte," he agreed, "but you need not think to put me off by changing the subject. Why were you suddenly unhappy, Sophia?"

She remained silent, her love for him almost bursting within her. A lady does not love a gentleman who has not shown his esteem first, she reminded herself. Ramsey was simply sorry for her. Or maybe he was using her simply to save his sister. He probably found the situation diverting. "Come, Sophia, speak. You are not usually so reticent."

She could hear the laughter in his voice, but before she could think of a reply he turned and wrapped his arms about her and pulled her close. She attempted to draw back, a feeble attempt that was at war with all her instincts, then allowed herself the rapture of being molded against his hard, muscular body.

Incapable of resisting further, she lifted her face to him and when his mouth found hers she responded with her whole being, and the floodgates of her passion released her imprisoned love.

Ramsey lifted his head and swore softly. "Damme, but I wish I could see you properly. Your eyes shine like the very stars. Sophia, do you care at all for me? Is our engagement to be only a masquerade?"

Hope leapt in Sophia's heart and she consigned all her mentors' teaching to perdition. She could contain herself no longer. "I hate it *because* it is false, my lord. And in the conservatory—I wept at the pretense. I so wished it was real."

The strong arms were suddenly braced around her like iron bands containing her in a welcome gaol. "Sophia, my darling, my own brave, clever, beautiful woman, I love you more than you can ever know. I shall need a lifetime proving my love to you."

Sophia gave an inarticulate cry of joy and her hands went up to draw down his head. The coat slipped from her shoulders and dropped to the ground, as their lips met in a kiss in which all doubts and uncertainties were drowned in ecstasy. Ramsey tenderly wrapped Sophia in his coat again and they walked together, stopping often to embrace and to recall the past.

"You bought a poor, ugly serving girl a meal," reminded Sophia. "I should have known then that you were kind and not at all the reprobate decribed to me."

"Reprobate?" His lips found hers again and his hands slid down the satin of her gown. "What a superb shape you have, my love. And how ridiculous were those pads."

"Ridiculous!" Sophia was outraged, then she giggled. "When did you know about them?"

"As soon as I touched you, you foolish woman. Your disguise did not fool me for long."

Sophia said, "I am so happy, I want everyone to share. Poor Charlotte and Edwin are still having to pretend."

The viscount gave a shout of laughter. "Poor Edwin! Poor Charlotte! They are very much in love with each other. Charlotte's protest was shaped in the same mold as yours. She is profoundly impressed by his gallantry in being prepared to fight for her. And so am I!" His voice was solemn as he continued, "The night I saw you and Edwin leave that private parlor, both looking so flushed and guilty, I believed you had been making love. I was wickedly jealous."

"We were quarreling," said Sophia. "I can't recall why now."

"Edwin will make Charlotte a splendid husband. It was because she feared she had forfeited his esteem forever that she ran off with Crawley. I am very fond of my sister, but have to confess that she is bird-witted. Thank God she soon realized her dreadful mistake. Edwin appears to have the power to control her. I never thought to see the man who could. Love makes all the difference."

"All the difference," said Sophia fervently.

"We shall enjoy helping their courtship along." Ramsey sighed. "We must go back to the house. I have no doubt that our departure was observed. The duchess will probably be exceedingly rude. Her temper has been exacerbated by her nephew's announcement. She wanted you in her family."

"God forbid! I feel sorry for Miss Willis!"

"I think you need not. His Grace of Chiddingley is beetle-headed but stubborn, and he loves his Annabel."

"Did you feel at all disturbed by all the playacting this night, sir?"

"It was immensely amusing," he replied cheerfully. "But I must remind you that I was not acting a part. Charlotte's mad elopement hastened my plans, but I marked you for my own an age since."

"What brazen conceit!"

"Yes, wasn't it! But not misplaced, my dearest, you must confess."

She stood on tiptoe to put her arms about him and bestow a lingering kiss.

"Wonderful girl," he whispered. "How I shall enjoy awakening your body to love."

Sophia shivered with delight.

"We really must return," said Ramsey regretfully. "Are you ready to face the *haut ton*?"

"Your beautiful coat may have grass stains on it."

"So might your gown. And your sandals must be ruined. My dear Lady Sophia, what will people think?"

"They may think what they please."

"Just so long as it is what suits us," said Ramsey.

Sophia laughed softly. "You are incorrigibly arrogant, my love."

"How beautiful that sounds. I truly am your love. And you are mine. My love, my one and only love, my future wife." He kissed her with infinite tenderness and murmured, "Let our wedding be soon."

Sophia thought that in the history of the world there had never been more beautiful words.

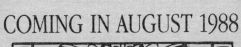